Marheh of the Silberay, Book 1.

I0460495

Water Road Apprentice

By
Rosalind Kentwell

L'Optimisme
Melbourne

Acknowledgements

My thanks to those friends who have read and made comments especially Elwin, Noni and Elenor.

Thanks too to my family who have likewise contributed their time and comments.

I am also grateful for the help I have received from *Varuna* and the *Victorian Writers' Centre*.

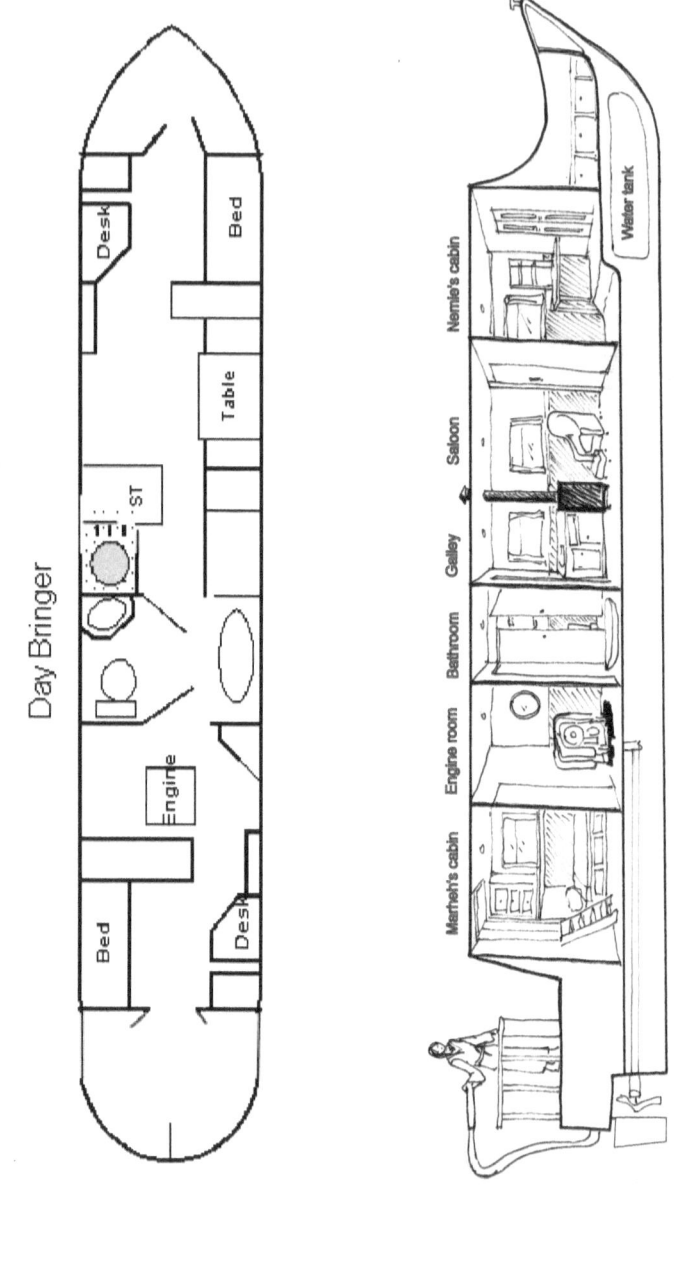

Day Bringer

Desk

Bed

Table

ST

Engine

Bed

Desk

Martlet's cabin   Engine room   Bathroom   Galley   Saloon   Nemle's cabin

Water tank

"BIRTHS – to Margaret and Stephen Carron a daughter"
Deerford Gazette, March 1910

Chapter One

March 1930

Nemle chose a seat in the front row. She was not normally a front row person, but today she had a job to do. Today she would become a mentor. Today she would take an apprentice who would be her charge for the next twenty years.

She had met her yesterday, a slim, dark-haired child with enormous brown eyes.

"Not a child," she rebuked herself inwardly. "A young woman."

But she seemed a child. She had only just scraped into this year's intake. Yesterday had been her twentieth birthday. If it had been tomorrow she would have had to wait until the next Gathering two years hence.

"And she wouldn't have been mine," Nemle thought with a little flutter of... what... apprehension, excitement, anxiety? She didn't know. Perhaps a mixture of all three.

The last night of the Gathering was always a grand celebration. For three weeks the ninety Silberay had been together to discuss problems, to share joys, to obtain their next assigned route and for apprentices to attend formal classes. In the morning they would take to their boats and spread out around the water road perhaps not to meet again for two years. Even more important than the celebration though was the ceremony and now the tables of food were moved to the side, the music and the talk were dying down and others were assembling behind and around her..

The Harbour Master and the Apprentice Master mounted the low dais and the gathered Silberay grew silent. In the ceremony to come the progress of the apprentices would be acknowledged. Until they reached their tenth year they were required to attend formal classes during the three weeks of the Gathering and satisfactory results were rewarded by the presentation of a new tunic in the colour of their new level.

Apprentices were the future of the Silberay so it was important to mark their progress at every level but for Nemle, as for many of the others, the two most important parts of the ceremony were the graduation of the final year apprentices and the induction of the first years.

This year five apprentices would graduate, five new Silberay take possession of the boats they had lived on with their mentors, five mentors retire to live their last years at the Harbour. That was a sobering thought. Today she would become a mentor. Would she be ready, twenty years hence, to leave the water road for ever? When she was twenty, seventy had seemed old but it did not seem so now she had reached it. Twenty years a mentor … again the flutter of apprehension, or was it anticipation?

The apprentices were gathering beside the dais. Nemle could see them moving into position all alike in their white shirts and loose brown trousers. There were three first years.

Nemle watched with interest as the first two, a young woman and a young man, were welcomed, spoke the words of commitment and received their tunics, gold-coloured for first year. Then came the third. This one was hers. The girl moved forward, back straight, chin up, ardent, glowing like a candle flame. She turned a little towards the Harbour Master and revealed a thick plait of long dark hair hanging neatly down her back.

"That's the Carron youngster." Nemle heard a man behind her. "She'll be a handful."

Nemle frowned.

"I, Marheh Carron, promise myself to the Silberay." The young woman's voice rang out. "I choose for my life the active pursuit of goodness and beauty."

"All that passion and melodrama. I don't envy her mentor."

"They say she's very talented." This new voice sounded a little doubtful.

"All the more reason to come down hard then. Don't want her to get above herself."

Nemle went forward then to sign the indentures and welcome her apprentice but the man's words hung in the back of her mind. "Come down hard" was that how she must treat this shining child?

Marheh stirred and stretched as the morning light crept into the little cubicle where she had slept during the Gathering. Then she remembered what day it was and flung back the covers. Today she would move onto a boat and her life as Silberay would really begin. The three weeks of classes had been, not boring exactly but not exciting either. After all she'd already been on lots of Silberay boats because of her Uncle Jik. He had even let her steer Autumn Wind once or twice on short straight stretches. The other two first years had been older, Tippa was months past her twenty first birthday but they had not really known very much at all.

Jik had told her lots about the history of the Silberay and what they believed so she had found it hard to sit and listen to someone else telling her the same thing when what she really wanted to do was to meet her mentor and start boating. Sometimes she had wanted to argue with the Apprentice Master who seemed to think she was a child who knew nothing but mostly she had remembered to hold her tongue. Jik and both her parents had warned her against showing off.

Last night had been glorious. She had been too excited to eat much of the party food. She couldn't keep still long enough. She had spotted the woman who was to be her mentor. Jik had told her she was very lucky but watching as she moved quietly among the older Silberay Marheh could not see why. She was just a little old woman in Silberay uniform.

She had said her promise with all her heart, loudly, so they would know how much she meant it.

She scrambled into her clothes and re-did her plait. Now she had her tunic she looked like Silberay. The soft bag which held all her belongings was almost packed. She tucked her nightdress into the top then stripped the linen from the bed. That had to be taken to the laundry. She gathered it all into her arms and whisked off with it.

She was going to be the best apprentice that ever was. Nemle was pretty lucky really.

Nemle was up early too, dressed and breakfasted and ready to take Day Bringer around to the loading dock by the time the sun was fully above the horizon. She would need to get diesel and water before they set off but that could wait until Marheh was on board and become part of her first practical lesson.

Usually the tasks associated with setting out, the engine checks, the careful untying of mooring lines were second nature but today everything was done as if for the first time, knowing she would be teaching these skills. Manoeuvring out of her mooring she noticed how she used the throttle as well as the tiller to help her reverse and felt Day Bringer respond as she moved slowly and easily through the quiet Harbour waters.

She was just tying up at the loading dock when Marheh appeared from the building which housed the accommodation, extra bathrooms and the laundry. She was carrying a large soft bag and trying to run but the bag kept banging into her legs turning the run into a hop and a skip. Nemle watched her for a moment then bent to finish her mooring.

When she straightened again Marheh was in front of her, eyes shining, a little breathless, the bag clasped in both arms. Nemle smiled a greeting and hoped it would hide the sudden surge of panic that swept over her. What did she know about being a mentor? The advent of this eager young woman would change her life and now, suddenly, she didn't want her life to change. Then she realised that Marheh was looking not at her but at Day Bringer.

The girl stood transfixed for a few moments then she put her bag down very carefully and stepped across it to touch the dark green hull and trace around the decorative letter D.

"Day Bringer," she said softly, turning to Nemle. "She's beautiful."

"She is a pretty boat," Nemle said, keeping her voice matter-of-fact. "You'll be able to help care for her." She stepped onto the back deck and turned to Marheh. "Come on board and get settled. There's a bit to do before we can set out."

Turning, she led the way through the open door and down the four steep steps into the back cabin.

"This will be your cabin," she said. "Put your bag down here and I'll take you through the rest of the boat."

A sudden flash of resentment surprised her into the realisation that she did not want to relinquish her cabin to this new comer, did not want to have to occupy the new cabin that had been created for her in the bow, the work space it replaced gone forever.

She led Marheh through the cabin to the engine room, the big engine shining with her care, just waiting to be awakened. Then they passed the tiny cubicle that housed the toilet bucket and reached the galley with the saloon beyond it. She heard Marheh's little gasp of delight as she took in the neat, compact space. The morning sun bounced off the water and filled the boat with light. The kettle gently steamed at the back of the stove. Everything that could possibly sparkle did so. The sink and the stove defined the small corner that was the galley. The chimney for stove and fire reached to the roof, black and shining. There were green curtains at the windows with a pattern of wildflowers. The lower sides were panelled in light golden timber, the lining of the roof and topsides was painted a very pale grey-green. There was a big green armchair and a matching footstool by the fire and a small table and two little benches built against the opposite wall. Beyond that was the door to Nemle's cabin, firmly closed.

After a few moments Nemle turned to look at Marheh.

"Your new home," she said.

Marheh's face shone.

"She's beautiful," she said again.

Nemle smiled then.

"She is, isn't she?"

A moment of silence while Nemle hunted for some more words.

"Would you like to unpack now, or shall we get under way?"

"Get underway," Marheh said, in no doubt. "But I just have to get my box of clay."

Nemle stared after her as she turned and hurried away, watched through the window as she bolted towards the accommodation building and disappeared inside then shrugged, went to get the hose and started filling the water tank.

"Maintain firm discipline, instruct the apprentice in obedience and service and expect both at all times."

Guidelines for mentoring the young apprentice

Chapter Two

Six weeks later Nemle stood at the tiller of *Day Bringer*. Part of her mind was on her steering, the other part, the major part, was attempting, not for the first time, to address the problem of her new apprentice. Marheh was at present sitting on the boat's roof, half heartedly dabbing at the brass ventilator caps with a polishing cloth, a sulky expression spoiling her lovely face.

Things had begun quite well. Marheh had seemed eager, too eager perhaps. Even on their first day of boating she had wanted to talk and been surprisingly forthright in her opinions. Nemle had not expected that. Neither had she expected how wearing a constant presence could be. She had snapped at times, sending the child and her chatter away to her cabin.

Her cabin. Nemle caught the thought and forced herself to examine it. The cabin that was now Marheh's had been her own for fifty years. No matter that she now had a new cabin, the old one had fitted her like a glove. She knew where everything was. There was a place for everything and never a wasted moment hunting for some ordinary necessity.

She mourned her workspace too, gone to make room for her new cabin. None of that was the child's fault.

Then there was the problem of the clay, something her father had given her to practice with, though practice what she did not know.

The landscape slowly eased past as *Day Bringer* moved steadily onward. The countryside had a pleasant, homely feel about it. The silver ribbon of the water road uncoiled in easy curves between low hills. Nemle saw Marheh pause in her polishing, saw her face soften as she took in a farm cottage nestled amongst trees. A trickle of smoke drifted from one of its several chimneys and almost like a reflection, a drift of greyish white sheep fed in the field below.

She is beautiful. It must make a difference.

Nemle had no illusions about her own looks. She had always been short and stout even when she was the age of this girl. Now, at seventy, she was stocky and strong with a face that hid her thoughts behind the weathered look of old wood.

She pushed the tiller a little way from her so *Day Bringer* moved easily into the curve ahead.

"Bridge!"

She called a warning to Marheh and received a venomous look in return.

"I saw it."

She stayed where she was a dangerously extended moment before swinging nimbly down to the gunnel.

Nemle bit back her instinctive anger, understanding that Marheh was being deliberately provoking. She supposed she must bear some responsibility for that too, remembering how she had lost her temper in the first week of their journey.

She had been woken while it was still dark by the movement of the boat. At first she had simply waited expecting the movement to cease when Marheh returned to bed, but then there had been stealthy sounds from the galley and she had got up to investigate.

She had found Marheh crouched on the floor feeding the fire with little pieces of coal. Keeping it alight was one of her jobs. The fire door was open but the damper was still partly closed so there was smoke in the saloon and the galley. She did not like to remember the scene that followed.

Marheh had looked up at her from the floor. She had not bothered to put on her dressing gown or slippers and her white nightdress was streaked with coal dust, not only her nightdress, but her hands and face also.

"The fire was going out. I thought I might be able to rescue it."

At that point Nemle had still been in control of herself. She had put her candle on the bench next to Marheh's and tightened the belt on her dressing gown. Marheh had returned to her fire, carefully positioned another couple of pieces of coal and shut the door.

"I think it's caught now," she said, beginning to stand up and stepping on the hem of her nightdress.

She put out a hand to save herself and caught the rack of dishes she had left to drain the night before. They crashed to the floor. A couple of plates, a mug and a bowl shattered on the hearth, cutlery skittered into corners and a saucepan tumbled into the sink then rocked itself gently into stillness.

Nemle remembered a moment of shocked silence before she exploded, hurling her anger at Marheh in a stream of ugly words that cut across her attempts at apologising. She had grabbed Marheh's wrist and held her, berating her, then hauled her off to the bathroom.

There was barely enough room for them both in the tiny space, but she crammed them in and began to pump water into the basin with her free hand. Marheh tried to wrench her wrist free.

"What are you doing?"

"Scrubbing some sense into a stupid, spoilt child."

She had dropped Marheh's wrist and seized her plait at the nape of the neck instead. Then she had grabbed the nailbrush, stabbed at the soap with it and begun to scrub at the black smear across Marheh's cheek.

"You're hurting me!"

"I'm punishing you. Keep still."

She had scrubbed until the black smear was gone and Marheh's cheek was bright red then she had handed her the nailbrush and stood over her while she scrubbed away every last speck from her hands.

Marheh had been monosyllabic ever since.

Nemle watched her, still standing on the gunnel, looking ahead, one foot kicking restlessly at the paint work.

She had apologised of course, later when Marheh had dressed and cleaned up the mess. She knew her apology had been stiff and unpractised but she had not dared to reveal how appalled she was at her own outburst.

Marheh had shown clearly in the weeks that followed that her apology had not been accepted.

"I'll be mooring in a few minutes Marheh. Take the front line please."

A boating task such as this was the only time Marheh showed any enthusiasm for her new life and now she moved obediently into the well deck and picked up the coiled rope.

Time and patience, Nemle thought, hoping she had enough of the latter.

She eased back the throttle and guided *Day Bringer* carefully towards the bank. The bow touched lightly and Marheh stepped off with her rope, a mallet tucked into her belt and a mooring pin in her other hand.

She can learn when she wants to. Nemle pushed the tiller over and allowed the stern to ease in. A short burst of reverse halted the forward motion and a moment later she too had stepped off. She held *Day Bringer* steady with the centre line while Marheh worked with mallet and mooring pins at bow and stern. She did not in fact need Marheh's help, having managed alone for the past thirty years, but since this was help Marheh actually wanted to give she was glad to take it.

"This is Fairdale Wood." Nemle was coiling her line as she spoke. "We'll stay here tomorrow."

Marheh shrugged, returned her mallet neatly to its home and disappeared below.

Later as they ate their evening meal together, Nemle offered a cautious word of praise for her quick understanding of the process of mooring, but Marheh had not forgiven her yet and only tossed her head and scowled. Nemle held onto her temper and tried to continue calmly.

"I'm going plant hunting in the woods tomorrow. Would you like to come with me?"

"I'd rather go by myself."

"I thought you might like to learn about some of the plants."

"No." Marheh stood up to take their bowls to the sink. They had not yet been able to replace the broken plates. "I'd rather go by myself."

Nemle watched her fill the sink and begin on the washing up.

"If you wish. Perhaps you could collect some wood for the fire on your way home."

Marheh said nothing only scrambled through the dishes and disappeared into her cabin. Nemle sighed and went to clean up the sink. Her one burst of temper had had catastrophic results and she was determined not to lose it again but sometimes she found it very hard.

She spent the evening making quiet preparation for her plant hunting and sorrowing over a relationship broken almost before it had begun.

"Your new environment may seem
different and challenging, but domestic
chores are the same everywhere. Use
these to centre yourself in the familiar."

The Silberay apprentice : a handbook

Chapter Three

Marheh spent the evening grumbling to her journal. "I hate her and she hates me," she wrote scowling at Nemle's back, bent over her work in the galley. She scribbled a little drawing of a fierce Nemle face. She would have preferred to be in her cabin but the only lamp was in the saloon. "I just want to go home and be Marheh the Great again." The next sketch was of her three younger brothers saluting a very grand Princess Marheh. "I want to learn to make a difference in the world and all I get is more washing up."

She finished by drawing a cruel caricature of Nemle with a dandelion in each hand and deliberately left her book open on the table when she went to bed.

"It will be her own fault if she sees it. It's my book and she shouldn't look at it."

In the morning when she rose, dressed in her uniform and came out to make up the fire and attend to the other morning chores Nemle had given her it was still where she had left it.

"Clear the table for breakfast please Marheh," Nemle said when she came out, that was all.

After breakfast she set out with her baskets and an old trowel and some clippers in a sack leaving Marheh to complete her morning chores.

"Old witch," she said aloud as she watched her trudging across the field towards the wood.

"Old witch," she said again, louder, as she finished the washing up and cut herself a sandwich.

Everything was spoilt. Nemle wouldn't teach her to steer or look after the engine, only made her wash up and polish the brass. She thought she'd be sick the first time she'd had to empty the toilet bucket. It was disgusting even when there was a proper place for it, but last week she'd made her dig a hole in a field.

"Old witch, old…" but there wasn't a word bad enough.

She stuffed her sandwich into her rucksack and slung it over her shoulder. Too bad about the mess on the bench, she wasn't going to waste the day cleaning up when she could be out and away exploring as far from Nemle as possible.

Since Nemle had gone across the field she kept beside the water road. When she was little she'd thought everyone could see the water, then she'd thought she was special because she could see it and her brothers couldn't. Later she'd begun to understand that seeing was a privilege, but it didn't seem much like a privilege now. She just wanted to go home.

The morning was cool and fresh. Walking was something she could escape into, feet finding the way even when the going was difficult, stepping over roots, swinging around tree trunks, making progress. There were birdsongs and bluebells in the woods and starry white wood anemones and she paused sometimes to gaze and listen. Then the woods gave way to fields and she left the water road, climbing the hillside where the trees and fields met.

At the top of the hill she stopped to eat her sandwich, to gaze out over the countryside and to sprawl on her back on the grass.

Did she really want to go home? Father would let her resume her apprenticeship with him in the pottery, but he'd be disappointed and she'd feel a failure. The boys wouldn't call her Marheh-the-Great any more. She was already a failure really. She'd promised herself to the Silberay and now she wanted to go home. If only she'd had a different mentor. She couldn't bear to think of all the years she would have to live with Nemle.

The sky was high and wide above her and a bird sang. Rough grass prickled her neck and tickled the backs of her hands. Lying there she could be empty, feeling nothing, only being.

At last she got up and turned to enter the woods.

The narrow path was strewn with leaf litter. On either side were straight, slim trunks. New green coloured the branches. It was quite light, the leaves too new to provide much canopy. Birds shouted with joy, bluebells reflected the sky, celandines the sun. A small pool lay still and silver. She moved quietly, lightly to be part of the beauty around her.

The path forked and she paused to consider her way. A sound from behind swung her round. A large man stood filling the path, shaggy beard, matted hair.

She gasped a little and groped for a smile, but none were available.

The man stayed watching, inarticulate, urgent.

"Do you want to pass?"

But no, he wanted her.

"You come."

He seized her upper arm, tightening his grip as she tried to pull away.

"You come."

He thrust her ahead of him on the narrow path, panting breath, feet that tripped and tangled and the painful band of his fingers, hard and relentless. 'Please' and 'No' and 'Let me go', even the whimper were lost in her gasps. She had time to be afraid.

Then suddenly it ended in a small clearing. He pushed her forward and let her go so she fell sprawling on the ground. He shouted something incomprehensible. By the time she had got her breath back enough to look up, she was surrounded.

Nemle spent her morning on the edge of the wood fossicking for the plants she used in her medicines or propagated for sale in the small towns and villages she visited. She could lose herself in the work and was grateful for the respite.

At lunch time, her baskets filled, she went back to *Day Bringer* to eat and to care for the roots and cuttings she had gathered.

She frowned to see the mess Marheh had left.

How could she get through to the child? Well, she wasn't a child really, but she behaved like one sometimes. Her mother would have beaten her for insolence and slovenly behaviour if she had behaved like Marheh, but then her parents hadn't really wanted a daughter. She'd been cheap labour to them and they had rejected her when she had left them to become apprenticed to the Silberay.

It hadn't mattered. Hafa, her mentor had been everything to her. She could do for her all the things her parents had demanded as of right. Hafa never demanded but gave her affection and appreciation. She'd been glad then that she had been so thoroughly trained in the domestic arts and could serve her well.

As she worked with her plants, carefully potting and watering, spreading leaves to dry, her thoughts drifted back to the happy years of her own apprenticeship as well as the solitary, sometimes even lonely, middle years after Hafa had gone. She had looked forward to having an apprentice as a return to the happiest time in her own life, but so far it had been anything but happy.

She finished her work and set out again with her baskets. There was a marshy pond she knew of where a small group of alder flourished and she collected leaves and bark for her medicines. Half way across the field she paused, lifted her head like an animal scenting the breeze.

Marheh was afraid.

Catching her breath she quickened her step and plunged into the wood. Marheh's fear had caught her and was reeling her in. She paid no heed to pathways but tramped steadily onwards, straight to the source.

Marheh looked at the faces around her and tried to scramble to her feet. A big boot landed on the centre of her back, pressing her down. She went sprawling again. The breath went out of her and she spat out a mouthful of leaves. For a moment she lay still, stunned and frightened, while around her the watchers exclaimed and remonstrated. She could not distinguish words but there was anger and distress in the sounds she heard.

She tried to struggle. The big boot held her down like an insect pinned to a board. A scream required breath she did not have. Her mind shouted despairingly. "Get off me. Let me go." Abruptly the foot was withdrawn.

She sprang up, ready to run, but the people surrounded her, individuals reaching out to hold her as she turned and twisted.

When Nemle reached the clearing she saw her in the centre of a group of Travellers. Someone would try to hold her only to snatch their hands away, then another would try and another.

"Marheh," she called, trying to reach her.

This wasn't like the Travellers. They had always respected her, knew who she was and what it meant. They helped her with finding plants she wanted. She helped them with knowledge of how to use them and the medicines she made.

"Marheh!" she called again and added a word of greeting in the Travellers' dialect.

The noise and confusion stopped.

"What are you doing? You're frightening my apprentice, my daughter."

13

"Mama Nemle." The big man reached out to her, swept her into a hug that lifted her off her feet then put her down carefully.

"Mama Nemle. You will help us."

"Of course, if I can Barntredor."

She patted his hand and gently removed it from her arm.

"You must let me talk to my daughter first, then we'll talk together."

She looked around for Marheh and held out her hand to her.

"Are you alright?"

A curt nod and a lifted chin. The child had panicked and now she was ashamed of it.

Nemle looked around at the Travellers.

"What's the matter? Why have you done this?"

A burst of speech answered her. She lifted her hands.

"Let's sit down shall we, then we can talk."

She looked towards one of the older women.

"Fliandre, what's wrong?"

Small, apologetic movements, silent withdrawal and in a moment she was standing alone with Marheh and Fliandre.

"I'm sorry Barntredor frightened you child," Fliandre said to Marheh. "He is desperate to recover his son."

She gestured towards the small fire and the silent Travellers seated around it. Nemle saw Marheh hesitate and sit cautiously a little apart. She sat down herself, not too close, with Fliandre on her other side, then she turned to Barntredor.

"Your son is missing?" she asked gently.

The big man poured out words in an anguished stream. The dialect was not always easy to follow but his last words were easily grasped even though half choked with pain.

"Since three days," he said. "Since three days."

Nemle looked at him compassionately.

"Of course we will help if we can, but why did you think my daughter would know anything of this?"

"My son is like you," Barntredor said. "He sees the water."

"I long to believe that those of us who can
live in the other dimension might find a way
to share ourselves and our different
understanding."

Sila's Journal : the early years

Chapter Four

Marheh, still aloof and trying to distance herself, saw a side of Nemle she
had never before allowed herself to see. The Travellers loved her. What
ever their trouble it was clear that she was a comfort to them. Scruffy, sun
brown children showed her their treasures and she admired them carefully.
She had a sympathetic word for the elderly among the group and
exchanged smiles with the others and all the time she listened to
Barntredor, asked questions and consoled.

At last she stood up with some difficulty. She held out her hand to Marheh,
grasping her wrist when she was slow to respond and pulling her to her
feet.

"My daughter and I will watch and listen with our hearts."

She rested her other hand on Barntredor's shoulder.

"Be hopeful."

Marheh twisted her wrist out of her grasp as soon as they left the clearing,
but continued to follow her. Nemle's drab green back, her sturdy legs in
their uniform trousers, the worn boots, her ordinariness, mocked her all the
way back to *Day Bringer.*

"Did you understand what they were telling me?" Nemle asked once they
were back on board.

"Something about a missing boy." Marheh shrugged. "For three days, I got
that bit."

"Barntredor's son. He's only ten. He was collecting wood for the fire and
didn't come back. Barntredor lost his wife two years ago and he's frantic
about the boy. He didn't mean to frighten you."

"I wasn't frightened."

She tossed her head and met Nemle's gaze defiantly.

"Why did you say I was your daughter?"

"Because it is a way of expressing our relationship that they understand."

"We don't have a relationship. I'll never be your daughter."

She'd hoped for a reaction, but Nemle only pressed her lips together and took a deep breath. She let it out very slowly then spoke quietly.

"Did you understand what they said about the boy?"

"You'll tell me whether I understood or not."

"Don't you think you are being rather rude?"

"Yes."

She turned to leave.

"What ever your feelings about me." Nemle bit off the words. "For the sake of the boy you will come inside and listen and stop behaving like a spoilt child."

Marheh shrugged and strolled insolently ahead of her into the saloon, pleased to have provoked her. She thought about sitting in the armchair but was not quite game to usurp Nemle's place so she slid into a seat at the table and waited.

She watched Nemle pause in the doorway then move about the galley for a few minutes, checking the kettle, taking down mugs, making sperit. She enjoyed the knowledge that Nemle was angry. It made her feel powerful. The longer she took fussing with the sperit the better. It was like watching a kettle come off the boil.

A nasty little smirk found Marheh's face as she pictured steam gradually subsiding from the top of Nemle's head as well as from her mouth, nose and ears.

A mug of sperit appeared in front of her then Nemle was sliding into the seat opposite with her own drink.

"Barntredor thought you would know about his son because the boy can see the water road. He has the potential to become Silberay."

"So?"

"So he is very vulnerable. So he is a target for our enemies." She paused and looked hard at Marheh. "Stop thinking about yourself for a moment and think about a father who has lost his only son."

Marheh flushed, bit her lip and looked away.

"Sorry," she muttered.

She pulled back from the hand Nemle reached out to her and stared into her mug to avoid meeting her eyes. She heard her sigh before continuing her explanation.

"The little boy, Trodkali, was with two of his friends in a corner of the wood near the water road. The other two confessed they were teasing him because he kept talking about the water that wasn't there. He got angry and shouted at them then he laughed. 'There's a boat'. He pointed, greeted someone unseen, held out a hand and disappeared."

Marheh looked up at Nemle, interested in spite of herself.

"He's been gone three days, so it wasn't one of us giving him a ride. I can't help feeling the Yareblis have him."

"Who are they?"

"Our enemies."

There was a short silence as if Nemle was trying to decide whether to continue, how much to say.

"I didn't know we had enemies, not enemies who can see the water road."

"Yes, I'm afraid so."

Marheh waited.

"Sometimes it's up to us to undo the things they've done."

"Like taking the little boy?"

"Yes. It's part of our work."

Marheh forgot who was speaking. This was more interesting than polishing the brass.

"So we can look out for him if he's on a boat because we can see the water and his father can't?"

Nemle nodded.

"They must be ahead of us otherwise we would have seen them."

"That's probably the way of it, but their boats are small and fast like canoes. They don't live on the water like we do. There's a chance that they passed us while we were away today, or even during the night, though I think I would have sensed something."

"What are we going to do then. We can't go after them if we don't know which way they went."

If they went after them they'd have to boat longer than their usual two or three hours a day and Nemle might let her steer.

"We'll go slowly along as usual and watch carefully. The important thing is to try with our hearts and minds to listen for Trodkali's distress."

Marheh leaned back and looked scornfully at Nemle.

"What sort of use will that be?" She felt Nemle's gaze assessing her and pushed her mug away impatiently. It seemed a long time before she spoke.

"When you were afraid today I heard you. Did you think I'd arrived by chance?"

"I wasn't afraid."

"Don't lie Marheh." Nemle's voice was sharp. "Not to yourself, what ever you say to me."

"I don't lie!" She heard herself shouting. "I never lie."

She pushed herself away from the table, looked around wildly and ran out of the saloon and the galley, through the bathroom and the engine room, through her cabin, onto the back deck and away.

She ran until she could run no more and then she walked. Something was pursuing her, but it was nothing she could escape. She had almost walked herself to a standstill when she turned into a field and collapsed under a big old tree. She stayed with her face to the ground, her breath jagged and unshed tears pressing behind her eyes. She didn't lie. She didn't. Marheh the Great wasn't frightened ever. She pushed herself to a sitting position her back against the tree trunk, held by the big spreading roots. A little distance below her was the water road, the life she had chosen.

Jik, her Silberay uncle, had shown her the life as something rare and precious, something to aspire to. He had spoken seriously of simplicity and self discipline too but that had seemed like a fascinating challenge, not house work and doing what she was told. Especially not doing what Nemle told her.

It was getting dark. The last rays of sun slipped below the hills as she watched leaving only a clear pearly twilight. She hoisted herself to her feet. It was a long way back. She began to make her way out of the field. Too bad if she was late, nothing mattered. The water road was ahead of her, dark steely grey in the half light. She was almost there when it came, swift and silent near the other bank, a canoe with two paddlers. She stopped.

Breathing was suddenly difficult. Then they saw her. She felt their attention. This was the enemy.

She knew better than to go with them, not like the Traveller child. She would go back into the field, walk away and wait for them to go. So why wasn't she? Why were her feet taking her forward, closer and closer to the water, closer to the silent paddlers in the silent canoe. Another step and she would be in the water. She wouldn't take another step, she wouldn't. She would not. Her feet stayed where they were and she thought she had won.

A mocking laugh, attention re-focused, and instead of stepping she threw herself, face forward into the water.

The cold was like a blow. Beneath the surface the water was dark, thick and bitter. She came up choking, spitting, not quite comprehending where or how. Another mocking laugh floated towards her and dwindled into the distance. She struggled upright and found some kind of footing. At least her feet were her own again, but she was up to her armpits in the freezing water. Her boots were glued to the bottom. As she tried to move towards the bank she felt the sucking mud dragging against every step. The bank seemed enormously far as she battled towards it her breath coming in short gasps, her teeth chattering with the cold and when she reached it the struggle was not ended. The sides of the water road dropped sharply. She still had to fight the weight of her waterlogged clothes and the mud's grip on her boots and pull herself up and onto the path.

It was almost too much effort to stand up then and for a few moments she lay on the path. She was so cold and so far from home and it was nearly and dark and she was so tired and she couldn't stay here. She had to get up and walk whether she wanted to or not. She pushed herself to her hands and knees and staggered to her feet. For a moment she couldn't remember the way she needed to go and took unsteady steps in a circle until she oriented herself and set off along the path, freezing cold and already exhausted.

For a time the movement warmed her a little and she managed to trudge along thinking of nothing except putting one foot in front of the other, but she had lost any sense of how far she had come and soon every corner was a new disappointment. No *Day Bringer*. What if Nemle had gone without her? Would she have deserved that?

She caught her breath in a sob and stumbled into a run, but she could not keep it up beyond a few steps. The darkness was complete now and the bumps and potholes in the path made new difficulties but she struggled on, tripping sometimes but never quite falling until at last she rounded a bend and saw ahead the soft lamplight shining from *Day Bringer*'s windows.

Nemle had sat and listened to Marheh's pounding feet running through the boat, felt the dip and rise as she left it and gazed at Marheh's mug on the table, still half full of sperit.

It was a special mug, made for her by her father as a farewell gift. It had been kept in Marheh's cabin and so had escaped when so much else had broken. It was a gift of love, father to daughter. It represented a relationship that Nemle had seen and envied as a girl. She reached forward to touch it. In its way it too was beautiful; carefully crafted, fragile looking but surprisingly strong.

Surprisingly strong. They'd said Marheh was talented but they didn't know the half of it. They had not felt Marheh's terrified call for help. They had not seen her use her mind to beat away the Travellers' hands that reached for her. And she didn't even know she was doing it.

One day this talent would be channelled into the discipline of the mind and it was her job to teach her. Somehow she had to reach her. Right now she didn't seem to know the meaning of discipline. She'd been protected from even the knowledge of their enemies. First year apprentices always were if possible. First year apprentices didn't use their minds even unknowingly the way Marheh had. First year apprentices learned self discipline through obedience to their mentors and the ordered simplicity of a structured life. Hafa had not even introduced the subject until she was beginning the third year of her apprenticeship.

What would it do to her, how would she respond if she knew how much potential she had? If she was kept in ignorance would that damage her?

She had to reach her, she had to.

She closed her eyes, rested her chin on her hands and for a while let her mind hold an image of Marheh without questions or anxious wondering. Then she sighed, relinquished the gentle attention she was giving and went to begin preparing their evening meal.

When the stew was simmering on the back of the stove she took up her mortar and pestle and began grinding some of the day's gleanings into paste. It was a soothing, rhythmic task that helped to calm her thought and empty her mind of worries about Marheh and Trodkali. Only when she paused and went to light the lamp did she realise how long Marheh had been gone. She went out to the back deck and scanned the landscape but saw no sigh of her. The lamp in the saloon threw a neat golden square onto the path. The curtains could stay open. It would be nice for Marheh to see the light welcoming her home.

The stew would keep on the back of the stove. There was really no hurry for supper. Probably she had gone further than she realised. Marheh would hate her to go looking for her. Best to keep on with her work, there was plenty to keep her occupied. She hadn't been out as late as this before though.

Nemle went again to look out, listening with heart and mind for sounds of distress as she had told Marheh they would do for Trodkali. There was nothing like the panicked scream from the woods.

How dare she stay out so late? Could something have happened to her? If she wasn't back soon she might go a little way along the path to look for her, just a little way.

Then *Day Bringer* moved.

She's back!

Such a rushing release of tension Nemle felt her knees weaken beneath her.

How dare she! How dare she! How to punish her?

"Marheh!"

She appeared in the doorway, soaked and shivering, looking as if she could hardly stand.

"Marheh!"

Nemle was beside her in a moment supporting her to the fire.

"Quickly, off with those wet clothes, I'll go and get the bath."

She left her huddled on the floor by the fire and went to fetch the big tin basin they used to wash in. She emptied the kettle into the basin and filled it again. She would need plenty of hot water. She knelt to unfasten Marheh's belt and unlace the sodden boots.

"Good girl. Come on, help me now."

One boot and then the other were wrestled off her feet. The socks were easy after that.

"Good girl. That's my beautiful girl."

The tunic was pulled over her head.

"Come on daughter, you have to get warm."

More hot water in the basin, another filled kettle on the fire and Nemle back again beside Marheh who seemed unable to help herself. She sat and shivered as Nemle unbuttoned her shirt and took it off.

"Up you get. Hold on to me. Good girl."

Somehow she managed to get Marheh to her feet so she could pull down her trousers and pants and help her to step into the big basin of warm water. There was just enough room for her to sit. She rested her head on her knees, wrapped her arms around her shins and continued to shiver.

Nemle poured more warm water into the basin, scooped it up and poured it over her back. She built up the fire and brought out towels to warm. Gradually Marheh's shivering eased. Nemle undid her plait and washed the water road out of her hair. She wrapped her in the heated towels.

At last Marheh lifted her head and looked at Nemle.

"I was afraid," she said. "I did lie to you."

Nemle leaned forward, kissed her lightly and began to dry her hair.

Next morning they were already underway before Marheh awoke. Even the noise of the engine starting up had not disturbed her. She lay for a moment listening to its steady pulse. What was happening? Why were her curtains closed? She never slept with her curtains closed. She shouldn't still be in bed. Nemle would be angry. Then she remembered.

"Sleep as long as you want," Nemle had said.

Nemle had bathed her and fed her and tucked her into bed last night. She'd looked after her as if she cared. Probably she had drawn the curtains too so the light wouldn't come in too early. Nemle had called her daughter and kissed her.

Marheh wriggled uncomfortably and felt herself redden. She'd been so rude to Nemle and tried to make her angry. She rolled over to press her hot face into her pillow. Nemle was just doing her duty. Nemle hated her really and she hated Nemle. There wasn't any way back from hating Nemle. If she didn't hate her then she would have to hate herself and she was Marheh the Great, wasn't she?

She pushed back the covers impatiently and felt some unexpected twinges from the body she could normally take for granted. Her shoulders especially were stiff. It would have to be clean clothes this morning, everything she had on yesterday would still be wet and need washing out.

When she was dressed and her cabin tidied she pushed open the doors to the back deck and looked up to where Nemle was standing at the tiller. The morning sun was on her face and she looked as plain, brown and unreadable as she always did. Then she saw Marheh and smiled.

23

"You've had a long sleep."

Marheh said nothing.

"Your boots are by the fire, but I don't think they'll be dry yet."

Marheh said nothing.

"Why don't you get yourself some breakfast?"

Marheh still said nothing, then, in a rush before she turned to go. "Shall I bring you some sperit?"

"Thank you," Nemle said. "I'd like that."

"Be firm and decisive. The young apprentice may resist
discipline if the mentor is half-hearted or inconsistent."

Guidelines for mentoring the young apprentice

Chapter Five

Marheh's offer had seemed to hint at the possibility of a new beginning.
Two days later Nemle was still hopeful though she felt as if she was walking
on eggshells her dealings with her needed such care.

The village of Fairdale Lading was not far off. They would moor there,
perhaps for a couple of nights. The way was so familiar and the day so calm
and bright that steering was automatic and Nemle, as was so often the case,
found herself again reviewing her relationship with her difficult charge.

The incident with the Yareblis had awakened her curiosity about their
enemies and the power they had over the mind. Nemle had used this as an
excuse to test Marheh's own potential.

"Will you sit here and drink your sperit?" she said to her. Then she entered
her mind and instructed her to do the opposite.

Knowing it was a test, Marheh had seemed puzzled rather than frightened
when she was unable to obey Nemle's spoken request.

What Nemle had been coming to terms with ever since was the knowledge
that she had to find a way to reach Marheh, to build a real relationship with
her so that she could teach her to manage the extra ordinary potential she
had discovered in her.

Well, perhaps it was beginning to happen. There had been no
acknowledgement of her care of her, no word of thanks for the clothes
washed and hung in the engine room to dry, the boots stuffed with paper
and put by the fire but she had not expected that. It did seem as if she was
taking a little more care with the chores she had been given though and
there was even an occasional attempt at communication.

Nemle eased back the throttle a little as the small, round head of a water
vole drew an arrow of wake across *Day Bringer*'s bow. Marheh might have
been talking more but it was not always easy to negotiate the
communications without being provoked into argument.

"When will you teach me to steer?" was one recurrent theme.

"One day." Was all the reply she could give and that was not considered acceptable.

"It's not fair. Why not now?"

No answer was safest. She was not going to tell her that she was too arrogant and too immature.

"When will you teach me to steer?"

"One day."

When that was all the answer she got she resorted to cunning.

"If I could steer you could walk the bank and look for plants. That would be useful."

"If you could recognise the plants you could walk the bank. That would be more useful."

Nemle gave a wry smile as she remembered Marheh's response.

"I'm not interested in plants."

Neither was she interested in trying to understand what she meant by suggesting they listen with their hearts.

"We should go after the canoe" was her other theme. She relinquished that reluctantly after Nemle pointed out that the Yareblis canoes were not only faster than the long Silberay boats but could turn anywhere along the water road. They had no need to find a turning place.

Despite these potential disagreements she was presently, at Nemle's suggestion, sitting in the well deck with her mending. Although she had everything new six weeks ago the socks Nemle had removed from her feet and washed for her were in obvious need of attention and no doubt they were not the only items of clothing showing signs of wear. For all her twenty years she was still such a baby sometimes.

Her dark head appeared above the roof and Nemle sighed and squared her shoulders. She would not allow herself to argue, nor would she give in to pressure. She had to do what she thought was right even if the consequences were sometimes uncomfortable. She watched her walking carelessly towards her along the gunnel. She was leaning in to the hull, but barely holding on, a pair of socks in one hand and scissors in the other.

"Finished already? That's good."

No smile, but a little nod of acknowledgement as she leaned in through the open back door and tossed the socks and the scissors down onto her bunk.

"Only another half hour and we'll be at the mooring for Fairdale Lading. Why don't you have a little look at the chart before we get there?

That it seemed found favour and she swung down into her cabin, bypassing all four steps and disappeared in the direction of the saloon.

Marheh was outside again, holding the front line as they reached the village. A long sweep of green led down to the water road and at the top of the hill there was a cluster of cottages around a church and an old farm house. She was still dealing with her mooring pin when a girl came running down the hill towards them.

She wore a faded brown dress, worn brown boots and a blue pinafore, just the sort of clothes Marheh had worn before she became apprenticed. She viewed her comfortable, hardwearing trousers with a touch of complacency. The girl had dark hair in two plaits that bounced behind her as she ran. She looked to be about sixteen.

Marheh watched curiously as she raced towards *Day Bringer*.

"Mama Nemle," she cried out and flung herself into Nemle's arms.

Marheh stared at this obviously joyful reunion until Nemle pointed out that she had not finished mooring and the bow was now drifting out. She flushed, annoyed with herself and completed the job as smartly as she could. Then she walked along the gunnel on the side away from the bank, came to the back deck without passing Nemle and her friend and hovered in the doorway trying to simulate disinterest.

"Would you put the kettle on for sperit Marheh please."

She looked away, swung a little out and back over the water. Why should she? This was Nemle's friend. Then she clattered noisily down the steps and thumped through to the galley. When Nemle appeared with the girl the kettle was steaming and three mugs stood ready on the bench.

"This is Kithla," Nemle introduced the two girls. "Kithla, Marheh, my apprentice."

Kithla smiled and held out her hand.

"You are lucky. It was my dream to become apprenticed but I'm too young yet and now my father needs me."

Marheh barely touched the outstretched hand.

"I've known I'd be Silberay for ages. My father was happy for me to go."

"Sperit please Marheh."

27

"Alright, I'm getting it."

She poured boiling water into the mugs. Nemle had given her such a look. What had she done? Nothing! That girl was sitting on the footstool sucking up to Nemle. Let her. She would never be Nemle's apprentice.

She passed mugs to Kithla and Nemle and slouched against the bench with her own.

"Why don't you come and sit here?"

Nemle patted the broad arm of her chair.

"I'm alright."

She knew she was behaving badly but she seemed to have no will in the matter. That girl was talking to Nemle as if she liked her. No she wasn't, she was talking to her.

"I would have loved to be Nemle's apprentice, but I'm the wrong age for her so I always knew I couldn't be."

She probably wishes you were. I bet you'd do everything perfectly. She didn't say it though, finding enough restraint for that at least.

"Kithla and her father take young plants from me and grow them on to sell. In exchange we get lavender and some other herbs from them … and a basket of vegetables in season sometimes."

"Nemle's helped us so much since my father's accident."

She's even leaning against Nemle's knees, sitting on the footstool like she's the apprentice.

Kithla put down her drink and twisted round to look at Nemle.

"Dyti's disappeared."

"You don't think she's run away again?"

"We're friends now. I don't think she'd go without telling me."

Nemle looked across at Marheh.

"Dyti is twelve. She lives with her aunt. She used to get into trouble and run away every so often, but we've thought she was happier lately, haven't we?

Kithla nodded.

"She's learned not to talk about the water road except to me so she doesn't get teased like she used to and Nemle has helped us both to understand what the water road is about and what it means to be able to see it."

28

"Doesn't everyone know about it, even if they can't see it," Marheh said.

Nemle shook her head.

"You've been lucky. Not many people have a family like yours. For lots of us it's just something we stumble on by ourselves. Dyti's aunt didn't want to talk about it."

She turned back to Kithla.

"She said nothing to you? Nothing about seeing a boat or meeting any strangers?"

"Nothing, and her aunt hasn't seen her for days. I'm sure something has happened to her?"

"There's a Traveller child missing from Fairdale Woods. He can see too. I'm afraid this might be connected."

"Why? What difference does it make that they can see?"

Nemle looked from one girl to the other. She patted the arm of her chair again.

"Come and sit down Marheh. I think it's time I told both of you something about our enemies."

"Enemies?" Kithla said.

"Yareblis?" Marheh asked, still lolling against the bench.

"Yareblis," Nemle agreed. "Marheh will you tell Kithla about what happened to you two days ago?"

Marheh raised her chin and looked at Nemle. Then she hoisted herself up to sit cross legged on the bench, surveying the lesser beings below her.

"I went out by myself," she began. "Just for some exercise and I saw two people on the water road in a canoe. When they saw me they did something in my mind and made me fall into the water. They thought it was funny."

"I thought only Silberay could see the water," Kithla said.

"In a way these are Silberay, at least they began as part of us. Now they call themselves Yareblis because they've chosen to be the reverse of what we try to be."

Nemle turned to Marheh.

"Why don't you remind us about some of the history you learnt at the Gathering?"

"You mean about Sila and the making of the water road?"

29

"Yes, Kithla has never had the chance to hear about that."

"Well it is quite interesting really."

She sat up straighter, opened her eyes wider and raised her eyebrows a little.

"Sila was the person who had the idea for the water road. She thought it could be like a bloodstream for the land. Silberay all give a drop of their own blood to show that they are part of it. The water road carries the Silberay, so it carries goodness and beauty because that is what we promised."

She stopped abruptly and flushed.

"And we call ourselves Silberay, Sila's people," Nemle said.

Kithla sighed and looked at the floor. Nemle touched her shoulder lightly.

"People can be Silberay if they can see the water road, but it's a choice. At first everyone wanted to follow Sila's dream, be catalysts, helping people and giving them power to choose how they live their life, only trying to show what goodness and beauty could be like. But things changed so slowly that some Silberay became impatient and wanted to force people to be good instead of showing them a choice. In the end there was a division. Ten people left and became Yareblis. They had good motives but they forced people and because they **could** force them they stopped respecting them. Then there was nothing to stop them using more and more force and developing that mental power that Marheh experienced.

They try to get more people by recruiting children and young people who can see the water road but are too young to make a choice, or don't know there is one to be made."

A little silence followed Nemle's exposition.

"So you think they've recruited Dyti and the Traveller, don't you?" Kithla asked at last.

"I fear so. Nothing else makes sense of what we know. We need to find them, but I can't see where to start."

"I told you we should have gone after the ones I saw." Marheh tossed her head. "It's probably too late now."

"It was never a possibility."

"I don't see why not."

"But you don't see very far yet, do you Marheh?"

Another silence. Kithla looked at the floor. Marheh glared at Nemle who took a deep breath and began again.

"Best we just go on with our everyday activities. We'll take the pallets of cutting off the roof and up to your cottage Kithla. Then Marheh can go to the farm for milk while I talk to your father about what is needed for the garden and you go and pick me some borage and some comfrey. We can do all that and still be keeping our ears and eyes open and listening with our hearts."

Marheh raised her eyebrows and shrugged. That's just stupid, an excuse for doing nothing. She levered herself off the bench and bent to fossick under the sink for the milk pail. She watched Kithla help Nemle up from the armchair and saw them go off together into Nemle's cabin. Why would she care if they shut her out? She grabbed the pail and stomped through the bathroom, the engine room and her own cabin then out to the back deck.

"Good," Nemle said when she appeared. "If you take this one we won't need to make two trips."

A tray of seedlings was thrust into Marheh's hands.

"Off you go. Follow Kithla."

"Youth is a season of extremes. There will be storms and sunshine."

Guidelines for mentoring the young apprentice

Chapter Six

Follow Kithla. Why should she follow little miss perfect. She didn't want to know anything about plants. It was enough she was expected to water them.

Marheh grumped her way up the hill to the neat little cottage where Kithla lived.

"Here we are."

Kithla put down her load on the low stone wall that edged the front garden. She opened the gate and smiled a welcome. Marheh put down her pallet of seedlings next to Kithla's.

"I'll go for the milk."

"Won't you come in and meet father. He loves a new face."

"Of course you'll go in," Nemle said, coming up behind, a bit breathless after the climb. "We've plenty of time."

Marheh shrugged and picked up her load again. Kithla led them around the side and through to a small greenhouse where they could leave the seedlings. Then she took them through the back door and into a big sunny kitchen.

A long, low bench ran the width of the room under the windows. It was covered with small pots and trays of seedlings. A man sat there potting up the seedlings. Marheh felt her face burn as he turned towards them and she saw the big wheels and bright knitted rug over his knees. She remembered how she had boasted about her own father.

It was Nemle's fault. She should have warned her.

She watched Kithla run to him, saw him hold out both hands to Nemle, responded to his smile of welcome with a small, tight smile of her own and held up the milk pail.

"Go for the milk," she said, backing towards the door.

Nemle frowned, but she ignored her. It made her sick all these people calling her Mama Nemle. They'd never had to live with her.

"I'll let myself out."

She let the door close more loudly than necessary and escaped to the garden. They could talk about plants and fawn over Nemle if that was what they wanted, she was going to look for clues that might lead to the missing children.

She wandered along the lane swinging the empty pail and kicking a stone ahead of her like a schoolboy.

It was a nice little village, bigger than it looked from the water road with a couple of rows of cottages curving around the church yard below the hill. She pottered amongst the grave stones, telling herself she was enjoying the sunny afternoon.

The farm was beyond the church on the edge of the village. There was no mistaking it, a comfortable looking house, a haystack and a couple of sheds. The front door was painted blue and sheltered under a canopy of vines. She knocked loudly. Nothing happened for some minutes or so it seemed. She was about to knock again when she heard footsteps and the door opened slowly inwards to reveal a rather stern looking woman wearing a long white apron over her plain dark dress.

"What do you think you're doing?" The woman seemed to be taking in Marheh's Silberay uniform and finding it unsatisfactory. "The back door's the place for your sort."

Marheh's jaw hung open, the words she had prepared died on her lips.

"Go on then. Take your pail around to the dairy and don't come bothering me again."

The door slammed shut with much the same tone as the woman's voice. Marheh put her tongue out. Back straight, chin up, she marched around the house. Nemle should have told her, probably she wanted her to get it wrong.

The farm yard was warm and sunny when she reached it. A few brown hens pecked at the dirt and a small black and white dog lazed in a corner. There was a rich, earthy smell, not unpleasant, made up of milk and cow and hay and silage. So which was the dairy, or was she supposed to keep on making mistakes until she found it? She took a couple of steps forward, then a couple more. There was a stable door, open at the top but dark within. It was not that. Then a girl who could only have been a dairy maid, blue clad, white aproned with a white mob cap, popped out of an open door to greet her. She held out her hand for the pail, popped back inside and in a few moments returned with it nearly full of creamy milk.

She held it out to show Marheh before pushing the lid on.

"Not quite full else you'll likely spill it on the way home."

Marheh held out the penny Nemle had given her.

"You one of them Silberay?"

The girl tucked the penny into her apron pocket.

"I'm an apprentice."

"D'you really live on a boat?"

"Yes, all the time and travel all over the place."

"Can't say I'd fancy it really."

Marheh shrugged. From where she stood she could see that a farm gate led into fields and down towards the water road.

"Is it alright if I go that way?" She pointed to the gate.

"Don't see why not. It might be a bit mucky though. You don't mind cows then?"

"I like exploring."

She made for the gate. As she turned to shut it after her she saw the girl was still watching her but as their eyes met she nodded and disappeared back into the dairy.

Marheh set out across the field. There was nothing to find here, just daisies and tufty grass, but at the bottom of the next field was a small copse close to where the water road lay behind a hedge. Nemle could talk all she liked about listening with her heart but as far as she was concerned action was better. She would go looking for clues and here was as good a place as any to start.

She reached the stile and crossed into the next field, spilling some of the milk in the process. Stupid pail should have a better lid.

There were cows in this field, black and white ones. She was not, of course, afraid of cows but these were quite large seen close to and seemed to be curious about her. She forgot to watch her feet and stepped into a moist and smelly cowpat.

Then she arrived at the edge of the copse. It was very dense with lots of ground cover, brambles, elder and hawthorn growing thickly around the spindly trunks of the coppiced trees. She forced her way in on tiny animal tracks that caught at her legs and threatened the milk pail at every step.

The field and the farm disappeared surprisingly quickly. Looking around showed her nothing but vegetation and the constantly flickering spatters of light filtered through the spare, springtime canopy. She stood still, listening, but once the noise of her own passage was silenced there was nothing to hear. Brambles snagged her clothes and her skin. She stopped again to suck at a bleeding scratch on the back of her hand. Why was she doing this? There was nothing here, nothing, nothing. So why did she think there was something to be found?

She just did. Maybe she had heard it with her heart. Wouldn't Nemle be amazed if she found something.

On she went. There seemed to be the hint of a path now, just a slight thinning in the undergrowth. She followed as best she could, once or twice seeing something that might even have been a footprint. Someone had come this way she was sure and there was the proof of it.

She stopped and stretched out to reach for a bright orange ribbon snagged on a thorn bush to one side of the path. It was a bit beyond her reach and as she grabbed for it her foot slipped. She looked down to find she was on the edge of a puddle that seemed to extend to right and left.

Stuffing the ribbon into her pocket she pushed her way along the edge of the puddle which seemed to grow deeper as she went. Within a few more steps it was no longer a puddle but a little runnel widening in the direction of the water road. More steps and there it was, a large dark shape lying on the water half hidden by overhanging branches.

She pushed closer, heedless of scratches and spilt milk and found not one, but two big canoes. They looked simple and harmless lying there. They were empty as far as she could tell. The paddles had presumable gone with the paddlers. This must be a Yareblis hiding place and she had found it. Fairdale Lading was obviously not the innocent smiling village Nemle thought it was.

A triumphant grin spread over her face. Nemle thought she couldn't do anything right, well Nemle didn't find the canoes, she did.

She stood a moment longer, half tempted to step into the nearest canoe, wishing there was a paddle so she could take one out onto the water road. Nemle would be furious. She could see how there was a little gap at the bottom of the hedge that edged the water road. A paddler would have to crouch really low but a canoe could push through. She couldn't though, not without getting wet. She battled her way out of the copse and half way across the field before finding a break in the hedge but when she emerged beside the water road she could see *Day Bringer* moored by the next field.

Nemle was not back but she could let herself in. She put what was left of the milk into the cold cupboard in the bilge, made up the fire and put the kettle on then settled herself in Nemle's armchair, put her feet on the footstool and gloated.

Nemle settled her rucksack carefully over her shoulder and set off back to *Day Bringer*. She'd enjoyed her afternoon with Kithla and Thad. It was nice to feel wanted for a change. Marheh's resentment was hard to bear at times. What sort of mood would she be in? Would she have arrived back with the milk? She seemed always to be considering Marheh, how she would respond, how she might be changed back to the ardent young woman she had glimpsed at the Gathering.

She was on board. The door to her cabin was open and a window in the saloon. Nemle took a few deep breaths and tried to prepare herself before stepping onto *Day Bringer*.

She made her way through to the galley and stood for a moment in silence looking at Marheh in the armchair. Her expression said as clearly as if she had spoken that she knew she should get up and give her the chair but she wasn't going to. Almost it seemed as if she was daring her to insist.

She wouldn't be drawn into that, but neither was she going to be manipulated into overlooking everything that had happened that afternoon.

"I'm sorry you didn't stay longer at the cottage. I think Kithla was disappointed."

"You told me to go for the milk."

"There would have been time for both."

Nemle moved to the bench, took her rucksack off her shoulder and began to empty it of the half dozen eggs Kithla had given her.

"Would you like custard for supper?"

"There's not that much milk. I spilled some on the way home."

Carefully Nemle unwrapped the newspaper from each egg and placed it in the basket on the bench. She kept her lips firmly together. Perhaps if she waited there might be the suggestion of an apology. Finally she spoke into the silence, quiet and controlled.

"Perhaps we'll have scrambled eggs then."

"I don't care."

Marheh drew her feet up into the chair so she was glowering at Nemle over her bent knees.

What was going through her head? She looked as if she was hugging something to herself.

"No, you don't care, do you? You don't seem to care about anything except yourself."

"I do so!" Marheh sprang to her feet, shouting. "I do care. It's you…"

She stopped abruptly.

"Yes?" The upward inflection made it a question.

"You make me feel like I'm always wrong. Nothing I do is ever good enough."

Nemle raised her eyebrows.

"And what do you think yourself about what you do?"

"I'm not allowed to do what I want to do." Her voice rose again. "Maybe you're afraid to teach me in case I'm better than you."

The air seemed to vibrate between them with thoughts unspoken, words unexpressed then Nemle sighed and began cracking eggs into a bowl.

"It will be scrambled eggs, take it or leave it."

The meal was eaten in silence. Nemle could not trust herself for more than a curt good night when it was over and she disappeared into her cabin as soon as Marheh had begun on the dishes. She sat on her bed, her head in her hands. Things seemed worse than ever between them. What had happened this afternoon? She had hoped Marheh and Kithla might have become friends. They could have spent a few days at Fairdale Lading. Thad would have appreciated her company and her help and the two girls could have talked about things girls talked about and done things girls did and Marheh might have been happier. Instead she seemed to have gone deeper into the hole of hurt pride and disappointed dreams she had dug for herself. If things went on the way they were it would soon be impossible for their relationship ever to mend and that didn't bear thinking of.

Although it was still very early she began to prepare for bed. She did not know how to talk to Marheh but she could enter the discipline of the soul and offer her song for her.

This was the true work of the Silberay.

It meant she did not sleep much and came to the new day more tired than she expected. Marheh looked tired too and there was an air of sly triumph about her that was something new. Unhappiness was twisting her.

The ordinary tasks of the morning were done in silence for the most part. It was difficult to maintain any kind of normal communication when Marheh mostly ignored any conversational overtures. She bitterly regretted her initial angry outburst but surely she had paid for it over and over.

The familiar routines of departure completed they were on their way. She tried to concentrate on her steering. Skills as natural to her as breathing were hidden in a thick fog today. Marheh had been openly rude to her more than once and was now standing on the back deck watching her, an intense scrutiny she found difficult and distracting. Perhaps she was sickening for something. She certainly felt very unlike her normal self.

She judged the approach to a bridge badly and barely got through without bumping, then was unable to avoid an encroaching bush as they emerged. Marheh looked at her, scornful and triumphant.

"You won't teach me to steer because you don't want me to be better than you. That's it isn't it?"

Goaded beyond enduring Nemle took a second to put the engine into neutral then she abandoned the tiller and grabbed Marheh. Years of single handed boating had given her a strength that her anger only enhanced. She thrust Marheh's head under her arm, gripped her waist and gave her a good hard smack. It felt very satisfying. She heard Marheh's gasp of surprise and felt her begin to struggle. A good hiding my girl, her mother's words came from somewhere, that's what you deserve.

When she finally released her she was breathless and her hand was stinging.

"I'll teach you to steer if and when you learn humility. Now get below and stay there."

Marheh stumbled towards her cabin and disappeared.

Nemle drew the doors closed behind her and stood stunned by what she had done. All those weeks of careful, patient forbearance wasted. She wanted to weep. What chance would there be for them now?

Slowly she looked around as if returning from somewhere else. The day was gentle, *Day Bringer* was drifting quietly, nudging the bank and easing away. It didn't matter how Marheh had behaved she should have been able to manage differently. She had done what her own mother would have done, something she thought she would never do.

Sadly she put the engine into gear and moved *Day Bringer* slowly onward until she found a place to moor. When everything was secure she took a deep breath and opened the doors to Marheh's cabin.

Marheh had managed to get down the steps somehow and flung herself face down onto her bunk.

How dare she! How dare she treat her like that. She would not cry, she wouldn't. She hated her. She was not a child to be punished that way. It wasn't fair. She had wanted so much to be apprenticed to the Silberay and it hadn't been anything like she thought it would be. She just wanted to go home. She wanted her father. He would hug her and love her and listen and take her part. Or would he? She remembered what she had said, how she had behaved. Could she tell him that? She had been rude on purpose. He would be sorry and disappointed. She pushed her hot face into the pillow and wished she could not hear herself mocking Nemle.

She was aware in some remote part of her mind that *Day Bringer* had moved on and stopped again then the silence registered. No engine. Nemle's feet sounded on the steps. She held herself so still and tight, stopped her breath as if she could hide.

Nemle didn't go past. If she opened one eye she could see through a tangle of hair that she was sitting on the floor beside her bunk. Then one hand reached out to lift her hair and smooth it back.

"I'm sorry little daughter. I'm so sorry."

Marheh heard the catch in her voice.

"It was wrong to punish you when I was angry."

Marheh gulped, felt the gentle hand on her head and began to cry. A dam had broken and she could not stop the flood. Nemle continued to sit silently beside her reaching out to stroke her head from time to time.

At last her crying eased enough for her to stammer out her own apology. Nemle stroked her head again and leaned in to kiss her lightly.

"We've managed to get off on the wrong foot haven't we? Do you think we could start again?"

Marheh lifted her head to look at her. Her face was damp and blotched, swollen with crying. Yes please, was what she wanted to say but all that emerged was a croak. Nemle seemed to understand though. She took her hand in a warm clasp. Gripping on felt like finding an anchor and she thought for a moment she might cry again at the comfort it brought.

There was a minute of quiet. Marheh began to relax then surprised herself with a big yawn. Nemle reached across to place her other hand over hers.

"I'll put the kettle on. Why don't you go and wash your face, then you'll feel better."

By the time she had finished in the bathroom and gone through to the saloon Nemle had prepared mugs of sperit and placed them on the table. She was sitting facing the door, her mug held loosely between her hands. She smiled. Marheh tried to smile back and went to lean against the table and pick up her own drink.

"Alright?"

Nemle's hand reached out to her.

She nodded, tears pricking again.

Nemle fumbled with her mug, changed hands, lifted it a little.

"A new start."

Marheh's smile was easier this time. She touched her mug to Nemle's.

"A new start."

She drank, her eyes meeting Nemle's over the top of her mug. She sighed deeply.

Nemle put her mug down awkwardly, steadying it with both hands. Marheh saw that the third and fourth fingers of her right hand were swollen.

"What have you done to your hand?" she asked without thinking.

Nemle looked at her quizzically.

"I'm surprised you need to ask."

"Oh!" Marheh's eyes widened. "You mean…?"

She reached out to take Nemle's hand in both of hers, studied the reddened palm for a moment.

"Poor hand."

She gave a wicked grin.

"Do you suppose my behind looks all red and swollen like that?"

Nemle laughed. She hadn't heard Nemle laugh before, not properly. Was that because of her?

"Should I examine it and tell you?"

Marheh giggled.

"Perhaps not."

She rubbed her rear thoughtfully.

"I think I must have had more padding than you."

"I'm quite sure I got what I deserved."

Marheh shook her head.

"All of a sudden I realized how horrible I've been."

"Not horrible, just unhappy, but we'll both do better this time."

"In the eye of the mind
Hold a perfect flower
Small and sweetly growing.
In the eye of the mind
Hold a candle flame
Ardent and bravely glowing."
Songs of the Silberay

Chapter Seven

Tired after the emotions of the day, Nemle suggested an early night for them both. Sleep did not come quickly but it scarcely mattered. She spent time within the discipline of the soul holding Marheh in warmth and love. She rested in the deep thankfulness that filled her. When she had almost lost hope there was now a real chance for reconciliation and she would devote all of herself to maintaining and developing it.

She slept at last but woke early roused by the movement of the boat. Marheh was up and getting on with her chores. The thought made her smile a little. Then she heard the whistle of the kettle quickly subdued and a moment later a soft scratch on her door. This was something new. The door opened and Marheh stood before her holding out a mug of sperit. She looked troubled.

"What's the matter?" Nemle sat up. "What is it?" She eased herself back against her pillows.

"I should have told you yesterday. It went out of my head."

Nemle smiled and took the mug Marheh was offering.

"Told me what?"

"I found two canoes."

She blurted it out as if needing to be rid of it.

Nemle reached out to her.

"It's alright. Did you make a drink for yourself?"

Marheh shook her head.

"Why don't you go and get one. You can bring it in here and sit on the end of my bed and tell me about it."

Marheh's face lightened and she darted away. She had been afraid of rebuke. She too wanted their new understanding to continue. Nemle took a sip of her sperit. Two canoes, two, and Marheh had found them.

Then Marheh was back. She perched rather gingerly on the end of the bed and told how she had made her discovery.

"I should have told you that day I know," she finished. "I was being horrid. Then yesterday I forgot. I'm sorry Nemle."

"Never mind about yesterday, we're starting again remember."

Marheh made a little, relieved sound and lifted her mug to drink.

"Tell me, did you have any ideas about what we should do?"

She swallowed hastily and shook her head.

"I thought and thought." She blushed and looked down. "I wanted to be one up on you."

She said it so softly Nemle only just heard.

"Of course you did, but not now?"

"No."

"Good."

"So what shall we do?"

Nemle took a sip of sperit.

"You know I still don't have a better answer than the one I gave before. Perhaps it would be more honest to say I don't know, not yet anyway."

"But we can't do nothing."

"It won't be nothing. We'll stay here I think. It isn't a bad mooring. We can keep watch from here for a few days and you and I can begin to work on the disciplines. We can do that now."

Marheh looked down into her mug.

"I'm sorry Nemle. I... I know it was my fault we couldn't before."

"We were both at fault, not just you, but now we have forgiven each other we'll make sure things go better."

She pushed back her bedclothes.

"How about you go and start breakfast while I get dressed and Marheh..." She smiled as Marheh turned back to her. "Thank you for my sperit."

The disciplines.

Marheh found herself singing under her breath as she washed up the breakfast things and tidied her cabin. The disciplines were real Silberay, the discipline of the soul and the discipline of the mind. The words sounded themselves in her mind. At last she was going to learn about being Silberay, the special things.

"We'll go and sit in the well deck," Nemle said. "It's quiet and sunny there. Would you like to get a cushion?"

When she arrived in the well deck with her cushion Nemle was already there. She turned to smile a greeting. She looked quiet and purposeful. Like Marheh she wore the traditional Silberay dress, loose trousers and tunic held in place by a leather belt that served to hold a windlass when necessary. She didn't have to wear apprentice colours though and usually chose drab greens. Today it was as if she was seeing her for the first time. Why had she not noticed how disciplined she was? She had not wanted to of course. She had deliberately turned away from seeing anything good about her. Well she could look with new eyes now and see something beautiful in the way a rock could be beautiful, austere, enduring, strong, hard sometimes perhaps but necessarily so.

She sat down opposite trying to look as workmanlike as Nemle did, but not quite able to hide her excitement at the possibility of this new learning.

"We begin with the discipline of the soul," Nemle said, smiling at Marheh's eagerness. "This is where we relinquish our self into the soul song. We all have to find our own way in, but I'll help you. Silberay think this is the most important thing we do even though for many people it might seem like doing nothing."

Marheh nodded to show she was listening.

Nemle smiled.

"Don't look so anxious. It isn't a test."

She spoke a little more about the soul song, how it was first of all a way of becoming.

"If we can let go humbly, willingly, we begin to find the song that belongs to us. We don't try to sing the song, it sings us."

"But what does it do?"

"In the beginning it keeps us true."

Marheh saw Nemle go into herself looking for the words.

"Every time we sing we practice our own true music first. Then when we become more familiar with our own song we learn how it fits with other songs. Then if we're lucky and practice and want to enough there might come a time when we can sing further than ourselves and begin to push away the dark."

Marheh let out the breath she had been holding. She quivered with longing. This was what she had chosen for herself, without knowing, it was this.

Nemle laughed at her, a tender, teasing laugh that she caught so she laughed too.

"Relax child. The beginning is simple, gentle. It doesn't come with wanting but with letting go."

Not with wanting but with letting go. That was the hard thing when it was something she wanted so much.

Nemle helped her to a beginning, guiding her to choose the beautiful image that would become her portal to this new way of being. There were so many beautiful things that it surprised her when she found the one thing almost without having to think. Nemle wasn't surprised though, she had even brought a candle and a box of matches out to the well deck with her so she would have the real candle flame to look at as well as the image in her mind.

Nemle said the first time she saw her she thought of a candle. She had looked sad then and apologized all over again because she had put the candle out, but it wasn't only her.

Nemle said she had made a good beginning. It didn't seem like much in one way, but it was enough she could glimpse the possibilities. She knew she had worked hard.

She turned her face into the wind and looked out over the landscape. Nemle had suggested she climb to the top of the hill to stretch her legs and she had been happy to obey. She had been so stupid. It wasn't Nemle who put the candle out. She'd done it to herself. She stretched out her arms until she felt as if she was leaning on the wind and it was blowing through her, blowing away the weeks of unhappiness. She saw herself flying. Then she turned back to look down the green slope to *Day Bringer*. Nemle was still sitting in the well deck. She lifted her face and Marheh felt the warmth of her smile. She waved and Nemle waved back then she saw her stand and move inside. She'd promised there would be sperit when she got back.

And there was, not just sperit but one of Nemle's raisin biscuits to go with it.

They took them out to the well deck again.

"It's nice and sheltered down here, but the wind was good too."

Marheh gestured widely in the direction from which she had come.

"There's a lane just below the hill and I think I saw the spire of the church at Fairdale Lading over there."

"I expect that's what it was. Are you ready to start again?"

She gulped the last of her sperit and nodded.

"This time we'll work at the discipline of the mind."

"Like the test you gave me? Like the Yareblis did on me?"

"What we did first, the discipline of the soul, that is difficult, but practicing is always a step towards something bigger, something that will add to the sum of the world's goodness and beauty. The discipline of the mind is different, a two-edged sword that can be used for good or evil. Silberay are forbidden to use it against anyone except the Yareblis, though sometimes we may use it for self defense.

"But you did it to me, remember."

"Not without warning you."

Nemle smiled.

"That is the exception. You and I, apprentice and mentor, we can use it between ourselves so I can teach you and help you develop your skills"

"Like a pretend fight, but you'll always win."

"Sometimes like a pretend fight, but I certainly don't expect to win all the time."

She paused and looked thoughtfully at Marheh.

"Have you ever found yourself wishing hard that someone would do something and then all of a sudden they did?"

She was surprised by the question but really it was not so hard to answer.

"My brother Tep, my youngest brother. We're close. He often seems to know what I want without me saying."

"And what about wishing Nemle would make a mistake steering and then she did?"

46

"Oh Nemle I didn't."

She was aghast.

"I didn't do that, I didn't…"

"It's alright."

Nemle reached across and patted her knee.

"We've put all that unhappy time behind us, but I think you might be going to be very good at this. Perhaps you are already doing it without knowing."

"But… but…"

"But?"

"You said it is forbidden. What if I do it to someone I shouldn't and I don't even know I have?"

"I think perhaps when you know how to do it consciously you will know how to stop doing it if you need to. Try not to worry about it."

Marheh heaved a big sigh. How come she might be good at something that would probably get her into trouble? What if she couldn't stop herself when she should? What did it really mean if she was good at it?

"It's a big responsibility isn't it?"

Now Nemle could read her thoughts!

"That's why the discipline of the soul is the first learning. It helps to fit us for the responsibility."

Again Nemle reached across to touch her.

"But for now we'll forget all these serious things and just play."

She waited until Marheh was looking at her.

"I'm going to insist that you do something, just with my mind and you are going to answer with your mind 'No Nemle, I don't want to'."

Marheh grinned.

"Just as long as you don't make me jump into the water."

Nemle laughed.

"Nothing dangerous or unpleasant I promise, just something you might not choose to do right now because that will make it easier for you to refuse."

"Dangerous and unpleasant come later I suppose."

She could tell Nemle was trying to reassure her but that only made her more scared.

Nemle looked at her. She began to stand up then forced herself down. She wasn't going to stand up and sing Nemle a song, she wasn't. She didn't sing in public, not by herself. No Nemle no.

For perhaps five minutes she managed to refuse, then all at once she found herself on her feet and singing.

> "Sun on the water,
> Rippled by wind,
> This is the life about me.
> Help where I can,
> But never forget,
> Life will go on without me."

It was a traditional Silberay song she had learned at the Gathering.

"You won," she said when Nemle released her.

"So I did, and that was my prize."

She felt herself blushing. Nemle couldn't possibly mean she liked her singing.

"You did very well. I had to work quite hard."

"I did too. I felt it this time. I knew I was saying no."

They practiced for an hour. Sometimes Nemle waited receptively for a request from Marheh. Sometimes she commanded her, not allowing her to refuse though she tried for minutes at a time. It was light-hearted but tiring never-the-less.

She allowed Marheh to refuse to sing again.

"Enough! You've worn me out. You won that one and your prize is to go and make lunch."

"Some prize!"

Nemle watched her go inside. She was a different person when she was happy. How quick she had been to grasp the principles of the morning's lessons. Keeping ahead of her would soon become a challenge. It was pleasant here in the sun, restful. She felt quite sleepy, but lunch was ready so she'd better go in.

She stood up, entered her cabin then stopped. Well, well, here was Marheh trying her skills. Lunch was ready. How clever and subtle she had been. She resisted for a minute so Marheh would know she had not got away with it completely then made her way through to the saloon.

Marheh was watching the door. She looked anxious, but when she saw Nemle she gave a big grin.

"It worked! You got my message."

Nemle moved to her place at the table.

"Bad child, trying to put one over me."

"I wanted you to come for your soup before it got cold."

She sounded demure but the grin was still there in her eyes.

"I'm not sure whether I should spank you again for presumption or congratulate you on a lesson well learned."

Nemle smiled.

"Either way, I must thank you for my lunch."

"Nemle?" Marheh finished her soup and looked across the table. "Do you think I could do that with my mind, connect with you, even if we weren't near each other?"

"I'm sure you will be able to even if you can't yet."

"Could we try?"

"If you like."

She fiddled with her spoon and looked back to Nemle, not quite sure how to say what she wanted.

"What did you have in mind?"

"Do you think I could look as young as Kithla if I wore two plaits like hers?"

Nemle laughed.

"I'm sure you can, but why?"

"I thought I could be a kind of decoy. Let them find me and then I could tell you where I am."

She blurted out her idea in a rush and looked at Nemle, anxious to see what she thought.

"Let them find you. You mean the Yareblis recruiters?"

"Yes. I thought if they took me where the children are I could tell you and you could come and find us."

She could see Nemle did not look happy.

"I suppose it is a silly idea."

Nemle reached out and took her empty bowl and put it with her own.

"It isn't a silly idea, it's a very courageous one."

She was speaking slowly and Marheh saw she was troubled.

"I don't think it would work though. We've already been too visible. They know I have a young apprentice. They put her in the water. I think they would be suspicious if a strange girl suddenly appeared in Fairdale Lading."

She didn't know whether to be relieved or disappointed. She had not thought she was being courageous but perhaps it would be a bit scary.

"I just thought it might help us find the children."

Nemle stretched across the table to pat her hand.

"Never mind. Why don't you go for a walk this afternoon and try to reach me. It will be worth practicing even if we can't use it yet."

Her face brightened.

"Maybe I could walk back to Fairdale Lading."

She looked earnestly at Nemle.

"I could, I… I want to apologize to Kithla. I wasn't very nice to her."

She felt the warmth of Nemle's approval.

"I'm sure she would appreciate that."

Nemle slid out of her seat and took the bowls to the sink. Marheh saw she wanted to say something more. She gathered up the rest of the dishes and followed her. As Nemle turned to take them she stopped so Marheh had to look at her.

"You must promise me though, you're not to go looking for Yareblis."

"Couldn't I just see if the canoes are still there?"

"Absolutely not."

"Why not?"

It wouldn't do any harm and she might have an adventure.

"We don't want them to know you've found them, do we?"

"I suppose not, but what if they've already gone?"

"Then we've missed them, but it wouldn't help to know. We're not wasting time here. We've worked hard today. From what you told me they're likely to come and go from that spot."

She paused. Marheh found she had to meet her eyes.

"Please promise me."

She sighed.

"I promise."

Once the dishes were done she set off up the long green hill to the lane. This was just a cart track really but easier walking than the field. It was good to be striding out in the fresh air and good to know she wanted to return to *Day Bringer* and Nemle. Twenty minutes of energetic walking brought her to the village and she found Kithla's cottage without any trouble. She stopped by the gate. Maybe it would be best not to bother them. They couldn't want to see her, not after the way she had behaved, but she'd told Nemle she would apologize.

At last she plucked up courage and went to knock at the front door.

As she waited she remembered the woman at the farm. Maybe she should have gone around the back here too, but it would have felt like presumption. She raised her hand to knock again then lowered it awkwardly as the door opened and Kithla appeared.

"Oh," Kithla said.

Marheh blushed, aware that she had not made a good impression at their last meeting.

"Is everything alright?" Kithla asked at last.

Marheh nodded, feeling her blush deepen.

"I just... I just,"

Why couldn't she get the words out? Kithla was looking at her as if she was half-witted.

"I just wanted to apologize."

It was easier after that.

"I was horrid the other day."

"Not horrid, but I didn't think you wanted to be friendly."

Kithla still had not smiled. She couldn't blame her really.

"I was horrid and I got horrider."

Kithla's expression seemed to soften and she looked interested at least.

"I was really rude to Nemle." She couldn't tell her what happened then, she couldn't, but if she did it would prove she was sorry.

"Nemle spanked me." She knew her face was scarlet. "And I expect I deserved it."

"Well if you were rude to Nemle you did deserve it." Kithla gave her a friendly grin. "But I would have thought you were too big to be spanked."

"I thought so too, but I learned differently."

She grimaced. Kithla gave a little chuckle in response.

"Come in why don't you?"

"Are you sure?"

"Of course I'm sure."

She stood aside so Marheh could enter then pushed the door shut behind her.

It was quite dark in the passage but Kithla led the way through to the sunny kitchen where she had welcomed them before.

"Father is in the greenhouse. I was just starting to make our supper."

"Can you cook?"

Marheh looked around then focused on the bench where Kithla was starting to make pastry.

"You are clever. Nemle is trying to teach me, but I don't seem to be learning."

"My mother taught me. Then I had to learn after she died."

Marheh thought about her own easy, comfortable home and how foolishly she had allowed herself to behave the first moment something disturbed that comfort. Here was Kithla, four years younger, not complaining, just getting on with things even though her dreams for her life had had to change. "I'm sorry," she said, though not aloud, an apology to Nemle and to her parents as well as to Kithla.

"Do you mind if I go on with this?

Kithla reached out to pick up her apron and put it on.

"It will spoil if I leave it too long."

"Of course not. What are you making?"

"We're going to have a vegetable tart, with vegetables from the garden and eggs from our hens."

Deftly she rolled out her pastry and covered the base of her pie dish and slid it into the oven.

"I'm just going to cook it a little bit before I put in the filling."

Marheh watched as she assembled her ingredients, the vegetables already partly cooked, the eggs beaten. Before very long the tart was complete and back in the oven.

"I bet Nemle would like it if I could do that."

She sighed, thinking of how uncongenial she found cooking and how Nemle's efforts at patience sometimes showed.

"I thought you would be far away by now."

Kithla washed her hands and took off her apron.

"Is everything alright?"

"I found two Yareblis canoes on my way home with the milk. We wanted to watch and see if they are still around."

"I think maybe they are," Kithla said. "I think they might be interested in me."

Marheh looked across at her, waiting for her to continue.

"Father said a couple, a man and a woman, were asking about me. They had some story about a scholarship but he was not very happy about them. I think perhaps they saw me run down to meet Nemle."

She pulled out a chair from the table and sat down, indicating to Marheh to do the same.

"Why wouldn't it be a scholarship?"

If anyone deserved a scholarship surely Kithla did.

"Father said I couldn't be spared, but they were really persistent, unpleasantly so he said. I try not to show I can see the water road, but sometimes I forget."

She sighed and put her elbows on the table, her chin in her hands.

"Dyti is still not back and I'm really worried about her. Almost I wish they would come for me if it wasn't for father."

"Do you really?"

"If it would help find Dyti I do."

Marheh took a deep breath and looked at Kithla.

"Do you think they saw you close to?"

"I doubt it. Surely I would have known. Why?"

A grin spread over Marheh's face, her eyes gleamed.

"You can't go because of your father. I can't go because they know Nemle has an apprentice. Why don't we change places?"

"Here are already some dozen of us, of like mind, gathered together to explore ideas of living, to share the fruits of our past solitude and to learn from each other."

Sila's Journal : the early years

Chapter Eight

Kithla looked at Marheh in surprise. "Change places! What do you mean?"

"We're about the same height," Marheh said. "We both have dark hair. If we changed clothes you could go and stay with Nemle on *Day Bringer* and be me and I could be you and stay here and let them give me a scholarship."

"Why should you do that?"

"I wanted to pretend to be younger and try and get them to find me, but Nemle said they would be suspicious of a strange girl. This way I'm not a strange girl, I'm the person they've already spotted."

"I'd love to pretend to be an apprentice Silberay," Kithla said slowly. "But what about father and what would Nemle say and wouldn't it be dangerous for you?"

"I would be with your father as you until they came for me. Then you would come back as me. It would be just like Nemle to offer help and it couldn't be her because she would have to come after me."

"Slow down a minute," Kithla said. "You're getting ahead of me."

"I'm sure it would work." Marheh was on the edge of her seat with excitement. "Why don't we go and find your father and tell him?"

"I think I would rather *ask* him," Kithla said steadily. "He might not like the idea."

Marheh flushed, understanding the reproof. "I'm sorry, ask him, of course. I got a bit carried away."

Kithla stood up. "I'll just go and find him and have a talk."

"Shall I come?" Marheh stood up too.

"No," Kithla said. "I'd like to talk to him by myself first. We'll come back in here when we've talked." She looked at Marheh who had been about to protest. "I'm sorry, but I don't know you very well yet and … well, father did not get a good impression of you last time."

Marheh watched as Kithla left the kitchen then she sank slowly back onto her chair. She could not help knowing that Kithla's reaction was her own fault. Nemle's words about humility came back to her. Was this what she meant? She was so sure this was a good idea that she had been prepared to run over Kithla's feelings and her father's.

She did not have long to reflect. Kithla and her father were back in minutes, Kithla almost running beside the wheeled chair.

"No father, it isn't like that" Kithla said, but her father spoke louder.

"So you're not too good for us now that you want something."

"She came to apologise father," Kithla protested. "And she wants to help Dyti."

Marheh bit her lip, suddenly realising she was near tears.

"Well, where's this apology then. I suppose Mama Nemle sent you."

Marheh gulped and tried to speak.

"She was pretty uncomfortable about the way you brushed us off and my Kithla was really hurt."

"No father," Kithla protested.

"Yes Kithla. So I want to hear this apology."

"I'm sorry," Marheh whispered, scarlet faced and almost unable to speak for fear she would cry. Then she took a deep breath and tried again. "I'm really sorry I was rude," she said. "Nemle punished me, but she didn't send me, I wanted to come."

There was a moment of silence while Kithla's father looked searchingly at Marheh then he held out his hand. "Well done lassie," he said. "Apology accepted."

Marheh put her hand in his and the firm, enveloping clasp was so like her own father's that tears threatened again.

"Now let's have a drink of sperit and you can tell us again why you want to pretend to be my daughter."

Kithla went to put the kettle on and she and her father tactfully avoided noticing Marheh's mopping up operations.

After a suitable pause, once they were gathered around the table, Marheh began again to explain her idea that she and Kithla might change places.

"It wouldn't be right for Kithla to go with the Yareblis," she said. "Because we might not be able to follow, but because Nemle's my mentor she can hear me even when we are apart."

"Won't it be dangerous?" Kithla's father asked.

"I don't really know," Marheh said honestly. "But not as dangerous for me as for Kithla and if I don't do it they might take Kithla anyway."

"Why don't you go up to Kithla's room and change clothes, then I'll tell you what I think," he said. "Then if it seems practical to me you can go and talk it over with Mama Nemle."

Marheh followed Kithla up the narrow staircase to her bedroom. It was quite a large room, having once been her parents and held a desk, a comfortable chair and a bookcase as well as the double bed. Marheh sat down on the chair and began to undo her boots, too impatient to bother much about the room.

Kithla looked curiously at her.

"Surely we don't need to exchange our boots," she said. "They probably wouldn't fit anyway."

"Haven't you ever worn trousers?" Marheh asked, a hint of superiority in her voice.

Kithla flushed.

"No, I haven't and I don't expect you had either until you were apprenticed." She sat down on the bed and stared at Marheh.

"I suppose you can't get them off or on while you're wearing your boots," Kithla said. "Is that it?"

Marheh nodded. "Sorry," she muttered.

Kithla ignored her and began to unfasten her own boots.

Soon both girls were standing in chemise and knickers looking awkwardly at each other.

"I'm sorry," Marheh said, holding out her pile of clothes; trousers, shirt, tunic and belt. "These are not all that clean, but you can get fresh things from my cabin on *Day Bringer*."

Kithla smiled then and held out her own things. "You haven't forgotten how to wear a dress I presume," she teased, and Marheh smiled knowing she was forgiven.

There was a bit of giggling then as they transformed themselves.

"I feel like a different person," Marheh said, swishing the skirt of the brown dress and feeling the petticoat move against her legs.

Kithla fastened Marheh's heavy belt over her tunic and stuck her thumbs in it. "So do I." She put her hands in the pockets of Marheh's trousers and swaggered a bit, laughing. Then she pulled out her hands and with them the orange ribbon Marheh had tucked away there.

"Where did you get this?" she asked, suddenly serious.

"I found it near where I saw the canoes," Marheh said.

"It's Dyti's," Kithla said. "She must have gone with them."

"I'm sure we'll find her," Marheh said. "At least we know now."

Kithla nodded. "I suppose so. I gave her the ribbon. She'll be upset to have lost it."

Marheh held out her hand. "Why don't I take it? When I find her it will be a way of reassuring her."

"You're very confident," Kithla said, passing over the bright strip of silk.

Marheh tucked it away. "Of course," she said. "Now let's finish getting ready."

Hair was next and Marheh, looking at herself in Kithla's small mirror, felt like a schoolgirl again when a long dark braid hung on either side of her face.

"I always wore only one after I left school," she explained. "Because of keeping it out of the way of the wheel when I worked in the pottery at home."

Kithla examined herself in her turn. "It isn't very tidy," she said. "I'm not used to starting behind my back."

They grinned at each other.

"Come on," Kithla said. "Let's see what father thinks."

"Well, well," he said as they stood side by side in front of him. He looked from one to the other, his eyes resting longest on Kithla who looked both proud and self conscious in the unfamiliar garb. Then he reached out and gave one of Marheh's plaits a little tug. "You mind you behave yourself seemly daughter, or I'll put you across my knee." Marheh bobbed a schoolgirl curtsy and he laughed. "Now put your pinny on and go and see Mama Nemle."

"Are you sure father," Kithla asked, going to him.

"Yes I'm sure."

"If you give me the pinafore I'll wait for you in the garden," Marheh said awkwardly.

Kithla showed her where it hung behind the door and Marheh quickly grabbed it and let herself out into the garden. Once alone she tried to remember her lessons of the morning. Closing her eyes she reached out to Nemle in her mind, picturing her on *Day Bringer*, picturing herself and Kithla arriving and Nemle's greeting. Still and concentrating she held the image for a couple of minutes then opened her eyes, not sure whether she had been successful, but knowing she had done her best.

Five minutes later Kithla joined her. She was wiping her eyes, but she grinned at Marheh. "Come on," she said. "I told father he would have to teach you to cook or he wouldn't get fed, so mind you pay attention."

The two young women were quiet and thoughtful as they walked through the village, but once they reached the lane and open countryside they began to talk, haltingly at first but then with increasing confidence, sharing parts of their lives with each other.

On *Day Bringer* Nemle awaited their arrival with some anxiety. She had three mugs waiting as Marheh had pictured, but she was concerned about why Kithla might be joining them at this hour when she would normally be getting tea ready. When they arrived together she looked slowly from one to the other and her heart sank.

"No Marheh," she said. "No." But she knew she had lost. Marheh had countered all the reasons she could give.

"I have to Nemle," Marheh said, stepping eagerly on board. She looked back to welcome Kithla. "Come on, I'll show you where to find things in my cabin."

Nemle held out a hand to Kithla then stood back before following them into *Day Bringer*. She watched as Marheh opened drawers and cupboards for Kithla, offering her the use of her few possessions. She saw Kithla look wonderingly around the small space as if she could hardly believe she was to inhabit it. Marheh looked so young and so excited Nemle could hardly bear it. Marheh did not even know enough to feel afraid. The tour of inspection over Marheh led the way through to the galley, saw the three mugs waiting on the bench and smiled delightedly at Nemle.

"It worked! You knew we would both come."

Nemle struggled for a smile. "Yes it worked."

Marheh could not keep still. She almost danced as she prepared their spirit. Words bubbled out of her. "It feels so funny wearing a dress again. Do I look very young? Kithla can cook properly. I watched her make a vegetable tart. Kithla's father said he would spank me if I didn't behave myself seemly, but I think he was teasing."

"Marheh, Marheh stop!" Nemle said at last. She led her to the table and almost pushed her into a seat. "Sit here and drink your spirit and calm down you silly child." She plonked Marheh's mug down in front of her and beckoned to Kithla to come and sit opposite then she stood at the end of the table and looked from one to the other. "Now listen to me," she said. "This may seem like a great adventure, but it needs to be tackled with a degree of commonsense." She looked hard at Marheh. "Wisdom and humility too if that is possible."

"Probably not if you mean me," Marheh said cheekily.

Nemle looked at her and then at Kithla. She put her hand on one of Kithla's. "I think I'm going to have to scold this bad child," she said. "Suppose you go and investigate your new quarters while I get cross."

Kithla flashed a look at Marheh then slid from her seat and disappeared.

Marheh, eyes bright and cheeks flushed, gazed defiantly at Nemle. "I have to do it Nemle," she said. "Kithla's father said they came and tried to get Kithla, tried to make him have her take a scholarship with them."

"I know you have to do it," Nemle said. She slipped into the seat Kithla had vacated. "But I need you to understand that this adventure could be dangerous." She covered both Marheh's hands with hers and waited until she was looking at her. "Don't try to be clever. If they come for you they *must not* discover that you already practise the discipline of the mind. Your best defence if you should need one is to practise the discipline of the soul."

Marheh was solemn enough now. "But you'll come, won't you?"

"Of course I'll come, but sometimes things don't go quite as we plan and I might be delayed for some reason," Nemle said. She thought of the hundred and one other things that might go wrong and put them resolutely away. Marheh did not need to be too frightened to function, just sobered enough to take care. She squeezed Marheh's hands and released them. "Why don't you go and say goodbye to Kithla?" she said, sliding out from the table and standing up. "Best if you're back at the cottage before dark."

Marheh was much more thoughtful as she trudged back up the hill to the lane. She had not expected leaving *Day Bringer* to be such a wrench, though Nemle's enveloping goodbye hug warmed and encouraged her. Rather wistfully she imagined Nemle and Kithla sitting by the fire, Nemle in the big chair, Kithla perched on the footstool. It was a wistful time, this twilight hour when the air seemed full of good nights and good byes. Walking along the lane felt lonely, cut off from everything by the hedges that bordered each side. Why had she not noticed before how isolated it was?

At long last she reached the cottage and walked hesitantly around the back feeling unusually shy. Kithla's father called to her to enter almost before she had knocked. The lamps in the kitchen were already lit, the range provided warmth and good smells. He smiled at Marheh.

"Come in lassie," he said kindly. "You'll be feeling a bit strange."

Marheh nodded rather tremulously. She had leapt into this masquerade without thinking about how it would be, alone in an unknown house, with a man she hardly knew, facing a task she was beginning to realise held many more unknowns.

"How about I put you to work straight away?" Thad said. "I'm sure that pie of Kithla's is ready to eat. How about you dish it up? You'll feel better with something inside you."

He told her where to find crockery and cutlery and soon they were sitting together at the table. The warmth and the good food combined to make Marheh feel more like herself and after a while she was able to respond to her companion's kindly remarks, obviously designed to put her at her ease.

"I'm the oldest of four," she told him in answer to his question about her family. "I've three younger brothers."

"So tell me about them," he encouraged her. "I bet they teased you."

"Sometimes," she said, remembering. "Sometimes they ganged up on me if they thought I was too bossy." She stuck her chin in the air and her eyes flashed. "Mostly I was the leader." She grinned at him. "They called me Marheh the Great when we were little, now they just do it to tease." The grin faded. "I've never been away from them all for so long and it will be another year, may be more, before I see them again. I miss them."

"Of course you do. So what is it about this water road that my Kithla's so keen on and I can't even see? What is it that makes you want to leave home and shut yourself up on a boat for the rest of your life?"

Marheh looked at him seriously for a moment and saw that he really wanted to know. It was not something she spoke about easily.

"I've known the water road all my life," she said slowly. "It runs past the bottom of the garden at home and we even have a mooring there. Most of the family can sense its presence and see something of it. My Uncle Jik is Silberay and one of my earliest memories is of his boat. I could always see and I loved what Jik told me of the life he lived."

She stopped abruptly. Thad looked at her sympathetically. "And the reality has not been quite what you expected has it?"

"How did you know?"

"If you were happy you wouldn't be breaking poor Nemle's heart."

"What do you mean?" Marheh stared at him.

"You know very well what I mean, or you would if you thought about it."

Marheh was silent for a moment or two. "But she scolds me … and she won't teach me to steer."

He looked at her and laughed. "Are you really such a baby as that? You obviously have a loving family. Did your parents never scold you?"

"Yes of course. They love me."

"And you think Nemle does it for fun do you?" He pushed his chair back from the table in a sudden movement. "Up you get girl, dishes time. I'll dry and put away."

Marheh stood up slowly and began to gather up their dishes.

On *Day Bringer*, Kithla was washing dishes too. She had insisted that Nemle sit and rest and she was enjoying the familiar task in the unfamiliar surroundings. The galley was so small and compact compared with the big kitchen she was used to. From the sink she only needed to stretch out a hand and the kettle was there, hooks for mugs, cupboard for crockery, all within reach. She made everything tidy and went to perch on the footstool beside Nemle.

"You're worried, aren't you?" she said softly.

Nemle smiled at her. "Thank you for doing that."

Kithla waited.

"Yes, I'm worried," Nemle admitted. "But I'd best try not to be, because it isn't very useful."

"Marheh seems very … young," Kithla ventured.

Nemle put out a hand and patted her shoulder. "You've had troubles that have made you grow up very quickly," she said. "How do you like your trousers?" she added, wanting to turn the subject. She would not discuss Marheh with Kithla.

"I don't feel like myself at all," Kithla said. "But I like it."

Nemle smiled. "What would you like to do this evening? Marheh sometimes goes for a walk after tea, but it is a bit dark for that now."

Kithla looked at Nemle. "Would you be too tired to tell me about *Day Bringer*, when she was made, what she has done, things like that, as if I was really an apprentice?"

"Not a bit tired," Nemle said. "Are you comfy there?"

Kithla leaned back against the arm of Nemle's chair and stretched out her legs to the fire. "Very comfy," she said.

There was a moment of silence while Nemle gathered her thoughts. Then she began.

"*Day Bringer* was the third Silberay boat to be built. First was Sila's boat, *Morning Star*, then Lor's boat, *Tempest*. *Day Bringer* was built for Rinteh." She paused a moment then continued. The names of the women of the Silberay who had lived on her and loved her were so familiar she scarcely needed to think; Rinteh, Tala, Hafa, Nemle and now Marheh. Perhaps one day Marheh would want to know of her predecessors too. The old log books in Rinteh's elegant cursive script were there in the archive at the Harbour. 'She is to be called *Day Bringer*," Rinteh had written on the first page. 'Each day a new start, fresh light, hope.' It would have been different then, only three boats. Even with a new one in the water every couple of months it was years before that first pioneering group were all afloat. No engines either, the boats were pulled along from the bank with a line from the centre of the roof. You had to be strong to do that, but there was seldom any need for haste and there was much less water road to travel. An apprentice learned a lot about the disciplines trudging along in all weathers while the mentor stood on the deck and steered.

Nemle smiled to herself and wondered whether Marheh would have been happier under that regime. The women's boats on the whole had more peaceful, optimistic names than the men's; *Tempest*, *Storm Cloud*, *Autumn Wind* seemed to suggest the rougher aspects of the natural world, but just at the moment Marheh seemed more of a *Storm Cloud* than a *Day Bringer*.

"What was it like when you were an apprentice?" Kithla asked as Nemle appeared to be lost in thought.

"Well, I didn't have to pull on a rope, at least not often. *Day Bringer* was fitted with her engine by the time I joined Hafa, but she had pulled for

Tala. I loved being an apprentice. Hafa encouraged me and I wanted to serve her because she was always appreciative. I don't mean she was soft, or unwilling to work herself. She was perhaps more of a thinker than I am. I learned so much from her, and now I have an apprentice myself she is still teaching me."

The trouble was, Nemle thought, Marheh was so different to the apprentice she had been that some of Hafa's lessons were inappropriate. Times had changed too. Marheh seemed to have different expectations.

Marheh finished the dishes and wiped down the sink. She had a feeling that Kithla's father would not show Nemle's restraint if she skimped on the job. When she had finished he inspected her work quite openly. Rather as if she was a new maid, Marheh thought indignantly.

"Just give the table another wipe over," he said. "Then off to bed with you."

At the sight of Marheh's face he gave a short laugh. "Don't scowl at me lassie. You asked to be my daughter. I'm not going to spoil you."

"But it's too early to go to bed," Marheh said, giving the table a cursory wipe with her dishcloth.

"Well do your lessons, read a book, try on Kithla's clothes, but do it upstairs. If you're going to take my Kithla's place you will need to be down by six o'clock to start breakfast."

Marheh sighed rather pointedly and hung up her dishcloth.

Thad laughed again. "All the world is against you is it? You thought you were headed for adventure and all you get is more housework."

"It's always housework and I hate it," Marheh said passionately.

"Life has lots of housework of one kind or another," he said. "It isn't worth hating it. Do it as well as you can and get on with the next thing."

Marheh looked as if she wanted to throw something at him. "There's much more to life than housework," she said. "And I'll find it." She made for the door and turned back when she reached it. "Good night," she said emphatically. "And I don't care if you don't sleep well."

The sound of his laughter followed her up the stairs until she shut it out by slamming the door of Kithla's bedroom.

Kithla enjoyed the experience of Marheh's tiny cabin, lingering over her preparations for bed so as to savour every minute. It had been a quiet evening, interesting in an undemanding way, but she could see that she would miss her books if she stayed for long. Marheh only had room for half a dozen, though these were very well thumbed. Tomorrow she and Nemle were planning some plant hunting and Nemle would teach her more about the medicines she made. She took off Marheh's clothes and folded them carefully, slipped into Marheh's nightdress, blew out her candle and stood by the window looking out. There was a moon, not full, but on the way, and the sky was mostly clear. She could see the glint of light on the water as well as the pale fields and darker hedges on the opposite bank. You were so close to everything, she thought, not like the view from the bedroom window at home. She could feel *Day Bringer* rock gently as Nemle moved about in the saloon and was glad she was nearby. A moment later she stepped back from the window hastily, not quite believing what she was seeing. Across the water, hugging the opposite bank was a big canoe. As far as she could see it held only one person, paddling slowly and carefully. For a moment the paddler paused and stared at *Day Bringer*, a large pale face catching the moonlight, then the paddling continued faster as the canoe passed *Day Bringer* and disappeared into the night.

For a moment Kithla stood still gazing after the canoe then she began to make her way back through the engine room and the bathroom to Nemle who was still doing some quiet tidying in the saloon. The curtains were drawn and a single lamp gave a soft warm glow to the small cosy space. She looked around as Kithla appeared in the doorway.

"What's the matter? Can't you sleep?" she asked. "Is the bed too hard?"

"I haven't got into it yet," Kithla said, and told Nemle what she had seen.

"You're safe in *Day Bringer*," Nemle said. "She protects us."

"I didn't feel afraid," Kithla said. "But what does it mean?"

"Just that our enemies are watching us," Nemle said. "That they are still nearby."

"Perhaps Marheh will have her adventure then," Kithla said softly.

Nemle looked at her for a moment. "I'm afraid she will," she said heavily. "I'm afraid she will."

"Your mentor is both parent and teacher, especially in the early years of your apprenticeship. It is your responsibility to be both obedient and diligent. Thus you will ready yourself for the deeper understanding of the Silberay way your mentor will offer."

The Silberay apprentice : a handbook

Chapter Nine

Upstairs in Kithla's bedroom Marheh changed quickly into Kithla's nightdress, but she was much too keyed up to think of sleep. The nightdress was much prettier than her own very utilitarian garments and she spent a moment admiring her reflection in the dark window. She spun around and around and landed lightly on the bed, the biggest bed she had ever slept in, for even at home her room was small with just enough room for a little single bed along with a chest for her clothes and a small bookcase.

She bounced a little then sprawled out luxuriously. Kithla's father was mean to laugh at her but she would show him, show them all. They wouldn't laugh at her when she brought Dyti and the little boy home. She drifted into a dream of her success, picturing herself leading them, one in each hand and perhaps a trail of others behind, home to rejoicing parents and friends.

She was just listening to a speech in her honour when she saw Nemle's face. She rolled over to hide her own face in the pillows. Wisdom and humility, Nemle had said. Marheh felt herself blushing. Here she was admiring herself in the window and day dreaming when what she ought to be doing was practicing the disciplines. She got up, wrapped herself in Kithla's dressing gown and went to sit in the chair. Ten minutes practicing the discipline of the soul, Nemle had said that morning. Breathing deeply she closed her eyes and looked for the candle flame she had been working with before. It was slow in coming and she could not move beyond it, but the attempt steadied her.

When she opened her eyes again she was content to choose one of Kithla's books, climb into bed with it and read until she was ready for sleep.

Next morning she was only half an hour late getting down stairs. Thad had put the kettle on and was making porridge.

"Not good enough girl," he said when she appeared.

"I overslept."

She reached for Kithla's pinafore from behind the door, but he shook his head. "Pinafore for outdoors in the garden, apron for cooking. Come and stir the porridge."

Without trusting herself to speak Marheh put on the apron and took over the wooden spoon in the porridge pot.

"Cat got your tongue? What happened to 'good morning father, did you sleep well?'" Marheh looked scathingly at him and he laughed. "Come on girl, smile. I'm only teasing." He rolled his chair away across to the table and sat watching her in silence as she stirred.

After a few moments she looked at him. "Good morning father," she said, managing a little smile. "Did you sleep well?"

"Very well Kithla dear," he said, smiling now. "And you?"

"Too well," Marheh said. "As you observed."

She found the bowls, ladled a generous helping of porridge into each and brought them across to the table.

When they had finished eating Thad pushed back from the table a little and gazed thoughtfully at Marheh. "So what if they don't come back?" he asked. "They may not. I was pretty definite in refusing their offer."

"Then I suppose we'll have to try something else," Marheh said slowly. "But it is too soon to give up. Maybe they'll try to talk to me. They didn't see Kithla when they came before did they?"

"I don't like it," he said gathering up their bowls and wheeling himself to the sink. "Sperit?" he asked, putting out mugs without waiting for an answer.

"What?" Marheh asked. "What don't you like?"

"The idea of you going off with them. They looked very fine on the surface, but I just didn't take to them. I wouldn't think of telling them my soul name."

"I don't know any name for you," Marheh said.

He grinned at her. "Father will do for you," he said. "But you'd better know that Kithla is Kathleen for those who don't use the soul name."

"Kathleen," Marheh repeated. "Yes, I needed to know that. I don't think Yareblis use the soul name. They deny the soul." She took the mug of sperit he handed her and smiled her thanks. "What do you think I should do today? I don't know anything about gardening."

"Don't worry, I'll put you to work." He drew his eyebrows together with mock ferocity. "Don't cook, don't garden! What sort of useless female are you? You'll learn … or else!"

Kithla and Nemle enjoyed a quiet breakfast together sitting in the well deck in the morning sun. Kithla had not slept much, the bed was hard and narrow and the breeze that had developed over night caused *Day Bringer* to move gently against her moorings in a way that was quite disconcerting.

Nemle smiled at her. "The boat can take a bit of getting used to, especially if you are used to more space."

"I'm enjoying it though," Kithla said hastily. "It seems so much a part of everything."

Nemle nodded. She was quite pre-occupied, worrying about Marheh and wondering what was best to do while they were waiting for something to happen. She nodded again as if she had made up her mind about something then turned to Kithla. "Since they seem to be watching us we need to show we have a reason for staying here. It won't be a bad thing to be a bit nearer the village either, so we'll take a basket and a couple of sacks and go off for the day."

"What about *Day Bringer*?" Kithla asked. "Will it matter leaving her for so long?"

"I don't like doing it," Nemle said. "But in general they leave the boats alone. Their boats are so much more manoeuvrable that disabling ours is not much of an advantage. I'm more concerned that Marheh might come to find us, but it is a bit soon for that I think."

She sighed and held out her hand for Kithla's mug and bowl, but Kithla shook her head. "You stay here. I know you have things to think about." She stood up and took Nemle's dishes with her. "I'm happy washing up. It still feels like part of the fun of being here."

Nemle let her go. It would give her a few minutes alone to enter the soul discipline and work on some protection for Marheh.

Thad had set Marheh to work weeding in one of the herb beds. Although he had shown her what to look for it seemed to her that herbs and weeds had a great deal in common and she spent more time trying to decide whether a plant was to come out than actually pulling. Never-the-less she looked as if she was working so it seemed better to err on the side of caution and let Kithla complete the job later.

The day went past very slowly and Marheh was soon bored. When evening came and no return visit from the Yareblis she was disappointed and inclined to be restless and irritable. Thad tried to tease her out of her bad mood, but it was hard work and in the end he told her to grow up and sent her to bed. Kithla on the other hand was happy helping Nemle with the day's harvest and for her the time passed quickly.

The second day passed much like the first, but on the morning of the third day, when Marheh was once again making a half-hearted attempt to weed in the garden, there was a call from the side gate and a man and a woman pushed their way through.

Thad was out of the greenhouse and blocking the path with his chair before they had taken more than a step. "What do you think you are doing pushing your way in here?" he said belligerently. "I thought I told you we weren't interested."

The woman spoke sweetly. "We thought perhaps, for your daughter's sake you might have thought it over."

"I have and the answer is still no."

The man spoke then, looking earnestly at Thad. "It would be greatly to her advantage you know. Could we not speak with her?"

"No, she's busy."

"Is that her in the garden?" The woman lifted the fine net veil that covered her face and looked at Thad intently with unreadable eyes of very pale blue. "Why don't you call her?"

"Why should I? She's busy," he said, but it was difficult to say and he thought suddenly that resistance would be a battle. Just as well he did not plan to resist for ever.

"Such a fine daughter," the man said. "I'm sure she is a great help to you."

"Indeed she is," Thad said.

"Do call her," the woman urged. "At least let us meet her."

"Oh if you must," Thad said. "She can tell you herself that she is not interested." He raised his voice and bellowed. "Kathleen, Kathleen, I want you!"

Marheh had been staring at the visitors from the garden bed where she had been pretending to work. Now she dropped her tools and came running. "You called father?" she said, a little breathlessly.

He thought how young she looked, dusty pinafore, untidy hair and a smudge of dirt on her cheek. "Tell these people that you don't want their scholarship."

There was silence. Marheh's face fell. "Must I father?"

"What do you mean must I?"

"I thought perhaps after what you said last time…" She broke off.

"Come on then, what did you think?"

"'It, it might be … I might …"

"Spit it out girl."

"I'd like to go father, if you can spare me," she said.

The man and the woman looked at each other.

"And what if I can't spare you eh?"

"Then of course I won't leave you father," Marheh said, disappointment evident in her tone.

"A fine daughter," the man said again.

The glance Thad gave Marheh was a cautionary one. Don't over do it, he might have been saying.

"Suppose you tell us a little of what she might expect if I was to let her go with you," Thad said.

The man and the woman looked at each other again then the woman spoke. "We are just a small school," the woman said. "So we can offer individual tuition to talented students. The scholarship would be for three months at first and extended if she does well."

"As I am sure she will," the man slipped in smoothly.

"All our children have their own rooms and every facility to help them achieve," the woman went on. "I myself supervise their physical well being."

"Could I father?" Marheh said. "Just for three months."

"Supposing I was to say yes," he said. "When would you want her?"

"We would like to take her with us today," the woman said. "I know it is short notice but…"

"Impossible!" Thad interrupted. "She has jobs to do."

"Come now," the man said. "Isn't she worth a little sacrifice?"

"What would you know about sacrifice?" Thad said. "Kathleen. You go up stairs and put together a few things you might wish to take IF I let you go. I will talk a little more before I decide."

"Oh thank you father," Marheh said. She nodded to the visitors, her eyes bright and curious, then she hurried away.

"So!" Thad said when they had watched her round the side of the house and through the back door. "So what's in it for you?"

"What do you mean?" the woman asked.

"You can't tell me this all about philanthropy."

"But that is exactly what it is," the woman said, sweet and patronising. "We simply administer a trust set up to benefit young people who otherwise might not have a chance to develop their ability."

Thad gave a sceptical grunt. He was rather enjoying himself. "So where is this school? Why haven't I heard of it? I suppose I may visit her?"

"Not initially," the woman said. "We find that visits unsettle the children, but we will of course keep you informed of her progress."

"Well I don't know," Thad said doubtfully and lapsed into silence.

Upstairs Marheh was cramming some of Kithla's underclothes and a nightdress into a cloth bag she had found hanging behind the door. She was very excited, moving with little dancing steps and occasionally quivering all over. She knew she must communicate with Nemle, but try as she would she could not calm herself enough to find the concentration she needed. She had a moment of panic. She had to go now. What if she could not reach Nemle? She tried again, but focus would not come. Again a wave of panic, but she shrugged it off and ran downstairs with her bag. Surely she would have another chance to try.

Hugging the bag in front of her she came to stand before Thad. The man and the woman stood silently by.

"Please father," she said.

He looked up. "Three months, you want to go and leave me and the garden for three months?"

She nodded. "Please father," she said again.

"Very well," he said after a short silence. "Mind you're a good girl and study hard."

"Oh yes father," she said.

He took one of her plaits and gave it a little tug. "Well then, don't I get a kiss goodbye."

"Oh thank you father," she said, leaning down to him.

She stood up straight again and looked to the man and the woman.

"You've made a very wise decision sir," the man said.

"We'll take good care of her," the woman added. "Come along Kathleen."

Marheh moved with them towards the gate, looked back over her shoulder to Thad. Something in that look made him say gruffly. "I'm coming to wave goodbye girl. Three months is not forever."

Together they moved through the gate and into the front garden. There, standing beside the stone wall, was a horse and trap. Marheh gave a little gasp and looked again at Thad. How could Nemle follow her if she went off in a horse and trap?

"Chin up girl," Thad said. "It's an adventure."

"Quite right sir," the man said, taking Marheh's bag and helping her to climb into the trap. He helped his companion to a place beside her and then got up himself and took the reins. Slowly the horse moved off. Marheh, rather white and a little tremulous, looked back over her shoulder to where Thad sat. He waved once more then gave her a quick thumbs up sign.

Nemle and Kithla were just leaving *Day Bringer* to begin the day's plant hunting when Nemle felt Marheh's momentary panic. She paused, concentrating. Kithla was a few steps ahead. Nemle hurried to catch up as Marheh's second wave of panic reached her. Kithla turned and saw the trouble on her face.

"It's begun," Nemle said, answering her unspoken question. She stopped again, her hand on Kithla's shoulder, focusing in the hope of receiving some communication from Marheh beyond the knowledge of her fear. Then she shook her head. "Nothing," she said, more to herself than Kithla. "Nothing." She took a moment to steady herself then spoke evenly. "We must go to your father, find out what has happened."

Kithla nodded and together they made their way as fast as they could up the hill and into the lane. They had hardly gone more than a hundred yards along the lane when they heard the sound of hooves. They looked at each other then moved quickly to the verge, not really knowing what was coming, but wanting to avoid being noticed. Nemle grunted a little as she rolled under the hedge, but there was no time for finesse. They were scarcely hidden when the horse came trotting by, the trap rocking along behind on the uneven surface. They watched it out of sight.

"She looked a bit uncomfortable," Kithla said at last.

"We'd better keep moving," Nemle said. "Find out what your father knows." She looked at Kithla. "I think you'll have to help me get up. I'm too old for hiding under bushes."

Kithla scrambled to her feet and gave Nemle her hands. She grunted again and made a joke of it, but Kithla could hear her breathing hard and sensed a degree of discomfort as she struggled to her feet. However she would not rest and set a fair pace as they stepped out again, heading for the cottage.

When they reached the village they found Thad still in the front garden.

"I thought you might be along," he said.

Kithla ran to give him a hug and turned the chair to wheel it around the back.

"She's a good girl, your lassie."

"Yes," Nemle said, then smiled at Kithla. "And so is your lassie."

Kithla waited until Nemle and Thad were in the kitchen, sitting around the table, then she went to boil the kettle.

"They took her off in a trap," Thad said. "She wasn't expecting that."

"We saw her father," Kithla said. "They were going down Meadow Sweet Lane as we were coming here. We had to hide."

"The lane," Nemle asked. "It goes to Fairdale Rising doesn't it?"

Thad nodded.

"So they could be anywhere," Nemle said. "No reason for them to stay near the water road."

Kithla put mugs of sperit on the table. "What shall we do?" she asked. "We have to find her."

Nemle sat silent, staring into her mug so that Kithla and her father fell silent also. When at last she spoke however she seemed to have regained her strength and resolve.

"I'm sure Marheh will manage to contact me somehow, but in the mean time I think I am going to plan for some help." She looked from Kithla to Thad. "I'm sure the Travellers are still in Fairdale Wood," she said. "I don't think they would move on while they hope to find Trodkali. They can travel overland without any suspicion though. I'm going to find them and ask for their help."

It seemed to Marheh, as her journey went on and on, that she was getting further and further from any chance of rescue. She sat awkwardly, clinging to her bag with one hand and her seat with the other and tried to gain a sense of where they were heading, but the little lanes twisted about and they seemed to avoid any well travelled roads. Once they passed through a small village, but even there she only saw one or two incurious bystanders, otherwise it was as if they were alone in the world. Her companions were silent as if they needed to take no trouble now they had accomplished their objective. Marheh ventured one or two curious glances at the woman beside her, but she had replaced her veil and seemed remote and unreadable.

At last the trotting horse was steadied back to a walk and they turned and stopped before a farm gate. Beyond was a short drive leading to a big farm house.

"Shall I get down and open the gate?" Marheh asked tentatively.

The woman looked at her as if surprised that she could speak.

The man nodded. "If you think you can," he said.

Leaving her bundle on the seat, she scrambled down and went, a bit stiffly, to the gate. It opened easily and she pulled it back, glad to be on the ground again. The horse and trap moved slowly through and she fastened it behind them before climbing up to her seat again.

On they went, still at walking pace. The farm house was built from warm red brick. There were many chimneys sprouting from the sloping slate roof. The drive divided as it approached the house and they took the left hand branch which passed the side of the house and led into the farmyard. The horse stopped of its own accord and there was silence for a few moments. Marheh looked around curiously. The yard was enclosed on three sides by the house and two big barns. There were no animal smells here, no chickens pecking the hard, dry surface of the yard, no small black and white dog. Instead everything was swept and empty, but the most striking thing was not the rather sterile yard, but the doors, two in each building, each painted a strident, artificial green that shouted at the warm red bricks and leached what colour there was from the pale, sandy paving where they waited.

The woman turned to Marheh. "Here we are Kathleen," she said. "Your new home."

It ought to have been welcoming, Marheh thought, but it sounded more as if it was an appropriate expression imperfectly learned. The man got down and helped the woman to alight. Marheh scrambled down before he came around to her and stood hugging her bundle.

"Come," said the woman, and Marheh followed her through one of the green doors in one of the barns. They went into a wide hall, up a flight of stairs and into a neat, well furnished bedroom.

"This will be your room," the woman said. "You can settle in now and someone will come for you in half an hour."

She had gone, shutting the door behind her, almost before Marheh had time to acknowledge her remark. Left alone, Marheh stood for a minute looking around, her heart beating fast. Bed, chest of drawers, little table, chair, she catalogued the furniture in her mind then walked across to the window. Her room was at the back and looked over fields and a pattern of hedges. The countryside was flat with few trees and she could see a long way. Far on her right was a small dwelling, beyond it a copse, on the horizon were a couple of chimneys and a spire spiked the sky above a clump of firs, on her left was a line of trees in the distance that might have bordered a lane or a drive, but in the centre, far away, was something that glinted in the sun. She looked at it longingly. Perhaps, just perhaps, it might be the water road.

Turning away at last, she emptied her bundle into one of the drawers and sat down in the chair. Now perhaps she could find her focus.

Nemle was sitting quietly in the warm kitchen as Kithla prepared some food for them all. She was thinking and planning and reaching out to Marheh. Kithla and her father worked quietly around her, understanding her need for silence. Suddenly she looked up, smiled.

"Green doors," she said, surprised, puzzled. "Marheh has sent me a picture of green doors."

"We have discovered that our ability to
communicate between minds is something that
can be developed with practice, but along with
this comes the ability to control minds. I find this
very disturbing and fear that we may be tempted
to use this power for our own ends."

Sila's journal : the early years

Chapter Ten

"You can't go wandering around Fairdale Woods today Mama Nemle," Kithla's father said, as they sat around the kitchen table finishing their late lunch.

"I suppose it would be foolish," Nemle said. "I would not be back to *Day Bringer* before dark."

"Couldn't I go for you?" Kithla asked.

Nemle smiled her thanks, but shook her head. "The Travellers know me. I'm a kind of Traveller too. They can be a bit suspicious of house dwellers."

"So what will you do?" Kithla's father asked. "And how can we help?"

"I think I'll spend the rest of the day taking *Day Bringer* back to the mooring by the woods," Nemle said. "Then I'll have her protection tonight and be ready to go looking for the Travellers in the morning."

"Shall I come with you?" Kithla asked. "Could I be useful?"

Nemle was silent, considering. She knew she would be best alone overnight for she planned to spend time practicing the disciplines in the hope of reaching out to give Marheh protection, but she sensed Kithla would be disappointed if her part was to finish now.

"Will you come with me back to *Day Bringer*?" she said at last. "I'd be grateful for your company on the walk. Then you could help turn *Day Bringer* and travel back with me as far as the village mooring."

Kithla flushed with pleasure. "That would be alright, wouldn't it father?" she said happily.

Marheh sat in her room thinking of Nemle and the advice she had been given and hoping food would be on the agenda when she was sent for. She had not long to wait. A brisk knock and the door opened to reveal a boy of about sixteen, smartly dressed in a brown suit with a neat collar and tie.

"I'm Samuel," he said. "I'm to take you to the dining room."

Marheh stood up to shake hands and follow him down the stairs, across the yard and into the farmhouse. The door from the yard opened directly into a big room. Two long tables ran the length of the room and there was a shorter one running cross ways furthest from the door. Samuel obviously felt his work was done having brought her for he disappeared to go to his place at one of the long tables. Marheh stood awkwardly inside the door as the eyes of all the diners turned to look at her.

"Your place will be up here today Kathleen."

It was the woman who had brought her. Red-faced and feeling too conspicuous, Marheh walked the length of the room and sat down where the woman had indicated. A bowl of soup was placed in front of her and she was thankful to occupy herself with eating, ignoring the curious glances coming from the two long tables.

There were about twenty children sitting at the tables. Some looked quite young and Marheh remembered that Trodkali was only ten. She wondered which was he, and which of the girls was Dyti. So far nothing very threatening had happened and the thought crossed her mind that they had been mistaken in their ideas and this really was a school Kithla could have attended.

Her soup bowl was replaced by a plate with a lamb cutlet, mashed potato and green peas. She was hungry and the food was excellent so she gave it her full attention. This did not seem like any school dinner she had ever experienced. The room was quiet, the children neatly dressed and well mannered. The only adults present, two men and the woman who had brought her, had no need to exert their authority and ate quietly along with everyone else. The only difference in their menu seemed to be the opportunity to enjoy a glass of wine with their meal, whereas the children, Marheh included, had water or lemonade.

When the meal was ended there were some announcements which seemed to be about classes and other activities, then the children filed out with the two men. Marheh was left with the woman.

"Now Kathleen," she said. "First we need to find you some clothes."

Marheh looked up in surprise.

"How old are you Kathleen?" the woman asked.

"Sixteen."

"Much too old for these." The woman fingered the pinafore Marheh wore disdainfully. "And perhaps we can find you a more grown up hairstyle." She stood up. "Come," she said imperiously and set off with Marheh scurrying behind.

A few minutes later she found herself in a large room she thought could perhaps be described as a boudoir. It was luxuriously carpeted and furnished with a sofa as well as a large bed, mirrors, closets, dressing table and a pretty decorated screen in one corner. Marheh stood and stared as the woman rang a bell and waited, tapping one foot and studying Marheh impatiently.

Two more women entered the room, curtsied and stood to attention one beside the other. "Servants," Marheh thought, surprised. They were dressed alike in plain dark grey; both were of middle age, pale with strangely empty faces. Marheh tried a small, rather tentative smile, but it was not returned.

"She needs a bath," the woman said, still looking at Marheh.

"Me!" Marheh said indignantly. The two servants stepped one on either side of her.

"I washed this morning," Marheh said, trying to free herself from their firm, impersonal grip.

"Kathleen!" The woman's voice was sharp, imperious.

Marheh stopped struggling.

"Bring her back when she is clean," the woman said.

The two servants frog-marched Marheh behind the screen where there was a large tub and began to undress her.

"I can do it myself," she tried to tell them. "I can do it myself."

The pinafore and the dress were soon gone and one of the servants held her on a chair while the other dealt with her boots and stockings. Marheh was beside herself.

"How dare you!" she shouted and flung a command from her mind at the one who held her.

The servant stepped back hastily and Marheh was about to repeat her action with the other servant when she remembered Nemle's words. "They **must not** discover that you already practice the discipline of the mind". She hesitated. The first servant came back to hold her again. Surely Nemle did not expect her to put up with being humiliated like this, but Marheh knew that Nemle did expect it. Abruptly she stopped struggling.

"I'm sorry," she said, looking from one to the other. "Please may I undress myself?"

The blank pale faces did not respond and the firm, capable hands continued to strip her until she was naked, but although her eyes filled with tears her act of acceptance had given her back some dignity. She submitted to being put in the tub and washed, thoroughly washed as if she were a small child, face and hands, ears, neck, fingernails, nothing was overlooked. They even unfastened her plaits and washed her hair. She hated it, but strangely she found that she could not hate the two servants with their empty, impassive faces.

When they were satisfied they hoisted her out of the tub and dried her as thoroughly as she had been washed. Then they took her, pink and scrubbed, back to the woman, who had obviously spent the period of Marheh's bath in gathering up clothes. There was a pile of pretty, lacy underwear on the bed and a dress of rich, dark blue draped over a chair. She took no notice of Marheh, who, scarlet with embarrassment, was trying to shake off her two attendants.

"These should fit," she said, holding up white silk knickers and a matching chemise. She passed them across to the nearest servant who held the knickers for Marheh to step into and then pulled the chemise over her head. She felt a bit more comfortable after that and allowed herself to be attired in all the appropriate underwear without any further protest. They wrapped her in a pale blue dressing gown and sat her down to attend to her hair, applying curling tongs and gathering up the resultant curls with a loose blue ribbon. Then, at last, the dress was eased carefully over her hair and fastened. The fabric was soft and rich, with a sheen that gave the blue deep, mysterious folds as well as highlights of a brighter shade. The woman stood back and observed while one of the servants tweaked the neckline to reveal a glimpse of white lace and settled the low waist more evenly. At last she was satisfied.

"Now you look more appropriate," she said, leading Marheh to the long cheval mirror.

Nothing she had known before prepared Marheh for what she saw there. Mirrors had not been significant in her life to date. Neither at home, nor in her cabin on *Day Bringer*, had she had more than a small square that was enough to check her face was clean and her hair tidy. Now she did not recognise herself in the slim, beautifully clad figure that she saw in the glass.

"Very nice," the woman said. "See you continue that way."

Marheh was not given long to look at her new self for a moment later there was a knock at the door and Samuel was admitted.

"Samuel is our head boy," the woman said. "He will show you around and explain something of our philosophy."

Feeling completely unreal Marheh followed Samuel out of the room. He waited for her with rather distant politeness and they walked side by side down the steps and back through the now empty dining room into the yard. Half a dozen younger children were taking exercise there. They did not look unhappy, but their activity was conducted in unnatural silence and with a restraint that matched their neat attire. Only one young boy behaved as Marheh would have expected a child to behave, running and jumping, kicking at the dusty ground, pushing the child in front and giving an occasional yell that Marheh thought sounded like frustration.

"Trod is quite new here," Samuel said. "He will settle into our ways in a day or so."

"But he's just behaving like a boy," Marheh said incautiously. "What's wrong with that?"

"It is inappropriate," said Samuel, sounding more like sixty than sixteen.

Marheh thought perhaps he was also referring to her remark and told herself to be careful and keep her mouth closed. They stood and watched for a few moments more and Marheh saw the boy fall in behind the other children and keep step with them, but she was aware of resistance in every line of his body. Poor little prisoner, she thought and remembered suddenly why she was there.

"Come this way," Samuel said coldly and they went towards the other barn that Marheh had not yet entered. "These are classrooms," he said and they stood for a minute and looked in at another group of neat well mannered children, slightly older than the first group.

"We older ones meet here sometimes," he said, indicating an empty classroom. "But more often we have small tutorials or individual tuition."

He looked at her and she thought she detected a hint of malice. "I expect you will spend quite some time with SW, especially at first."

Marheh shivered unexpectedly. "Who is SW?" she asked, managing to keep her voice even and only slightly interested.

"Senior Woman," Samuel said. "You've just come from her room."

"Oh," Marheh said.

After lunch Nemle and Kithla walked back to *Day Bringer*. Nemle was tired and pre-occupied and Kithla slowed her steps on purpose, very conscious of her weariness. As they climbed the stile from the lane into the field Kithla reached up to steady her.

"Do you have to move today?" she asked anxiously. "You would be less weary in the morning."

Nemle took her arm and rested a moment. "I need to be doing something," she said.

Kithla nodded and they continued slowly down the hill to *Day Bringer*. As she stepped on board some of Nemle's weariness seemed to fall away and Kithla realised anew just how much her home meant to her.

"Shall I make a drink?" Kithla said. "While you have a few minutes rest?"

"I don't need a rest," Nemle said. "Best if we get under way, then you can make us a drink."

She went through to the engine room, Kithla following.

"Can I help with anything else?" she asked.

Nemle was already bending over the engine and checking the oil.

"I'll just finish here," she said, wiping the dipstick and putting it back. "Then I'll come and show you what to do with the front line."

Kithla glowed with pleasure. She felt sorry if Marheh was in danger, but she could not help enjoying being with Nemle on *Day Bringer*.

After a few more minutes Nemle finished her engine checks and led Kithla outside. She showed her how to extract the mooring pin, coil the front line and push out the bow as she stepped on board.

"But not until I've started the engine," she said. "We need to know we can control her before we let her loose."

Kithla was all serious attention, but her eyes were bright and happy as Nemle left her to go and start the engine.

Soon they were under way. Kithla coiled her rope and left the mooring pin in the well deck before edging her way along the gunnel to Nemle at the tiller.

"We have to go on to the turning place," Nemle explained. "But it isn't far. We'll have sperit after that."

She was pushing *Day Bringer* a bit faster than her normal walking pace, but she was anxious to reach Fairdale Woods before dark. Kithla saw the village mooring approach with regret, but she jumped off as Nemle pulled in and stood waving her out of sight. For a few more days she would continue to wear Marheh's apprentice uniform as Nemle had asked, but she felt as if her contribution was over. Slowly she walked up through the field to the village. Her father needed her although he was so independent and she loved him and wanted to be with him, but she could not help wishing things had been different.

Samuel led Marheh into a small, cosy sitting room on the floor above the classrooms. Although the day was not really cold there was a small fire in the grate and the late afternoon sun slanted through the windows onto a polished table and across a patterned rug before the fire.

"This is my study," he said complacently.

"It's very nice," Marheh said sitting carefully in a chair by the fire.

"It is one of my privileges."

He sat in a chair opposite and studied her, looking her up and down quite openly.

"It is very nice," Marheh said again trying not to show her discomfort at his scrutiny. He is only a boy, she told herself, just a rude little boy.

"You know why you are here of course," he said at last.

Marheh just looked her question.

"You can see the drain," he said.

Marheh looked puzzled.

"The water," he said. "We can all see it. That means we are potential leaders. We can control the others. We are the powerful ones." His voice rose with his enthusiasm.

Marheh said nothing, just continued to look questioningly at him.

He reached out and rang a bell. "I'll show you," he said.

A moment or two later the door opened and a thin grey man stood in the doorway. Marheh saw in him the same empty face she had seen in the two women. He stepped into the room and stood waiting.

"Our leaders have emptied his mind so that I can command it," Samuel said.

The man turned in a slow circle and left the room.

"You see," Samuel said, pleased with himself. "Of course I only do easy things so far, but I'm learning."

"But why?" Marheh whispered, her eyes large and dark with horror.

Samuel stood up and stretched. "We have the potential. We have been given the power to command. It is our right and responsibility to use it."

"Right and responsibility," Marheh echoed. She hardly knew how to respond without revealing herself.

"The farmer here was lazy," Samuel went on. "Our leaders saw that they could make better use of the farm and make the farmer productive. They took control. The farm is our school and the farmer our servant. That is responsible use of our ability," he finished proudly.

Marheh closed her eyes and thought briefly of Nemle's words 'the discipline of the mind is a two edged sword that can be used for good or evil'. No wonder Silberay were forbidden to use it except against the Yareblis. She opened her eyes to find Samuel looking at her strangely.

"It doesn't seem right," she said at last, knowing she could not hide her feelings completely enough to be convincing.

Samuel looked patronisingly at her.

"That's because you haven't thought about it properly," he said. "We learn how to behave, how to dress, good manners. We fit ourselves for power. One day you might be SW, I might be Senior Man. We have privilege now because we are born to it and later because we take the responsibility."

He's only a little boy, Marheh thought, looking at him. He doesn't know what he's saying and then she thought, but he has learned it very well. Despite the fire and the sunshine she felt cold all through.

"The leaders," she said, knowing she must say something. "Are they the three who were at lunch?"

"That's right, SW, SM and SP."

"SP?"

"School Principal."

"Don't they have names?"

Samuel gave her a condescending smile. "Of course not. Names would undermine the power. When we grow into our power we will relinquish our names too."

He went to the door. "Time to go," he said. "SW wants you."

Again Marheh caught a hint of malice. She passed through the door ahead of him and felt an almost overwhelming longing for Nemle and *Day Bringer*.

Once Nemle had said goodbye to Kithla, her thoughts turned almost immediately to Marheh. She was afraid for her as she had never been for herself. Steering did not require a great deal of her attention, but enough so that she could not lose herself in the disciplines as she would have liked. She could listen for Marheh though and absorb the golden afternoon as a source of calm and beauty to be called on when trouble came. She had always loved the slanting light and long shadows of late afternoon or early morning and she set herself to appreciate them anew as *Day Bringer* carried her through the landscape.

She reached Fairdale Woods just as the sun was setting, but continued past to the next turning place. By the time she had turned and come back to moor it was almost dark and beginning to be chilly. She moored quickly and hurried down to the saloon. Kithla had built up the fire and left a big pot of vegetables simmering on a low heat. Nemle was so tired she was almost past hunger, but she pushed herself to eat and was grateful. Now she had energy to enter the discipline of the soul and find protection for Marheh. She put out the lamp and sat watching the glow of the fire and drawing the darkness around her until she went beyond both fire and darkness.

Samuel escorted Marheh back to SW without speaking again. When she opened the door to them he made a little, formal bow.

"Kathleen," he said as if handing over a parcel.

SW thanked him gravely and stood back for Marheh to enter.

"May I stay?" Samuel asked and Marheh's heart turned over. What was he expecting to happen?

"Not today," SW said and he went without argument as she shut the door.

Marheh stood awkwardly in the centre of the room. SW walked slowly around her.

"Now Kathleen," she said, pausing behind Marheh. "What have you learned today?"

She continued to walk until she was facing Marheh, watching her searchingly.

"Power and responsibility," Marheh stammered at last.

"Good," said SW resuming her slow pacing.

"Whose power Kathleen?" she said abruptly.

Marheh's head jerked around to look at her.

"Stand still!" More pacing. "Whose power Kathleen?"

Marheh had no answer.

"Your power Kathleen and your responsibility."

She stopped again in front of Marheh.

"Whose power Kathleen?" she asked in a quiet, even tone.

"Mine," Marheh said when she could avoid it no longer.

"Your what Kathleen?"

"My power."

"And whose responsibility?"

"My responsibility," Marheh said, and her voice was firmer. "My responsibility for my own actions."

SW raised her eyebrows and nodded slowly. She moved away and went to take something from a drawer in her dressing table. It was only then that Marheh noticed one of the servants standing still and silent against the wall.

"Now it is time for you to take responsibility and use your power," SW said. She turned and Marheh saw she held a short wooden pointer. "Our servant needs punishment," she said. "This is your job."

As Marheh watched the servant raised her arm, extended her hand palm uppermost. Marheh looked at the blank face and for a moment thought she saw something imprisoned behind the empty eyes. SW put the pointer into Marheh's hand. "She is waiting Kathleen."

Marheh looked from SW to the servant and back to SW.

"No," she said, finding her courage. She looked at the pointer in her hand as if wondering how it got there then flung it away across the room. "No," she said again.

SW looked at Marheh, continued to look at her while the servant crossed the room to pick up the pointer, still looked at her as the pointer was put in her hand.

"You will give her punishment," SW said, offering Marheh the pointer again. "Or you will take her punishment."

Marheh looked at the servant, who again stood with outstretched palm. This was a woman who had held her, had stripped her, had humiliated her. She looked back at SW and the pointer she was offering. She took a deep breath. "No," she said.

There was a short silence. Marheh thought she could hear her own heart thumping.

"Your hand Kathleen," said SW.

For a moment Marheh thought she might resist, but her hand seemed to extend itself, her palm to stretch out in a parody of supplication. She waited for the blow.

It hurt, oh it hurt, and she gave a little, involuntary gasp. SW watched her impassively then held out the pointer again. Marheh did not trust herself to speak, but she shook her head and held her hand out again without waiting for SW's command.

Another stinging blow and again the pointer was held out to tempt her. She seemed to wait forever for the third blow, but it was the last.

"I'm very disappointed in you Kathleen," SW said coldly. "We will try again tomorrow." She went to put the pointer back in the drawer. "Go and stand by the wall until I'm ready to take you down to dinner."

Water flows clear, here, near, so dear to us.
Road runs slow, flow, low, aglow for us.
Sing the water,
Sing the road
Travel the water road.

Water shows blue, hue, true, anew for us.
Road bears boat, note, gloat, afloat for us.
Sing the water
Sing the road
Travel the water road.

Songs of the Silberay

Chapter Eleven

At first it was all Marheh could do to stand straight beside the impassive servant and keep back her tears when what she wanted to do was hide and curl up around her stinging hand and whimper for her mother or Nemle. As she began to get control of herself however she gradually became aware of the silent woman beside her. Who was she? Had she really seen a glimpse of something or someone imprisoned behind her eyes? What had they done to her? What had Samuel said, 'our leaders have emptied his mind so that I can command it'? If Samuel could communicate that way, perhaps she could too, not to command but to contact. Timidly, half frightened by what she was attempting, Marheh began to try to bring the woman into her mind as she had done with Nemle when they played with the disciplines. She did not dare turn her head to look at her for fear of SW, but she could picture the pale, blank face and the empty eyes and as she built that picture she found that she pictured herself on the edge of a vast, empty grey quadrangle. There was nothing to right nor left but far ahead a wall arose like the wall of a dam.

"Oh I'm sorry, I'm so sorry." Marheh found herself pouring a litany of passionate regret into the emptiness. "I'm so sorry for what has been done to you. I'm so sorry for what you have become. I'm so sorry, so sorry." And then, as she advanced by tiny stages into the quadrangle, "I'm so sorry for what I may do to you. I'm afraid for tomorrow. I'm sorry. I'm afraid. I'm sorry."

She advanced a little further, the pain of her hand not forgotten, but outside the focus of her concentration. Almost it seemed as if the wall had cracked a little. A fine thread of light crawled over the surface from top to bottom, but she could not stay to see if it was true. SW's cold, disapproving voice was calling for Kathleen. With a last "I'm sorry," Marheh came back into herself and followed SW meekly down the stairs to the dining room.

SW made it very plain during dinner that Marheh was in disgrace and when the meal was over she was made to stand before them all while SP scolded her for her failure to take the responsibility due to the power that was hers. SW escorted her to her bedroom and the two servants came to undress her and take away her clothes. Then SW bade her a chilly goodnight before departing, locking the door behind her. Marheh crawled into bed, lonely, hurting and frightened of what the morning might bring. She curled up under the covers and gave in to the tears that had threatened all afternoon, but the moment before she slid into sleep she thought she felt Nemle's arms around her and was comforted.

It was still dark when she awoke. In her dreams Nemle had held her all through the night and she longed to snuggle back into that warmth and love, but there was a new day ahead. For a few moments she rolled over, buried her face in the pillow and fought the fear, the tears and the knowledge of her helplessness. None of this had gone how she had expected. She had not even seen Dyti yet. The children seemed perfectly content, except the little boy, Trod, Samuel had called him. He must be Trodkali, and she had come for him.

She stretched under the covers, carefully opened and closed her swollen hand, acknowledged the fact of her nakedness and the possibility of new humiliation ahead. She had chosen this. Nemle had not wanted her to do it. Nemle would come, but perhaps not today or even tomorrow and when she did come would it be enough? She dared not think of that. The sky at her window seemed a little paler now. They might come for her at any minute. She must not waste these moments of solitude in useless regret. She stretched again, deliberately this time, reaching out, fingers and toes extended, and felt the energy run through her body. Carefully she pictured Nemle, drawing her image in her mind. Hopefully she offered the place where she was so Nemle would have knowledge of her. Then she went in search of her candle flame, trying to keep faith with Nemle, trying to enter the discipline of the soul.

She only glimpsed the place where she would go, but even the attempt calmed and strengthened her. She pulled the covers up around her and sat and watched the light spread over the sky, the colour come to life in fields and trees.

It was the two servants who came for her in the end, bringing the blue dressing gown, hustling her into it and escorting her across the courtyard to SW's room. The dining room was empty as they walked through it and

Marheh wondered whether breakfast had come and gone. When she was presented to SW however she discovered that she was to enjoy a cosy breakfast just with her. There was a small round table set in a sunny corner of the room and an enticing smell of bacon somewhere about. She was to eat in her dressing gown it seemed though SW was fully dressed. The servants retreated to the wall and SW beckoned Marheh forward to sit opposite her. There were polite inquiries about how she had slept and a bowl of porridge with sugar and cream. Bacon and eggs followed and hot chocolate. SW it appeared had already eaten, but she sipped at a cup of coffee and watched Marheh's every mouthful.

It was difficult to enjoy the food under the intense scrutiny, but Marheh was determined not to show it. She was about half way through her bacon and eggs when she realised that SW's occasional comments had become more frequent and more pointed.

"I think perhaps you did not quite understand Samuel's explanations yesterday," she said. "Or perhaps he did not explain very well."

Marheh looked solemnly over her lifted fork, but said nothing.

"You know you have been given a scholarship because you can see the drain and that means you have an extra ability."

Marheh said nothing.

"Perhaps you have learned to call it the water road," SW went on. "But here we call it the drain, since that is really all it is."

Marheh found that chewing carefully meant she could continue to avoid speaking although she sensed that SW was becoming impatient and that a response would soon be demanded from her.

"Here we teach you to develop your ability, but it seemed yesterday that you refused to learn. I think you have more potential for power than you know Kathleen. I would be failing in my duty to you if I allowed you to waste it." SW's voice was as smooth as cream, but it only served to emphasise the threat beneath.

Marheh choked a little on her last mouthful and gulped at her hot chocolate.

"Isn't that so Kathleen?"

Marheh put down her mug very carefully and looked innocently at SW. "But if I have potential for power," she said, making it clear that she was quoting. "Do I have to use it to hurt someone?"

SW gave her a condescending smile.

"That question just shows me how immature you are Kathleen," she said.

Marheh was suddenly glad that her name was not Kathleen.

"You are equating punishing someone with hurting someone, when really you are helping them."

"I know I'm immature," Marheh said, hoping she sounded humble enough. "But do I need to be powerful to help someone?"

SW sighed impatiently. "Now you are just being difficult Kathleen. Hurry up and finish your chocolate. It's time you were having your bath."

Expecting it did not make it any easier to bear, especially as SW decided to take a personal interest in her ablutions, but it was soon over and she was again attired in silk underwear and a pretty dress, this time of a deep wine red. Although she was curious about the attractive young woman in the mirror Marheh missed her Silberay trousers and the freedom of movement they gave.

"I wish father could see me wearing this pretty dress," she said as SW kept her standing before the glass. Obviously she was expected to say something and that was the best she could do.

SW kept Marheh with her all morning, petting her, making her feel important and expanding on Yareblis' philosophy. Marheh listened carefully, storing up information for Nemle and trying to appear pliant and docile. You are potentially powerful and you should develop your power in order to control seemed to be the main thrust of SW's message, but there was always the underlying threat of coercion should Marheh fail to comply.

The morning seemed to Marheh to be like an endless balancing act, tight rope walking over something dark and frightening, so she was pleased when she found she was to eat lunch in company with the other children. She was given a place at one of the long side tables and felt almost anonymous, just one of the group. As she waited to be served she looked curiously around wondering if she could pick Trodkali in the group facing her, wondering which of the young girls was Dyti. She was aware of Samuel sitting almost opposite and staring intently at her.

They had all been served with soup and were beginning to eat when there was a slight disturbance at the door opposite the entrance. Marheh looked up to see a small figure struggling in the grip of the thin, pale man servant. Behind these two hovered a woman servant holding a bucket and scrubbing brush. The struggling child was pushed into the centre between the tables and left there. Marheh saw that it was Trodkali, rather scratched, scruffy and belligerent. The bucket and scrubbing brush were placed beside him. As the servants left him he stood up straight and stared defiantly at the three adults.

"I ain't stopping here," he shouted. "You can't make me."

"Don't be silly Trod," SM said, and Marheh saw that Trodkali's feet were stuck where he stood, that he could not move, any more than she could have stopped when they put her in the water. He looked so confused and frightened her heart went out to him.

"Trod will spend his lunch time scrubbing the dining room floor," SM announced.

A few of the children tittered nervously. Samuel and one or two others smiled in a way Marheh found disturbing.

"I don't care," Trodkali shouted. "I'm not scared of work like you lot." He looked along the tables at the children. "Silly spoilt babies you are." He tried to move and found himself still stuck to the floor. "Let me get with it then," he shouted angrily.

A minute more of struggle and SM relented and released his feet. Trodkali crouched down over the bucket and picked up the scrubbing brush. He looked very small and awkward and Marheh could not restrain herself.

"It isn't fair," she said loudly. "What's he done to deserve that? He's only a little boy."

Trodkali looked around at her. "Who are you calling a little boy," he said angrily.

Marheh grinned at him and thought of her brothers.

"Kathleen, be quiet." SW's cold tones did not need to be loud to penetrate.

Marheh looked at the faces all around, angry, nervous, excited, disdainful, and then back at Trodkali, now busily scrubbing.

"I'm not afraid of work either," she said, throwing caution to the winds. "I'll help him."

For a moment the normally quiet dining room was buzzing with noise. Then there was a sharp crack and all sound stopped abruptly. Marheh stood looking at the three adults, her back straight, her chin up. Her brothers would have recognised Marheh the Great. The room was held in a tense waiting silence for what seemed like an age then SW spoke, her voice sounding bored and a little sardonic.

"Bring the child a bucket," she said. "Take her dress off and let her get on with it."

Marheh was not going to let herself be cowed. "Good idea," she said, leaving her place and offering her back to the approaching servant. "I'd be sure to get it dirty and it would be a shame to spoil it."

A few minutes later Marheh too was on her knees in the centre of the room. She lifted her head and winked at Trodkali as she came near him and was rewarded with a small grin.

"You're daft," he muttered, busily scrubbing.

It was unpleasant work, damp and dirty and hard on the knees, but for Marheh there was an unexpected bonus. Every few minutes as she and Trodkali moved in and out from the centre to the tables and back, she came close enough to him to mutter a word or two. At first she just joked and grimaced, but when she knew he was with her she mentioned Nemle and finally, cautiously, that she was coming for them soon. He grinned and gave her a small, hidden thumbs-up sign as they parted.

Scrubbing under the tables was the worst part of the task. Somehow there seemed to be a great many undisciplined feet that kicked restlessly or pressed hard on unprotected fingers.

Lunch was over before they had finished. When all the children had filed out Marheh sat back on her heels and looked at Trodkali.

"Why don't we sing while we work," she suggested. "Do you know this one?"

She began to sing a folk song with a good strong rhythm. It certainly made the work seem easier and Trodkali joined in after the first few lines. There were only the two servants left to supervise them now and obviously there had been no instructions issued about singing, so Marheh and Trodkali almost began to enjoy themselves. They finished one song and Marheh stopped work again.

"Your turn to pick," she said.

"You're daft," Trodkali said again, but he thought for a minute and began another song.

They got noisier and noisier, enjoying the freedom after the careful, controlled lives they were expected to live, but it was too good to last.

"Stop that noise," SW ordered from the doorway as they began on a final rousing chorus.

Trodkali fell silent at once but Marheh looked up at SW. "Why?" she asked. "We aren't doing any harm." She went back to her scrubbing and her song.

"Kathleen!"

Marheh stopped and looked up, then she felt herself moving towards her bucket, her head down. SW was trying to make her put her head in the bucket of dirty water. For a moment she remembered Nemle's instructions, but this was different she decided. She was not going to actually do anything, but she was going to resist. "No I won't," her mind said firmly, and kept saying it.

The battle of wills did not last long. SW was disconcerted by the strength of Marheh's resistance and stopped trying to control her before she lost face. Marheh gazed at her with round, innocent eyes. She knew better than to reveal any of her satisfaction in her success.

SW looked at Trodkali. "You've done enough. Go and change and get to class."

"What about her?" Trodkali said, getting to his feet.

"Go before I change my mind," SW said.

Trodkali looked anxiously at Marheh who gave him a tiny thumbs-up where SW could not see it. He scuttled off. Marheh was still on her knees gazing at SW.

"Shall I continue?" she asked.

SW did not reply but continued to look speculatively at Marheh. Then suddenly there was a servant on either side of her. SW nodded and Marheh was hoisted to her feet.

"We'll see how cocky you are after a few hours in a punishment room," SW said.

She motioned the servants who marched Marheh through the dining room and down a flight of stairs opposite the entrance. At the bottom they stopped. SW went ahead to open a heavy door. Marheh was thrust into a small, empty room. The servants retreated and SW shut the door. In the sudden darkness Marheh heard the sound of the bolts being thrust home top and bottom.

Nemle allowed herself to sleep for a few hours before dawn. She knew she would need to husband her strength if she was to find the Travellers once the new day had arrived. She went very early into the woods however and made for the place where they had been camped when she met them with Marheh. It was lovely in the woods in the early morning. The birds were singing and the spring trees were shimmering in their new bright leaves. Nemle was not tempted to linger and admire, but she could not help being aware of the beauty as she passed through.

She found the Travellers where she had hoped they would be, still breakfasting around their campfires. Fliandre stood up to greet her as she paused on the edge of the clearing.

"Come Nemle," she said. "You will share food with us."

"Thank you," Nemle said. "I've come to ask for your help."

"Sit," Fliandre said. "Food first and then talk."

Nemle smiled, nodded. "Thank you," she said, accepting a mug of sperit and allowing one of the younger Travellers to toast a slice of bread for her over the fire.

She was impatient to be explaining why she was there, but she knew it was important to accept the Travellers' hospitality and observe their way of doing things. It was probably no more than twenty minutes, though it seemed longer, before she was telling them her story.

"My daughter," she told them. "She has gone with the ones in the small boats. She went willingly. She wanted to find Trodkali. She showed me a farm yard and many green doors, but it is not very near the water and I do not know where it is."

"She wanted to find Trodkali," Barntredor repeated softly.

Nemle looked sympathetically at him and nodded. "She allowed the small boat ones to take her." She looked around at the group. "I thought perhaps you might have seen the many green doors as you travelled. They took her towards Fairdale Rising."

The group of Travellers looked from one to the other. There were short exchanges in their own dialect. One middle aged woman stepped forward.

"Perhaps I have seen this place with the doors," she said. "They did not want to buy my lace or my sachets of lavender." She turned to Fliandre and spoke quickly in dialect.

"It may be the place," Fliandre said slowly to Nemle. "You think Trodkali is there with your daughter?"

"I think it is likely Trodkali is with my daughter," Nemle said. "And perhaps it will be in this place."

Fliandre nodded and turned to address the group of Travellers then she turned back to Nemle. "We will begin our journey towards this place."

Nemle smiled. "You are very good. Thank you."

"And you?" Fliandre asked.

"I will return to my boat and journey with you as best I can," Nemle said.

"That will be best," Fliandre said.

Marheh closed her eyes and opened them again. Either way made no difference. She took a little, gulping breath and told herself not to be silly. She had seen there was nothing in the room before the door was shut. Darkness could not hurt her.

Carefully she stretched out her arms and edged sideways until she could touch the wall then she leaned against it and eased herself slowly down until she was sitting on the floor, her back against the wall. She was already a bit cold, wearing only her petticoat, but there was no reason to be frightened, or bored, she told herself. This was a perfect opportunity to practice the disciplines. She turned sideways and stretched herself out on the floor. She would concentrate on pursuing her candle flame.

It was not easy. She might tell herself there was nothing to be frightened of, but believing it was another matter. She might concede that she was a bit cold when in fact she was very cold and getting colder. She was determined however. Hadn't Nemle said the discipline of the soul was her best defence? Gradually she built her concentration, focusing on every detail of her candle flame until the work became everything and fear and cold eased into the background. Her beautiful candle became enveloping golden warmth and she was part of it, lifted out of herself to a place of wonder and delight. She rested there outside time and space only coming back to the cold dark room and the sound of the bolts being drawn.

"I tell you she is not there." It was SW's voice Marheh heard as the door began to open.

"Nonsense!" A man's voice answered her.

Marheh blinked as the light from the passage filled the little room.

"You see."

Marheh struggled to sit, drawing her knees up to her chest so she took as little room as possible. SW gazed at her from the doorway. Marheh shivered and hoped they would think it was because she was cold.

"Twenty minutes ago I came here looking for her to teach her a lesson," SW said. "She was not here then."

"She's here now," SP said. "And so are you."

"True," said SW.

Something in her voice sent Marheh instinctively reaching for her candle flame, but she was too slow. Pain flared, excruciating pain unlike anything she had ever felt. She writhed in agony. SW continued to watch her with a cool detached gaze. Marheh screamed, choked and screamed again, and then she fainted.

Nemle stayed talking with Fliandre as the Travellers finished their breakfast and began the task of packing up to move on. They were of an age and had known each other for many years so Nemle could share something of her fears for Marheh as well as explaining in greater detail what she believed had happened to Trodkali.

At last the Travellers were ready to move, fires out, tents folded, wagon packed. Nemle stood and watched them go before returning to *Day Bringer*. Soon she too was on the move, back towards Fairdale Lading and beyond. Fliandre had explained as best she could the location of the farm with the green doors and Nemle thought she knew where the water road was closest, though it was never very close. Neither she nor the Travellers were likely to reach their destination by night fall. She must just keep going as best she could.

The water road had been very solitary since the Gathering when she had set out with Marheh. In the three months they had been travelling they had seen perhaps half a dozen boats. Nemle had been quite content to be alone with Marheh during their initial struggles, but now she would be grateful for the sight of another boat and the possibility of some help beyond that which the Travellers could give.

She did not stop for lunch, but cut the throttle in a bridge hole and let *Day Bringer* drift whilst she grabbed a piece of bread and some fruit, more because it was sensible not to be hungry than because she felt the need of food. She passed the village mooring and the place where she had moored with Kithla and continued on, steering automatically, giving most of her mind to thoughts of Marheh. She had received Marheh's sending at first light, but that seemed a long time ago now. *Day Bringer* chugged doggedly onwards through the landscape, the sound of the throbbing engine a steady background to Nemle's thoughts.

Marheh's pain pierced her suddenly, without warning. She gasped and looked wildly around. There was no time for finesse. Marheh needed her and *Day Bringer* would have to take her chances. Choosing the place that seemed most suitable Nemle ran her aground and cut the engine. Even as she hurried below she was gathering herself, looking for the focus that would enable her to reach out to help her, hoping desperately that it was not too late.

"Practicing the discipline of the soul can never begin too early. Your apprentice may be encouraged to choose something beautiful to direct and focus thought although it is likely to be some years before the apprentice moves beyond this."

Guidelines for mentoring the young apprentice.

Chapter Twelve

The darkness was filled with hurt and confusion. Was she drowning or falling? Something within had been wrenched out of place and the dislocation was painful and profound. She seemed to be fighting for her life, but there was nothing to hold onto. She sobbed and struggled, clawing her way to what might be consciousness in what seemed like an endless fog of despair. She was Marheh, wasn't she? She was Marheh. She had so far to go but any progress she made could be measured in inches when the journey ahead seemed miles long. It would be so easy to let go, to drown or fall or lose herself, lose Marheh, lose Marheh, mustn't lose Marheh.

She seemed to have been struggling for hours when the light appeared, tiny and distant at first, but piercing the darkness and reaching for her. She reached towards it in her turn, a spark of hope lifting and encouraging her. The light grew, the spark of hope became a beacon, drawing her towards it with warmth and love and then she was enveloped in it and it seemed that Nemle's strong, boater's hand clasped hers and she was no longer drowning or falling, but being gently held in a place where she could recover herself.

Then the music began, a fine thread of melody weaving itself around her, healing, restoring. For a while she dwelt there in the sounds, wondering at their beauty. Then, tentatively at first but with increasing confidence, she began to make her own melody, over and around, between, beneath, like a dance that moved now in harmonious partnership, now spinning apart to exult alone, yet always complementing the other.

For a time there was a lightness, almost laughter in the song, but then the other singer steadied, the rhythm sobered and became more purposeful. The celebration was drawing to an end. They must separate and take up the task, painful and solitary though it may be. Marheh once again felt the clasp of Nemle's hands and was able to relinquish them, regretfully, but with determination.

She opened her eyes to the cold darkness of the punishment room. Her body ached as if after some strenuous labour, her face was wet with tears, but the memory of the song remained to lift and strengthen her. Sighing a little she curled up on the floor against the wall and fell asleep.

Some small sound awakened her, like scratching at the door. She was immediately alert, senses sharpened by fear. She heard a slow, quiet rubbing sound and a click first high and then low, near the floor. Then, with a little creak, the door eased open. The quality of the darkness changed and she saw a rectangle of grey widen with the opening door and then, silhouetted against the grey, the dark shape of one of the woman servants. As Marheh watched, the figure paused in the doorway for a moment then moved soundlessly out of sight.

For perhaps five minutes Marheh waited, crouched on the floor not daring to believe that the way had been opened for her to leave, then she got up carefully, painfully and crept through the open door. She had already begun to climb the stairs when a sudden thought made her go back and quietly close and bolt the door. Then she went again up the stairs and through the empty dining room. It was night, but she had no way of knowing how late. She paused at the door to the court yard then opened it a few inches and peeped out. It looked still and bright in the moonlight and she knew she would not dare to walk across it. One or two windows showed glimpses of light behind blinds or curtains but it was the black, empty dark ones she was afraid of. Her white petticoat, dirty though it was, would stand out immediately to anyone looking out.

She closed the door again and leaned against it, trying to make herself think and plan rather than run or hide. She couldn't just leave anyway; there was Trodkali to think of. Going without him would be admitting to failure as well as letting him down. If she thought really hard and pictured Trodkali coming out of his room, wherever it was, would it happen, she wondered? At last she made up her mind, opened the door again and slipped out.

Keeping against the wall she walked quickly and quietly around until she came to the door leading to the bedroom she had been allotted. She would go up and take a blanket from her bed if she could. The few minutes spent crossing the courtyard had shown her she needed something more substantial than a petticoat if she was to spend time outdoors that night.

As she climbed the stairs and slipped quietly along the corridor she concentrated on Trodkali. Surely this was where all the bedrooms were, but maybe he was locked in as she had been. She found her own room open and thankfully pulled a blanket off the bed and wrapped it around her. As she left she realised that there was no key in the keyhole inside or out. She walked slowly along the corridor, looking at all the doors and thinking of Trodkali. No keys anywhere. She reached the further end and turned around to come back. Where are you Trodkali she thought? I can't go without you.

She had almost reached the staircase when she saw it, the dark shape of a key casting a shadow across the door plate of a room only two doors from her own. She barely hesitated, so sure was she that Trodkali was inside. Quickly she unlocked the door and found him standing on the other side, wrapped in a blanket of his own, his eyes blazing with excitement. She grinned at him and put a finger to her lips. He gave her a scornful look and walked past her out of the room, waited while she shut and locked the door, then led the way downstairs.

He seemed very sure of himself, Marheh thought, as she followed him across the hall and out into the night.

Nemle struggled back into herself, exhausted and a little disoriented. It was a long time since she had needed the skills Marheh was demanding of her now. Had she become complacent, she wondered? She thought she knew this section of the water road so well, she had friends here and she had worked hard for them, but she had failed to prevent the Yareblis establishing themselves in the area. She lay quietly thinking, gathering the energy to go out and deal with *Day Bringer*, to get her floating again and continue the journey for at least as long as there was light.

Already the sun was very low in the sky and an evening chill was beginning to make itself felt. She pushed herself to get up and attend to the fire, drink a mug of sperit and eat a handful of nuts. It would not help anyone if she neglected her own needs. Fears for Marheh were constantly present beneath all her thoughts and actions, but she made a determined effort to focus on what needed to be done and not allow the fears to surface. Pulling on a warm jacket she went out to assess *Day Bringer*'s position and remind herself of where she was.

To her surprise she found *Day Bringer* no longer aground, but neatly moored against the opposite bank and behind her, another boat pointing in the other direction. She had barely time to take in her changed situation when a young man stepped off the other boat and came towards her. He wore the uniform of a Silberay apprentice, but he was older than Marheh, tall and broad shouldered. As he came closer Nemle recognised that he belonged to *Storm Cloud*. His mentor would be Sul then, Nemle realised, and smiled at him.

"You're Kel," she said. "I've managed to remember. I'm so glad to see you."

"We saw you were aground and busy somewhere else. I've been watching while Sul rested," Kel said. "It seemed there might be something wrong."

"My apprentice," Nemle said, and to her surprise found her eyes had filled with tears. "My apprentice," she said again, turning her head away. "I must keep going. She needs me."

Kel put his hand on *Day Bringer*'s stern rail and spoke diffidently. "Sul would be pleased if I could help you," he said.

Nemle looked at him. He was very big and very young, but it was not muscle she needed. "Yareblis recruiters have a base somewhere beyond Fairdale Rising," she said. "I need to get as close as I can." She stopped and put a hand over his. "If you and Sul would turn round and come after me in the morning that would be the best help."

Kel studied her for a minute then gave a rueful smile. "I'm not far enough along in the disciplines to give the right sort of help," he said, then as her expression changed, "It's alright. I understand."

Nemle smiled at him. "I'll just check the engine and light the headlamp," she said. "Then you can help me cast off."

She was soon underway, determined now to continue into the night until she reached the place she had identified as being closest to the farm with the green doors. The knowledge of support gave her new heart. She set off into the twilight still thinking about Marheh. She had so looked forward to having an apprentice, but she had expected the relationship to be one way, she the teacher, Marheh the student, but Marheh had upset that idea from the beginning. She had been polite, but not humble and then had come her own outburst of temper. Nemle still felt uncomfortable about that. Three months had not been enough to let her forget the look of hurt and fear in Marheh's eyes as she had held her and scrubbed her cheek. She though perhaps she never would.

Now Marheh's youthful idealism was confronting her. Despite her concern, she would not have actively followed up Trodkali's disappearance though she would have sought for him with mind and heart and spent herself to help him if she had found him, but Marheh had forced the issue and now here she was pushing herself to the limit and feeling purposeful, even invigorated by the challenge. One day she would tell Marheh, tell her and thank her, but first Marheh needed to be supported in her task and brought home safely to *Day Bringer*.

Trodkali moved like a shadow, Marheh thought as she followed him around the courtyard and into a patch of deep shade under a big tree.

"How did you do that?" he said, when she was close to him.

"What?" Marheh asked, surprised.

"I knew you was coming," he said. "I just knew."

Marheh shrugged. "I tried to tell you," she said.

He looked at her sharply but did not pursue the subject.

"Getting along to the gate will be the worst," he said. "Bright night and not much cover."

Marheh would have been amused by his assumption of leadership if she had not been so anxious.

"What do you suggest?" she asked, recognising his travelling life would have given him skills she did not have.

"Not too fast," he said. "Do what I do."

He pulled the blanket over his head and crouched over, his knees bent, his arms hanging. Then he walked out into the moonlight and moved, more or less directly towards the next patch of shadow. He could have been a grazing animal, especially if viewed from a high window. Marheh copied him as best she could and tried to restrain her urge to simply take to her heels. It seemed to take forever to reach the farm gate, but probably it was only half an hour or so. Marheh waited in a patch of shade while Trodkali climbed nimbly over the gate. Once he was out of the way she followed him, not quite as neatly, dropping her blanket in the process, but able to scoop it up again once she was in the road.

Here they did not need to hide, the hedges that lined the way were protection enough. Marheh paused to adjust her blanket and look around. How much night did they have? Would they get far enough away? Trodkali was already walking steadily up the road. He turned and looked at her, gestured for her to hurry, so she put the thought away and set herself to walk with him. For a while the walking was enough. There was pleasure in the sense of freedom, in the still, moonlit landscape, the starry sky. There was no need to speak and no decisions to be made about direction, not yet anyway.

Marheh could have wished for her boots instead of the light slippers she had been given to match the clothes they had dressed her in that morning, but Trodkali was barefooted. It did not seem to worry him though. He was full of purpose and seemed to know exactly what he was doing, where he was going. Marheh tried once or twice to speak to him, ask him questions about what he had experienced, but he only grunted in reply and she soon gave up. The silence left space for her own thoughts to come pushing in. They were not particularly comfortable.

She and Trodkali were away, seemingly free, but left behind were Dyti and the other children and the captive servants. What would they become in that atmosphere of perverted power? Marheh wondered too what would happen when they discovered her absence. Someone would become a scapegoat perhaps and suffer because of their escape. Trodkali could rejoin the Travellers and she would find Nemle and they would be safe, but the Yareblis knew where Kithla lived.

Marheh stopped walking. They know where Kithla lives. The words repeated themselves in her mind. They know where Kithla lives. Trodkali realised she was no longer with him and turned to scowl and beckon. Marheh hurried to catch up. She was free and she was going to stay that way. Even if they did go after her to Kithla's home they would soon know they had the wrong person. Her steps became slower again. They would probably take it out on Kithla or her father though, that was the sort of thing they did.

She stopped. Trodkali beckoned but she did not move. At last he came back to her.

"What d'you think you're doing?" he said. "We gotta keep going, far as we can by morning."

Marheh shook her head, opened her mouth, but she could not say the words.

He looked at her, grabbed at her wrist. "Come on," he said urgently.

She pulled away. "I have to go back," she said, each word dragged out of her.

His mouth dropped open. "You're daft!" he said, grabbing at her again.

"You go," she said urgently. "You go and find your people, then find Nemle, tell her where I am. I have to go back."

"They'll kill you," he said.

"Not if I get back before they discover I've gone," Marheh said, trying to persuade herself.

He argued with her and she longed to be convinced, but she held to her purpose.

"You go," she said again. "Promise you'll find Nemle and tell her where I am. She won't have gone far from Fairdale Lading."

"You're daft," he said again, but he made her the promise she asked for.

She stood for a minute watching him striding away, the blanket flapping round his ankles as he went.

"I can't bear it," she thought, longing to run after him, but instead she hitched her blanket higher on her shoulders and set off back the way she had come.

There was no freedom in the starry sky now, no magic in the moonlit fields, only her aching feet and the fear she was trying not to look at. She tried to plan what she would do when she reached the farm, but her mind refused to obey her. Now she was alone she was aware that she had had no lunch and no dinner, that mind and body had been punished enough that day. Several times she stumbled on the rutted lane and once measured her length on its dusty surface. She lay for a few moments, winded by her fall. It was tempting just to stay there under the blanket and melt into the ground, but she hauled herself up and continued on. At the farm gate she let herself in and walked straight down the track, too tired to attempt to hide, hoping only that the lateness of the hour would mean that all were asleep.

At last she reached the courtyard, let herself in and climbed up to her bedroom to return the blanket. The bed looked very inviting but she dared not stay there. Wearily she made her way back to the bleak chill of the punishment room. Since she could not lock herself in she decided to leave the door open. As she had not taken the chance to escape she hoped they would think she was sufficiently cowed by her punishment. She went to the farthest corner of the room and sat on the floor, wrapping her arms around her knees and making herself as small as she could, trying to keep warm. Then she closed her eyes and began the waiting.

Perhaps she slept in snatches for she was very tired, but it was a long, cold night and nothing much to look forward to in the morning. Almost, she thought, she would not mind if they dumped her in the bath again. She could endure the humiliation for the sake of the warmth. She knew she must look very dirty and dishevelled and she didn't need to pretend to be cold and miserable. Hopefully it would be enough to convince them of her contrition.

The first streaks of morning sun splashed down the steps and brought some light into the room. She watched the doorway and listened, too tired to look for her candle flame, too fearful to close her eyes and try to sleep.

At long last there were footsteps, brisk and purposeful at first, then quick, even agitated, as the fact of the open door was assimilated. SW strode into the room and stopped abruptly when she saw Marheh huddled in her corner.

"You do look a miserable little object," she said, all cream and satisfaction. "Get up."

Marheh scrambled to her feet, still sticking to her corner.

"Who opened the door?"

Marheh shook her head. SW walked towards her, took Marheh's chin in one hand and forced her face upwards.

"Who opened the door?" she said again.

"I don't know," Marheh whispered. "It was like that when I woke up."

SW continued to hold her face upward and gaze at her searchingly for a few moments. Marheh concentrated on looking innocent and beaten and prayed she would be believed. It seemed she was, for SW let go of her and turned to leave bidding Marheh to follow.

"Do not be disappointed if life is quiet and even pedestrian. A quiet life will give you time to learn without distraction. Obey your mentor and listen to his teaching. This should be enough to satisfy you."

The Silberay apprentice : a handbook

Chapter Thirteen

Trodkali and Nemle, each in their different ways, were enjoying the night. Trodkali knew exactly where he was going and stepped out energetically. Bare feet did not handicap him unduly and after several frustrating tussles with his blanket he found a piece of wire and gouged a hole for his head. That done he could wear it comfortably without feeling his movement impeded. He did not think much about Marheh's departure, but put it aside as just another example of female peculiarity. More important to him was the thought of his father and the welcome he would receive on his return. He had the Travellers' instinct for direction and never hesitated when a choice of road presented itself. The night was alive with interest and he spent his journey naming the stars and the night creatures who were abroad around him. There was a sense of pride in this satisfactory conclusion to his adventure. He was tired of course, and hungry, but he had no doubt he would soon be safe with his people.

When he reached Fairdale Rising he stopped to take stock. He thought perhaps he had about a third of the night left and knew he would not reach Fairdale Woods before morning. It was a shame, but he would have to find somewhere to hide during the day and put off the glad reunion until the next night. As he continued on he went over what he knew of the surrounding countryside and tried to picture a suitable hiding place. It was perhaps because of this heightened attention that he saw the thread of smoke where no smoke would normally be and glimpsed shapes in the moonlight that reminded him of home. Curious, he left the road and made his way carefully across a field towards the smoke. A hobbled pony grazed quietly, lifting his head to whicker gently as the boy came close.

"Palopah!" Trodkali could hardly believe his eyes as he recognised him. He fondled his ears, scratched his forehead and allowed the long muzzle to push into his chest. "Where are they then? Why are they here?" He rubbed his hand along the pony's neck enjoying the warmth and the familiar smell. "Just as well you found me, old boy. I would have gone right past."

A last pat and he left him to graze and hurried towards the camp, half hidden in the trees at the edge of the field. A few moments more and he had found his father.

Barntredor's joyful bellow as he clasped his son in his arms was enough to wake the rest of the Travellers, who were always light sleepers. Within minutes someone had revived the fire, Fliandre had organised some food and Trodkali was holding court from the safety of his father's side. He was rather pleased with himself and felt it spoiled the story to make much of the help of a daft female, but he did, in the end, pass on Marheh's message. Fliandre nodded, tweaked his ear and ruffled his hair.

"Bed for you my boy. We'll need to be moving early in the morning."

He wanted to protest, he was enjoying this moment of importance, but Fliandre was accustomed to being obeyed and he was rather tired. Barntredor led him away to his tent and he was asleep in minutes while Barntredor, too happy to sleep, watched by his side.

Nemle reached her planned mooring at about the same time as Trodkali found his father. Her journey had been uneventful and she too had spent time naming the stars and the night creatures, but mostly she had thought about Marheh. Already Marheh had been challenged well beyond the strength and skill of an ordinary first year apprentice. What had she overheard, back in the beginning when Marheh made her promise? "She'll be a handful," the man had said. Well he was right in one way, not just a handful, two handfuls, two good handfuls, two hands, full of opportunity, of challenge, of love. Nemle knew now she had been influenced by that man's casual remark. She had allowed a careless comment to colour the way she had treated Marheh, the way she had responded to Marheh's eagerness and inexperience.

Her own apprenticeship with Hafa could not have been more different. She had adored Hafa, given her all her love, obedience and service because Hafa had taught her she was valuable, but Marheh already had a sense of her own. Nemle smiled a little. Marheh had the opposite problem and needed to discover the world did not always revolve around her, but it was not her job to teach her what life would teach her soon enough. It was more important that she be there, be trusted to bathe the bruises and guide her as she tried to make meaning from her experiences.

The night journey slipped by surprisingly quickly and though she was tired by the time she had moored she felt as if she had accomplished more than just the journey. She stood on the stern deck and looked out over the fields towards where she believed the farm with the green doors to be. Then she went below to rest and prepare for tomorrow.

SW strode across the courtyard with Marheh trotting obediently behind her. It was earlier than Marheh had imagined and there was no one about. She wondered how soon Trodkali's disappearance would be discovered. As she expected, a bath was the first of the day's humiliations. She had not been so thoroughly scoured in so many intimate places since she was a babe in arms, but there was a different quality in the service of her attendants today. Before they had been firm and impersonal, but today, from one servant in particular, there was something she might almost call tenderness. She tried to look her appreciation and for a moment met a spark of recognition before the servant lowered her eyes.

They were just helping her out of the tub when there was a knock at the door. From behind the screen they heard SW open the door. A voice delivered some kind of message and SW responded, sounding annoyed. Marheh and the two servants froze as a short argument developed then they heard the door shut, the key turn in the lock and the click of SW's heels as she departed along the corridor with the messenger.

The servant wrapped Marheh in a towel, took her face gently in both hands and looked at her. From somewhere, with enormous effort, the woman found a voice.

"Help my sister too," she said, her eyes beseeching Marheh though her voice could not.

Marheh looked back, puzzled and concerned.

"How can I help?" she whispered, but the servant could not seem to manage another word.

The two women went about their task of drying Marheh, putting her into the blue dressing gown and brushing out her hair, but Marheh saw that there were tears on one woman's face. She looked questioningly from one to the other and remembered how she had tried to communicate with her mind. Was that what the woman meant? There would be no harm in trying anyway. With SW out of the way it should be easier.

She looked at the woman who was not crying, looked at her and tried to remember how she had reached the servant that other time. At first it would not happen though she understood that the servant who had spoken was willing her to succeed. She closed her eyes to blink back tears of her own and suddenly she was there, standing in a vast empty space as she had before. Ahead, far in the distance, was a wall, but from where she stood the emptiness was so desolate and so profound that she could only weep at the loneliness and pain of it. But her tears seemed to make a difference. She was coming closer and closer to the wall and the tears she wept were eating at its base. From the vicinity of the wall she felt a throb of hope. As she stood and wept, the wall seemed to bulge as though pushed from behind. Then as more tears met the base, the centre seemed to dissolve and light began to expand into the space.

Marheh was so astonished at the sight she almost forgot to withdraw back into her own mind, but once she had, she became aware of an almost miraculous change as life flooded into the face and especially the eyes of the servant. This was far more than the crack in the wall she had perhaps helped to begin for the other servant. Again she looked from one to the other and understood that somehow she had managed to trigger something leading to release for the two women. She smiled, offering them her pleasure in their freedom. For the first time her smile was returned. They were silent together for a few moments then, in a voice rusty with disuse, the woman who had spoken first said her name, "Joan", then as if she was discovering something, "Jona".

"Jona," Marheh repeated carefully, understanding this was her soul name. She saw the woman's face respond and said it again, "Jona." Then she added "I am Marheh."

Again there was silence and more exploratory glances between them, but Marheh felt anxious, burdened by their expectation. This release was a small triumph, but how much did it really mean. They were still locked in and if SW had imprisoned their minds once she could no doubt do it again. Probably she would want to imprison Marheh's mind also, or worse, if she suspected Marheh had been responsible for unlocking them. She longed for Nemle. It was all too difficult, she felt as if she was exploring unknown and dangerous territory with equipment imperfectly understood that could backfire on her at any minute.

She smiled at the women again and looked around the room. At least she could get dressed, she thought, trying to pull herself together. There were clothes on SW's bed. Marheh detached herself gently from the women's clasp and went to investigate.

"Nemle, my mentor, might come today," she said, beginning to dress. "We will have to pretend until then if we can."

She spoke quietly, thinking aloud. Jona came to help fasten her dress, but Marheh saw that neither of the women really understood much more than the fact of their minds' release.

"Pretend," she said again, this time to them.

"Yes," Jona said and the other woman nodded.

This woman still held the towel they had used to dry Marheh. Now she approached and carefully patted Marheh's face with it.

"Elizabeth," she said. "Lithi."

"Thank you Lithi," Marheh said, realising she had wept real tears as well as the ones that healed Lithi.

Jona took Marheh and pushed her gently onto a chair while Lithi went for the curling tongs.

"Pretend," she said, bringing them across and waiting while Jona tackled the knots in Marheh's long dark hair.

When they heard SW's heels clicking along the corridor they were ready, Jona kneeling at Marheh's feet putting on her shoes and Lithi curling her hair. Both of them were careful to be facing away from the door. Marheh alone looked up as the door opened. SW seemed annoyed, but not, it appeared, with Marheh or the servants.

"Quickly," she said. "You'd better come with me Kathleen."

Marheh got up obediently and followed without a backward glance. SW was walking quickly and muttering as she went. She was put out about something and Marheh gathered it was to do with Trodkali's disappearance. Out they went across the courtyard again and into the barn with the classrooms.

"I knew it was no use taking a Traveller," Marheh heard SW say. "Just trouble and now they expect me to sort it out."

She pushed open the door to the largest classroom. It was full. All the children were gathered there, with Samuel standing at the teacher's desk. They stood neatly behind their desks as SW entered with Marheh trailing behind. There was no sound and no expression on any of the faces. Even Samuel looked wary instead of self-satisfied as he usually did.

"Sit!" SW said abruptly, standing beside the teacher's desk. With a remarkable absence of noise they obeyed, Samuel scuttling away from his place on the dais to seat himself at an empty desk in the front row. Marheh hovered uncertainly in the doorway until she spotted another empty place near the back and hastened to put herself into it.

SW surveyed the room full of children with cold, unblinking eyes.

"Where is Trod?" she said.

No one spoke. SW nodded as if she had received the response she expected. With a snort of exasperation she pointed to a small boy at one end of the front row and ordered him out to her. Marheh thought he whimpered a little, but there was no other sound, yet it was clear that SW was interrogating him. After a couple of minutes she allowed him to return to his place, pale and a little stunned looking. Then she moved to the child in the next place and the next. Marheh realised she was interrogating each in turn and began to be anxious. She had no idea whether she could dissemble if SW entered her mind and if she kept her out that would in itself be suspicious. She was glad she was near the back of the room since it gave her some time to think, but at first her thoughts all seemed hopeless and inadequate. The only thing she could think of was to try and lie, but she did not believe her mind could lie. Then she began to wonder whether perhaps, if she was to be discovered anyway, she might try her own ability against SW now, while SW was occupied with other minds.

Cautiously, trying to be as gentle and surreptitious as Nemle had been, she began to focus on SW. Perhaps it helped that SW was using her mind elsewhere and that she was totally unaware that Marheh posed any threat, for Marheh found that she could slip unnoticed into SW's mind with little effort. She observed the harsh, aggressive questioning and realised that compared with the communication she had developed practicing with Nemle, SW was clumsy and not very skilful. No wonder the children whimpered and looked pale and stunned. It was not pleasant on the edge of SW's mind. There was no softness, no compassion or empathy. Marheh returned carefully into herself feeling soiled by the contact, but also a little more optimistic about her future.

Marheh's turn was close now and she needed to decide what she would do. She watched the child sitting next to her walk reluctantly forward and realised she could delay her decision no longer. Waiting until SW was engaged with the child, she breathed deeply in and out then edged into SW's mind again. It was not pleasant and she felt sorry for the youngster who was enduring the rough questioning, but it hardened her resolve to take the initiative and not wait to become a victim herself. It was difficult to remain aware of externals and she knew she was barely connected to the physical reality within the classroom, but she understood when it was her turn and managed to negotiate her way to the front.

Then came the moment she feared. SW realised Marheh's presence in her mind. Marheh felt her shock of surprise, felt her gather herself contemptuously to slap down this insect who had dared to invade her. In a moment of panic Marheh hit out with all her strength. It hurt and for a second she was stunned by the pain of her action but as she gathered herself again she understood that her frightened response had been enough to disable the unsuspecting SW. The mind where she found herself was blank, unconscious and unresisting.

Disconcerted and a little sick Marheh returned to herself. What had she done?

Around her the children were beginning to be restless, even a little noisy and she thought perhaps she had been absent longer than she knew.

Pushing down panic she recognised she had to take charge, now, quickly before SM or SP came back from where ever they were, before Samuel decided to try his skill.

"Come on," she said. "Let's go home."

There was a moment of frozen silence. Puzzled faces turned towards her.

"Trodkali's gone, we can go too," she urged, trying to rouse them.

Samuel's stare was malevolent, knowing.

"They'll be back soon," he said. "Then you'll be sorry."

Marheh thought he was probably right, but she had to try.

"Let's go," she said again.

Ignoring Samuel she took the hands of two of the children, drew them from their places and pushed them towards the door.

"Go, go, wait in the courtyard. We'll all come."

But they wouldn't pass SW's frozen form, her blank blue gaze.

Marheh took her arms and turned her to face the wall then things went better. With much urging the children sidled past and out into the yard until only Samuel was left gazing at Marheh with such hatred that she shivered.

She thought to leave him with SW but he followed her out at a little distance, watching. She understood suddenly that he was trying to enter her mind and snapped up her defences so that his little probe slunk away though he remained.

The children were clumped together in the middle of the courtyard, silent, drifting in little formless eddies. Marheh thought she knew what a sheep dog must feel like, but a sheepdog had someone to tell it what to do.

"Just wait," she called and darted inside to race up the stairs and release Jona and Lithi.

Back she came to the children.

"Everyone take hands," she cried and was glad to see Jona and Lithi gathering the smallest.

"Let's go!"

It was hopeless, she thought, even as she urged them forward. They'd be caught in the narrow lane even if they managed to get up the drive to the gate. Then she remembered the sliver of water she might have seen from her bedroom window and turned away from the drive and into the field beside it.

"Come on. We'll go and find the water road," she said, trying to sound as if she believed in the possibility.

Jona and Lithi helped her to get all the children through the fence and into the field, all except Samuel who smiled mockingly.

"You'll be sorry when they catch you."

Marheh ignored him. She couldn't let herself think of capture.

Far too slowly the group straggled across the field. It was not difficult walking. The difficulty lay in the kind of malaise that seemed to hang over the children, sapping their energy.

Marheh felt her energy flagging too. She had had no dinner and no breakfast and not much sleep in between. Even so she could have danced with impatience at the slow progress across the field.

A stile gave access to the next field. Jona and Lithi helped the small children. Some of the older ones were beginning to enjoy themselves as they got further from the farm. The three twelve year olds even ran ahead of her to the next fence. Marheh pushed herself after them, reaching out to Nemle with all of herself that she could spare from the task at hand.

As they crossed into the third field, Marheh looked back and saw the pony and trap moving briskly along the drive towards the farm. Her heart sank. They were back, and much sooner than she had hoped. She and the children were far too close and Samuel would alert them to what had happened but all she could do was keep going. She led the way across the next field. They would have to follow on foot, which meant a little delay and perhaps they were not used to walking. Marheh knew she was clutching at straws, but nothing was going to make her give in, she would fight them with all her strength.

The children seemed to be moving a little faster now and some were talking, even laughing. Shoes and legs were getting dirty, but no one minded. As they climbed the stile into the next field Marheh waited for Jona and Lithi.

"Keep going," she said as they came up to her. "No matter what happens just keep going. I'll come last."

They looked at her anxiously, but did not argue.

Marheh watched them all moving across the field. She saw that they were beginning to feel their freedom from the unnatural restraints imposed in the farm. A tall boy was chasing a smaller one across the field, both were laughing. Two of the older girls had joined hands with a couple of younger children and the three twelve year olds were still running and skipping. When they had nearly all crossed the field and climbed over into the next one Marheh ran across to join them. She climbed last over the stile and turned to look back before stepping down. The pony and trap had disappeared and there was no one in sight, but she had no doubt there would be pursuit. Perhaps some of them would get away and surely Trodkali and the Travellers would find Nemle soon. It was worth continuing, she told herself fiercely, trying to ignore her hunger and weariness.

It was as she climbed the next stile that she saw them, two tall figures and a smaller one, striding out across the first field. Her heart sank. They were moving much faster than the children could, already they were nearly at the first stile. She jumped down and waited behind the hedge, guarding the stile until all the children had climbed the one ahead before crossing the field herself. She knew there was no possibility of concealment, there were too many of them and the fields were too open, but perhaps they might not notice that she did not cross with the rest and she would at least have the advantage of surprise.

As she mounted the next stile she saw the three figures had already gained on them. She jumped down quickly and crouched behind the hedge. Lithi was looking back anxiously but Marheh waved her on. She had got them into this and she would do her utmost to prevent them from suffering because of it. She watched the others into the next field and sat down wearily, waiting for the sound of footsteps and trying to prepare herself. SW had been surprisingly easy to deal with, but she had been unaware and otherwise occupied. The two men would have been warned by Samuel and were stronger physically too. She caught her breath in a little sob.

"Nemle," she whispered. "Where are you?"

She took a deep breath and lifted her chin. They would be on her soon and she would not let them see she was afraid.

She got to her knees and turned round to peer through the hedge. Nothing yet. Then as she watched she saw them, one at a time, climb over the stile on the farther edge and into the field adjacent.

"Your goal in the early years is to guide the
apprentice towards the necessary humility,
patience and thoughtfulness for the later progress
towards wisdom."

Guidelines for mentoring the young apprentice

Chapter Fourteen

Nemle woke with the light feeling anxious, heavy with worry. Marheh had
been silent for too long since they had sung together and Nemle had
helped her to return to herself. She dressed quickly and ate a sketchy
breakfast, listening all the time. She would have liked to send her mind to
Marheh's but refrained, knowing she must wait until Marheh called her.
Instead she set herself to work at the disciplines in preparation for what
might lie ahead. It was focused, concentrated work and time passed
unnoticed. Still there was no communication from Marheh and she had just
made up her mind to set out for the distant chimneys she understood to be
the farm with the green doors when she heard the throb of an engine.
Eagerly she hurried through to the stern and watched as *Storm Cloud*
chugged slowly into view.

Kel was at the tiller. He brought the boat neatly alongside *Day Bringer* and
greeted Nemle.

"I am glad to see you," she said, helping to tie *Storm Cloud* against *Day
Bringer.* "You must have made an early start."

Sul greeted her from the well deck where he too was busy with ropes. "We
slept in turn," he said. "It seemed important to be with you as soon as
possible."

"It makes such a difference," Nemle said.

She pointed out the chimneys she had identified earlier and explained that
she had been about to set out.

"Kel will go with you," Sul said firmly. "I will keep the boats, but my mind
will go with Kel."

Nemle nodded. That would be best, a combination of Kel's physical
strength and Sul's mind would support her in every possible way. She
reached out to the young man, touched his arm.

115

"You must eat something then we will go."

Within minutes they were setting out. There was a rough path leading away from the water road only a few feet from the mooring.

Nemle spoke quietly as they walked long together. "It looks to be a couple of miles away, perhaps more, too far for any of my maps of the water road. I've never needed to stop here before."

"Distances are deceptive when the land is so flat," Kel agreed.

The little track spilled into a narrow lane with high hedges on either side.

"Which way?" Kel asked, looking from right to left.

"There ought to be a path," Nemle said. "I don't think the lane goes in the right direction."

They separated and hunted for an opening, a stile or a gate that would allow them to continue.

The Travellers too had started early. Fliandre had a reasonably clear idea of where Nemle might be found and once they had packed up their camp they set off, wandering the narrow, little-used lanes that wove their way through the countryside from Fairdale Rising towards the water road and beyond. It was not in their nature to hurry, but their journey was more purposeful than usual even if only Fliandre was aware of the fact. She was driving Palopah in the wagon and she had invited Trodkali to come and sit beside her. He found this to be a mixed blessing as she set about turning him inside out with matter of fact efficiency. He told her how he and his two friends had been collecting wood by the water road when the canoe came by and the two paddlers had offered him a ride.

Although not naturally Silberay, Fliandre had learned to see the water road through her long contact with Nemle. She was curious about the canoe and its occupants who were so different from *Day Bringer* and Nemle.

"It was fun in the canoe at first," Trodkali told her. "We went really quickly through the water and quietly. Only we went on for a long time and I knew I should be getting back." He was silent, remembering the moment when he understood they were not going to take him back. "They did something in my head and I couldn't move. I could see we were getting a long way from home and I was…" he hesitated.

Fliandre looked at him. "No shame to be frightened," she said casually. "Anyone would have been."

He nodded. "Then they took me to this farm place. Nice little pony and trap they had. Food wasn't bad but too many baths and always inside so I wanted to come home." He kicked his bare, dirty feet against the front of the wagon. "They said I had to stay and learn stuff like the other kids, but it was boring and the other kids were just silly babies. I yelled and ran about so they got mad."

He stopped again. "And," prompted Fliandre after a short silence.

"It was like they could do stuff in my head and it hurt," Trodkali said.

Fliandre watched the pony's plodding patience and moved the reins a little though there was no real need. "And then you escaped," she said at last.

"Yeah." His face brightened. "They wasn't going to get to me! I was ready for them."

"All by yourself?" Fliandre asked, with nicely judged scepticism.

"Yeah 'course…" he began, then thought better of it as Fliandre looked at him. "There was this girl," he said at last. "Bigger than me. I told you. She said we had to tell Mama Nemle where she was. She's daft, she coulda got away with me, but she said she had to go back." He paused to contemplate the folly of this action.

"She went there on purpose to find you," Fliandre said quietly. "She helped you so now you're going to help her. Will you try and remember everything that happened, even the bad things, so you can tell Mama Nemle?"

"Is she grown up really?" Trodkali asked.

"Not quite," Fliandre said. "Will you Trodkali?"

He looked down at his feet pushed hard against the wagon. "Yeah," he said at last. "She's not bad for a girl."

Kel found the opening they were looking for, an old stile, half hidden in the hedge. He helped Nemle to climb over, watching the rotting wood carefully as she stepped up. Then they moved off together across the field. The path was barely distinguishable and the field was weedy and overgrown but the walking was not difficult. They walked in silence, Kel matching his pace to Nemle's. She was walking as fast as she could, increasing anxiety pushing her onward. She had a sense that Marheh was wanting her, but the communication was confused and unfocused.

The next opening was in the opposite corner of the field and so overgrown that Kel needed to hold back the foliage to let Nemle pass. She waited while he battled with it on his own account and took his proffered arm for support as they continued.

"You are worried?" he commented quietly as she urged him forward.

"Marheh is worried," Nemle said. "But she is not taking the time to find me. It's as if she is only giving me half her mind."

As they approached the next stile they heard voices and the sound of running feet. A boy of about twelve appeared in the opening, stepped up onto the stile and turned to look back.

"I won!" he called as two other children of similar age thundered up behind him.

They were all over the stile by the time Nemle and Kel were ready to cross. They looked curiously at Kel and Nemle and responded with wary smiles when Kel greeted them but ran on once politeness was satisfied. As she climbed the stile Nemle saw that there were more children spread across the field ahead, quite a lot of children, seemingly in the care of two women. One held two small girls by the hand, the other brought up the rear and kept looking back as if anxious about something or someone.

They were half way across the field, mingling, passing with polite, distracted smiles when Nemle received Marheh's frightened plea. She began to run, then stopped suddenly so that Kel almost bumped into her. Then he understood, running was no good, she needed to be still and focused. He stood quietly beside her, warding off the last of the approaching group, allowing Nemle space to enter the discipline of the mind.

Marheh was just trying to control her fear enough to practice her own mental discipline when she felt Nemle with her. It was as if she suddenly found firm footing when she had been expecting quicksand.

Confident now, she stood up behind the hedge and watched through the leaves as SP and SM came closer, Samuel still trotting behind them. SM was leading and she eased herself into his mind as he approached the stile. Like SW he was unprepared, not expecting to need to defend himself from this form of attack and Marheh found it was already becoming easier to be quick and invisible. Nemle felt her little gloat as she succeeded in stopping him in his tracks and held herself back from a small admonition on the subject of pride.

"SP next." Nemle almost heard her say it and held herself ready. Marheh was too confident now. SP had stopped when SM did and stood warily, walking stick firmly planted, ready to defend himself. Marheh, excited by her previous success, stepped out to stand in front of the stile, challenging SP openly. He looked at her contemptuously, seeing only the young Kathleen scrubbing the dining room and lying on the floor of the punishment room writhing under SW's chastisement. She felt his surprise when she entered his mind, but he was not unprepared and her previous guerrilla tactics would not serve against this more practiced and powerful mind. Almost immediately she found herself struggling. It was as if she was being squeezed in a giant fist. Exerting all her strength she could loosen the grip on one finger only to find it gripping tighter than before as she left it to work on the next. Desperately she fought him, afraid that he would squeeze her out of shape into a new shape that he could control, or even into a lump of nothingness.

Nemle had been taken by surprise at the suddenness of Marheh's action and it had taken her a few minutes to find her in SP's mind. When she did her strength was more than a match for his and she folded back the fingers to release Marheh and slapped them lightly to keep them from returning. Bruised, whimpering a little, Marheh clung to her and was drawn back onto her own mind. Nemle stayed there with her for a moment or two, allowing her to expand into her body, then gently detached herself and withdrew.

When Marheh found herself again, she was still standing in front of the stile. In the field beyond stood SM and SP, unmoving and unseeing, while Samuel hovered behind them. She took a deep breath and turned to follow the children, wondering whether Nemle was nearby. As she set out across the field she saw a large young man just climbing into the field from the other side. He was paying attention to someone behind him, but suddenly he looked straight at her and shouted something. She stopped and he shouted again. "Behind you," it sounded like. Marheh turned in time to see Samuel wielding SP's walking stick. He was swinging it ferociously, a look of hatred on his face. As she faced him he brought it down with all his strength.

Instinctively Marheh ducked and raised her arms to protect her head. Her movement deflected the blow a little, but it landed on her right arm with sickening force. Marheh fell to her knees feeling as if she might vomit with the shock and pain. Samuel raised the stick again. Marheh watched him warily wondering whether she would be able to avoid the next blow. Then she saw his face change, the look of hatred was wiped from it, the stick fell from his hand. She sighed a little. Somewhere was the sound of running feet. She tried to turn her head to look and subsided gently onto the grass. Clinging to consciousness in some distant part of her brain she was aware that the young man who had shouted was now crouched beside her. She opened her mouth but no words came.

119

"I think she's fainted," she heard him say.

Then, like manna from heaven, she heard Nemle's voice, a little breathless, a little anxious, but calm and steady.

"It's the shock," she said.

Marheh stopped struggling and let herself drift. Nemle would take care of her. From far away she felt gentle fingers probing her skull, words came and went.

"Not her head."

"She needs warmth."

She flinched as the gentle fingers touched her arm, opened her eyes and tried to smile at Nemle's concerned face hovering over her.

"Just my arm," she said, pleased to be able to get the words out.

Nemle took her hand, felt Marheh's fingers respond to her touch.

"Not broken I think," she said, pushing her gently back as she struggled to sit. "Kel will carry you."

She didn't really want a strange young man to carry her, she thought as he gathered her carefully into his arms. Getting off the ground was a bit jerky and she tried not to wince as he struggled awkwardly to his feet, but then it felt warm and safe to be carried in strong arms, especially with Nemle walking along side. It seemed a long time since she had felt safe. He lifted her over the stile and placed her gently on her feet where she clung unsteadily to Nemle for a minute while he climbed over. Then he scooped her up again.

"After the next one I'll walk by myself," she promised herself, but when the time came her protests were easily over-ridden and she enjoyed the feeling of warmth and safety for a bit longer.

"My legs will carry me now," she said, with reasonable firmness, the next time he put her down and this time she was allowed to continue on her own feet with only his arm for support. She decided the action of her legs must have prompted action in her brain because it was only now that she remembered Jona and Lithi and the children and wondered where they were.

"We saw some children," Nemle said, before she could frame her thought. "They'll be somewhere ahead of us."

So Marheh just muttered something to show she had heard and concentrated on where she was putting her feet.

It was not until they reached the lane that they found them, milling about, wondering where to go next. Jona and Lithi looked so anxious Marheh forgot the pain in her arm and called to reassure them. They all came running, gathering round her demanding explanations until Nemle took charge. She had barely begun however when the sound of hooves reached them and down the lane came the Travellers' wagon with Fliandre and Trodkali on board and the rest of the Travellers straggling behind. There was more noise and greeting, more demand for explanation, children running excitedly about and Marheh in the centre of it growing whiter and whiter.

Nemle nodded to Kel, who scooped Marheh into his arms again and set off for *Day Bringer*.

"Follow," Nemle said to the surprised crowd. "We'll have a picnic and plan what to do."

So slowly, with much excited speculation, they went along the lane, found the track and came to the grassy bank where *Day Bringer* and *Storm Cloud* were moored. Most of the Travellers could not see the boats or the water road, but they were happy enough to stop for a rest after their early start. Lithi and Jona could not see the water road either, though all the children could and caused more confusion as they chattered excitedly about the boats. One or two of the more enterprising hopped on and off the gunnels, disappearing and reappearing, to the great alarm of those adults who could not see *Day Bringer* and *Storm Cloud* floating there.

Knowing that the combined resources of *Day Bringer* and *Storm Cloud* could not hope to produce a passable picnic for such a crowd Nemle had a strategic word with Fliandre before following Kel and Marheh into *Day Bringer*. She met Kel coming out and asked for his help with the picnic then went into the saloon to Marheh.

She sat in the big chair, her eyes closed, her dark hair loose and dishevelled about her pale face. The stylish blue dress they had clothed her in that morning had been subjected to rougher treatment than it was designed for, the neat blue shoes were scuffed and dirty. Nemle thought she looked like a tired child after a dressing up party. She opened her eyes as Nemle came closer, tried to get up, to smile, to behave as if everything was fine and instead burst into tears. Nemle was beside her in a moment, holding her carefully to avoid hurting the sore arm, feeling her shaking as she sobbed in her arms, her face buried against her chest.

The storm of tears did not last long. Marheh lifted her head, blinked and sniffed.

"What made me do that?" she said, sounding rather aggrieved.

Nemle smiled, touched her cheek lightly with one finger and offered her own clean handkerchief to assist with the mopping up operations.

When she had composed herself Nemle handed her a mug of sperit.

"Drink it slowly," she said. "I'm going out to check on the picnic. When I come back I'll have a look at that arm."

Marheh sipped gratefully, scarcely realising how much she needed it. Holding the mug in her left hand felt awkward, but her right arm throbbed painfully even when she was not using it. She let herself drift, sipping her drink, listening to the chatter outside, feeling the dip and sway as *Day Bringer* moved under the activities of the exploring children. They had all got away. She felt a little surge of pride. They sounded happy. They were playing. They were free. She didn't think to wonder what would happen next.

Nemle was not away long but she had taken time to introduce herself to Jona and Lithi as well as speaking to Fliandre and handing over *Day Bringer*'s entire stock of bread, butter and eggs. Kel was out with the children and Sul was keeping a watchful eye on Jona and Lithi and listening to their halting explanations of what had happened to them. When she returned Marheh had finished her drink and was looking much brighter. Comfrey ointment, a bandage and a scarf for a sling made her arm more comfortable and she wanted to join the others.

"I think I'm hungry," she told Nemle. "It's ages since I ate."

Nemle looked at her searchingly. Her colour was better and she had regained something of her determination and chin-in-the-air assertiveness.

"I dare say you won't come to any harm," Nemle said dryly. "Just be sensible – if you can."

A Marheh-the Great look was flashed at her, but Nemle was unimpressed. She helped her to her feet and gave her a quick kiss.

"Off you go," she said, and followed her out.

The children stopped their chatter for a moment when she appeared on the stern deck. She smiled, blushed and put her chin in the air. When she stepped off the boat there was a little buzz of greeting which she accepted graciously, then Trodkali bounced up to her and demolished any inclination to grandeur.

"I could have told you not to turn your back on that Samuel," he said. "You're daft."

"Daft yourself," Marheh said, descending rapidly to his level. "I got them all out didn't I?"

Nemle watched this exchange with an inward smile. Sul came to stand beside her.

"Your young lady is feeling pleased with herself," he said.

"And so she should be," Nemle said. "But …"

"But she'll be neither to hold nor bind for a few days," Sul finished. "Don't worry; anyone can see you're her rock."

Nemle smiled, grateful for his understanding and continued to pay attention to the exchange with Trodkali.

"You might have got them out," he said. "But what are you going to do with them now?"

"They can go home," she said grandly.

"I knew you was daft," he said scathingly. "Half of them haven't got homes."

"What do you mean they haven't got homes? They must have come from somewhere."

"Them three used to pop around the children's homes and pick out the ones they wanted," Trodkali told her. "Nice lady and gent all ready to adopt, who would care?"

"I don't believe you," Marheh said.

Trodkali shrugged. "Don't matter what you believe."

"Well it's still better than being shut up with them," Marheh said, but she looked troubled.

As they were speaking, the picnic had been taking shape around the Travellers' small cooking fire. Each child had been given an egg, fried hard and a rasher of bacon between two slices of bread. Marheh sat down with the others and graciously allowed Nemle to cut hers up and put it on a plate so she could eat it with one hand. The adults were given their share and the noise and activity died down as the food was enjoyed.

Nemle sat with Fliandre and looked over the assembly. "What **are** we going to do with them all?" she asked at last.

Lie sleeping sweetly,
Water borne, floating,
Dream of your journey
Peacefully boating.
Lie sleeping safely,
At rest on the water.
Nothing to harm you
Silberay daughter.

Songs of the Silberay

Chapter Fifteen

Marheh looked down at the plate that had held her sandwich. She thought about licking her forefinger and pressing to gather the few crumbs that remained but somehow the thought got away before she could act.

The others had all finished eating. There seemed to be children everywhere, exploring the boats, patting Palopah, making daisy chains or just pottering about. Kel was watching the children on the boats, a quiet presence to keep them from being too adventurous. Most of the Travellers were gathered around the fire, some smoking, some talking quietly in their own dialect, some simply gazing into the glowing coals. Nemle was with Fliandre. Lithi and Jona were together. She was alone.

She put her chin in the air and blinked hard.

"Marheh."

Nemle's voice reached her. She was smiling and beckoning.

Marheh struggled to her feet and made her way across the grass.

"Come and help us decide what to do next."

At least Nemle had remembered her.

"Or would you like to go and have a lie down?"

For a moment the image of her neat, cosy little bunk beckoned. It was almost irresistible, but if she went to bed now they would decide things without her.

"I'm alright."

Nemle smiled and patted the ground beside her.

She sat in a small, awkward silence, aware that Nemle thought she should go to bed. Her arm throbbed uncomfortably.

"We are so happy to have Trodkali with us again. Thank you."

She looked up and saw Fliandre meant what she had said.

"I wanted an adventure. I got a bit more than I bargained for really."

"I'm very proud of you."

Did Nemle say that? Marheh flushed and bit her lip. Nemle nodded slightly and patted her knee.

"But now there are all those children and I still don't know which one is Dyti."

"So that's why you brought us all of them," Nemle said.

"I couldn't leave them there."

"Of course you couldn't."

Sitting with Nemle and Fliandre made things better. For a while she had almost forgotten she wasn't one of the children and part of the problem. Now she could be involved in the solution. She looked up and smiled a greeting as Jona and Lithi came to join them. The older man with them she knew was Sul, Kel's mentor.

"Sul."

She was surprised at the warmth of Nemle's greeting.

"I don't think you have met my apprentice. This is Marheh."

She smiled at him, feeling unusually shy.

He was perhaps five or six years older than Nemle and like her he wore the Silberay's traditional uniform, trousers, tunic and loose leather belt. The dark earth colours he had chosen were soft and unobtrusive but the collar of his shirt was decorated with a pattern in fine blue thread that exactly matched his penetrating blue eyes. His grey hair had receded revealing a high forehead. He had a short grey beard.

"Marheh," he said.

She felt his attention and blushed.

"Lithi and Jona have been telling me what you did for them. That was well done."

She blushed deeper as they told it again for Nemle. This was something she had done that was almost too personal to be spoken of, only they wanted to tell it and Nemle, Nemle was proud of her. She was surprised at how much that mattered.

Children's voices, laughter and racing feet, so different from the unnatural restraint at the farm, but soon they would be hungry again and need a place to sleep. Why had she assumed they would have homes to go to? And what about the Yareblis?

"It's difficult isn't it?" Nemle said, answering her unspoken question. "We can't just leave them littering the field like so many scarecrows. They'll free themselves from the command in a day or so anyway. If we imprison their minds permanently like they do then we are no different from them. How do we stop them from starting up all over again somewhere else?"

There was a short silence as Marheh began to comprehend the problem. She looked at Nemle and back to the ground.

"Oh," she said, pushing at the grass with one finger.

So it wasn't over, not really. Perhaps it would never be over. Whatever they did would be only temporary unless they became like the enemy.

"Oh," she said again. "But we had to stop them."

"Of course," Sul said.

He sounded very kind, concerned for her. She might have resented it only she saw he understood. Nemle too. They had felt as she was feeling, been confronted with the knowledge that the difficult task, the challenge met was never the end.

The tempestuous arrival of Trodkali brought a welcome change of mood. She looked up to grin at him, but his attention was elsewhere.

"Can Bernard come and live with us?" he demanded of Fliandre.

"Are you Bernard?" Fliandre greeted the taller, quieter child who hovered behind him. "Would you like to live with us?"

"He's got nowhere else to go," Trodkali answered for him.

"Trodkali," Fliandre said. "Remember what I asked you?"

Marheh saw him mentally change key.

"To think about all the stuff what happened?"

"That's right. Will you tell us about it carefully so we can understand."

He didn't seem to mind being the centre of attention and held forth importantly about the canoe that had taken him from his people, his treatment at the farm and the children who had been his companions.

"Just babies they are," he said scathingly. "They wouldn't know how to make a fire even, or snare a rabbit or anything useful. I tried to talk to them but they didn't want to know. They didn't even want to play outside. We had to just do exercises and marching, nothing interesting." He kicked at the grass. "I got into trouble 'cause I tried to get away and after that I mostly shut up. You can find out stuff better if they don't notice you. When they left us on our own sometimes kids would talk about wanting to go home, but some of the poor buggers liked it there cause there was always plenty to eat and not much work – just lessons."

"What kind of lessons Trodkali?" Nemle asked as he paused to take breath.

"Reading and stuff," he said. "And learning stuff about being strong and powerful so we could have servants and boss people." He scowled. "They made us do weird stuff like try and boss the servants just by thinking." He looked at Lithi and Jona. "You was different then," he said. "But you never brought me me own clothes. That's what I kept wanting you to do."

"You weren't there very long," Nemle said. "But did you find any friends?"

"Her," Trodkali nodded at Marheh. "She even helped me scrub the floor. Only she said I was a little boy."

"Poor thing, she didn't know any better," Nemle said, carefully not looking at Marheh. "Anyone else?"

"Not really," Trodkali said. "Cept maybe Bernard. He sat next to me in lessons. He could even read. He'd been there ages. He liked it there 'cause he always got enough to eat. He's pretty smart too, just went along with what they said and then did what he liked."

"Can you tell me about any of the other children?" Nemle asked.

Trodkali thought for a minute. "Couple of girls always wanted to boss the little kids. Used to give a nasty pinch if they didn't like you and tell on you to that SP. That Samuel what hit her. Real mean. He could even boss the servants sometimes, like they wanted us to do. Always crawling to them he was." He paused. "Most of them was just ordinary I s'pose … just ordinary, but they used to go on about how we could get to boss the world if we did what they said." He turned to go then looked at Fliandre. "But we did get pudding every day."

Fliandre laughed. "Off you go Trodkali. Thank you for talking to us."

The two boys raced off. Fliandre looked around at the others.

"That seems to be one taken care of."

"They'll all need feeding again soon," Nemle said. "That's the trouble."

"There is plenty of food at the farm," Lithi said hesitantly. "You could go back. It would be different without them." She paused and looked at Marheh and Nemle. "You could release Min," she said, a catch in her voice.

Min, it seemed, was the true owner of the farm, Lithi's husband, Jona's brother. Marheh tried very hard to follow the discussion that ensued. The farm or not, food, Min, the children, the farm, servants, room for the Travellers, deal with the Yareblis, return to the farm. It was all too difficult, the pain in her arm too distracting. Then it seemed a decision had been reached.

Nemle got to her feet and held out a hand to her.

"Come with me to *Day Bringer* for a minute."

She followed her on board, too tired to wonder why.

"Will you stay here and have a sleep?" Nemle asked quietly once they were standing together in the privacy of Marheh's cabin. "I'll only be gone a couple of hours and Sul will be staying with the boats."

"But I want to come with you," Marheh cried. "It's not fair to make me stay behind."

"I want you to stay behind," Nemle said. "But I shan't make you."

"But why? It isn't fair!"

"You're very tired, your arm is hurting." Nemle wanted to touch her, to comfort her, but she refrained. "Listen to yourself, you're not making sense."

Marheh stared at her stubbornly and began to cry, tears running down her cheeks. She rubbed them away angrily.

"I keep crying," she said. "I never cry."

"You're exhausted," Nemle said softly.

Marheh stood looking confused and lost. Nemle pushed the dishevelled curls gently back from her face.

"You have a sleep now and when I come back we'll turn you into a proper Silberay apprentice again."

Marheh stood still while Nemle helped her out of her dress then allowed herself to be guided onto her bed. Nemle knelt to take off her shoes and pushed her gently down to her pillow, drawing the covers over her. Marheh closed her eyes, then opened them again.

"My boots," she said. "They took away my boots."

Nemle gave a little laugh and bent to kiss her.

"Go to sleep," she said. "I'll find them."

Marheh gave a small sigh, closed her eyes and was asleep before Nemle had finished drawing the curtains.

As Nemle stepped off *Day Bringer* her eyes met Sul's. She gave a nod and a smile.

"I'll take care of her," he promised.

"I know," Nemle said.

The others were ready to go. Kel had already set off with some of the Travellers and some of the children. Jona and the two smallest children were squeezed onto the front of the wagon with Fliandre who would drive Palopah through the lanes. Everyone else would go via the fields.

Nemle's task was to command the Yareblis and she knew it would take all her concentration. Kel had promised to try and deal with Samuel, but his skills were not very highly developed as yet so Nemle would perhaps be needed to release him from the command she had placed on him to prevent him attacking Marheh. She was grateful that she did not have to watch out for Marheh though she would not have used that to persuade her to stay behind. The others moved off slowly ahead of her, only Barntredor stayed beside her ready to help with climbing stiles or to give her an arm should she need it. She tried to explain what she needed to do once they reached the field where SP, SM and Samuel still stood waiting.

"I will need to enter their minds and give them a different command," she said.

Barntredor looked puzzled, but nodded. "I'll just stay by you," he said. "It doesn't matter if I don't understand."

She put her hand on his arm and let him help her over the first stile. It would be a tiring journey and she needed to husband her strength.

They soon reached the still figures of the Yareblis. Kel waited by Samuel, looking back to Nemle for guidance. Ahead Lithi and the Travellers were progressing with the children, slowly and steadily towards the farm. It was lucky the day was fine and sunny. Nemle paused to collect herself before turning her attention inwards.

"Try to release him," Nemle said to Kel as she came up beside him. "You'll need to watch him though if we leave him to come with us of his own will."

She waited, ready to help if Kel needed her, but he had Sul's support and was able to draw on that as he entered Samuel's mind and released him from Nemle's command.

Before Samuel had a chance to act of his own volition Kel had taken his arm kindly but firmly and began to talk to him. Nemle watched with Barntredor as Kel led the boy past SP and SM and moved briskly ahead, catching up with the others.

"D'you think you can undo the damage?" Barntredor said. "Or will he grow up twisted?"

Nemle shook her head. She did not know but she could not help feeling doubtful.

"I think Sul and Kel are planning to keep him with them for a while," she said. "If anyone can straighten him they can."

She paused, breathing quietly, glad of Barntredor's solid, unquestioning presence as she focused on SP. It was not difficult to enter his mind while he was still under the influence of her previous command and she had no trouble directing him to walk to the farm and wait for her there. She sensed his anger at his impotence and reinforced the command for him to wait for her, giving him no chance to escape once he reached the farm.

Next she turned to SM, wondering what she would find. He stood, still and vacant, where Marheh had left him. Cautiously she approached his mind conscious that what ever Marheh had done had been more by instinct than acquired knowledge and could perhaps be insufficient to hold him for much longer. She need not have worried. Her difficulty was to find what was left of his mind and give him a simple enough instruction to get him moving the way she wanted.

She withdrew and watched as he plodded after SP, moving in a straight line, unseeing and unknowing. Now she had a new problem. Reacting in fear, with no understanding of her own strength, Marheh had given his mind a blow from which it was unlikely to recover fully. Nemle put her hand on Barntredor's arm and together they moved slowly onwards. She hardly dared think of the consequence to Marheh resulting from what she had done. Not only would Marheh herself feel a degree of guilt and regret even though she had acted unknowingly, but the Silberay had sanctions against the excessive use of force. There would be enquiries, perhaps even punishments imposed and what ever the outcome Marheh would be hurt.

She put one foot firmly after another and resolved that she would say nothing to anyone. As long as it was possible she would keep her knowledge to herself and spend all her energies teaching Marheh to understand and control her power. One day, Marheh would know enough to understand what she had done, but by then she would have the maturity to cope with the knowledge. She sighed and leaned more heavily on Barntredor. She felt tired and old and all of a sudden there seemed to be a long way to go.

The children and the other Travellers were quite a way ahead and would have reached the farm well before Nemle and Barntredor if they had continued at the same pace. It seemed however that there was a degree of reluctance on the part of some of the children to continue to the farm. The pace slowed, the running and laughing died down then stopped. Lithi and the children waited with some of the Travellers two fields away from the farm. Nemle and Barntredor caught up with them and understood the problem, but reassurance could only help to a limited extent. The children would only understand that things had changed when they could experience that change for themselves.

Nemle and Lithi urged them onwards, the Travellers teased and encouraged and the Traveller children, especially Trodkali, set an example of confidence. At last they were all standing in the courtyard with the green doors. Nemle remembered how Marheh had shown it to her.

Also in the courtyard stood SP, SM, Kel and Samuel. Nemle could see that if she was to have any help from Kel she would need to restrain Samuel with another mind command, but for the moment getting her bearings was the important thing and Lithi and Trodkali could help her best with this. The wagon with Fliandre and Jona would no doubt arrive soon and then the Travellers could set up their camp in the nearest field which would give them a focus. Perhaps some of the children would enjoy helping.

Nemle called Trodkali to her and looked from him to his father.

"I need to go with Lithi," she said. "Will you stay with the children, talk to them, find out which ones have homes to go to and whether they know how to get there?"

Trodkali nodded importantly. "I'll introduce them to my father and we'll find out together."

Nemle smiled and turned to Lithi. "Where will we find Min? The first thing is to release him."

"I expect he'll be in the scullery," Lithi said, leading the way. "We had to go there when we weren't working."

Nemle followed her in through the green door that led to the dining room. In the opposite corner from the entrance a doorway gave onto the kitchen, empty but warm from the stove, and then through another door and down a couple of steps to the scullery. There was a fireplace, but no fire, a couple of big sinks, racks, shelves, benches and an old wooden table. Sitting at the table, his back straight, his face looking blankly ahead, was the person Marheh would have recognised as the male servant.

Lithi ran to him, knelt by his side, but his face did not change, nor did he move to greet her or acknowledge her presence in any way. Nemle looked at him sympathetically and spoke his name before moving her mind into his. Unlike Marheh, she knew what to expect and how to deal with it, and she knew his soul name. Reaching the wall which imprisoned him she placed her whole mind against it and called to him. She felt a tremor run through the wall and placed herself more firmly against it. Then she called his name again, her mind magnifying the tremors so that when she moved away the wall had crazed and begun to come apart. Once more she spoke his name and felt him respond. She slipped back into her own mind. She had begun the process and he could finish it, that was better for his recovery than doing it all for him.

She saw him smile at Lithi and squeeze her hand. Lithi looked from him to Nemle and spoke her thanks before turning back to Min. Nemle left them and went quietly back out to the courtyard. Trodkali and Barntredor were now the centre of a group of children. The rest had gathered around Fliandre and Jona who had just arrived in the wagon. She couldn't see Kel and Samuel, but SP and SM stood blankly by the west wall of the farm buildings. She looked at Fliandre, met her eyes, raised her eyebrows. Fliandre nodded. "It will all get sorted one way or another," she seemed to be saying. Nemle smiled. It would of course, but the task seemed rather large just now.

"Is it possible to have power and put it aside? Is it responsible to do this? I sometimes think of the discipline of the mind as a destructive practice, yet there are times when I feel I have used it for good. Thankfully practicing the discipline of the soul seems to offer guidance, developing my compassion and my ability to love. These can govern the use of power. At least I believe so."

Sila's journal : the early years

Chapter Sixteen

Kel had kept hold of a sulky and difficult Samuel during the walk to the farm. He had tried his best to encourage the boy to talk to him and, as they drew nearer the farm, he began to succeed. Samuel was only too pleased to boast about his place as favourite, his ability at manipulating the servants and his destiny as a person of power. He hated Marheh not so much because she had pitted herself against the leaders, his leaders, but because she had questioned the way power should be used. It seemed to Kel that he envied her, yet wanted her to admire him. He spoke almost as much about Marheh as he did about SP, SM and SW and his life with them. Kel listened without much comment, wanting to try and understand the values he had been encouraged to develop and not to alienate him with criticism, but he could not help feeling that the task of showing him a different way with different values would be difficult and discouraging and unlikely to succeed.

When they reached the farm, Samuel was keen to show Kel around. He showed him the bedrooms, the dining room, the classrooms and finished up in his study. There was no fire today and although the sun still shone on the polished table and the patterned rug and there had been no time for dust to gather, the room seemed to Kel to be uninviting, though Samuel apparently saw nothing amiss.

"I brought her here," he told Kel. "That traitor. SW told me to show her around. She sat there, where you are sitting and all the time she was mocking me. I hit her, didn't I? She was on her knees. I remember that. I hope I hurt her."

"Why do you call her a traitor?" Kell asked, worried by the degree of hatred the boy seemed to be cherishing against Marheh.

"She betrayed us to the Silies," he said. "She came here and tried to destroy us."

"She didn't come to destroy, she came to rescue," Kel said.

"Rescue who?" Samuel sneered. "That fool Trod and the servants, and to do that she destroyed us, but only for now. The Silies are soft. I'll get even with her and she'll be sorry."

"You know I'm Silberay," Kel said quietly.

"Of course," Samuel laughed, not the kind of laugh Kel expected to hear from a child. "You're soft too. Silie, Silie, Silie," he jeered.

Kel stood up and looked at Samuel, realised that the boy was trying to enter his mind. His skills were barely beginning to be developed, but he knew enough to deflect Samuel before taking hold of him again.

"Stop that," he said severely. "It will get you nowhere."

Samuel giggled. "Not this time perhaps," he said, and refused to say another word.

Out in the courtyard Nemle and Fliandre, with Barntredor's help, were beginning to feel as if they were getting things under control. Jona had gone to the kitchen with a couple of the Travellers and one or two older children. The Travellers were engaged in setting up their camp. Lithi and Min had taken charge of the other children for the time being and Barntredor was planning the use of the pony and trap to convey those children with homes to go to. Nemle knew she alone could deal with the Yareblis and there was still one more to see to. She was half afraid of what she would find, knowing how Marheh had dealt with SM. Trodkali showed her where to find SW, still locked in the classroom staring blankly at the wall. Nemle could see her through the glass panel in the door. There was no resistance at all when Nemle entered her mind and, like SM, she would not recover from the blow Marheh had given her. Both of them would need to be placed where their physical needs could be cared for and where they could be protected from invasion by other minds. Nemle turned away. SW could stay where she was for a bit longer, she could do no more harm nor could she come to harm there.

It seemed to Nemle that she had been hours at the farm, much longer than she planned when she had left Marheh to sleep on *Day Bringer*. At last however she was ready to return, the children were cared for, the Yareblis under control for the time being and she could leave and go to Marheh. Barntredor drove her and Kel in the trap and she was glad of the half hour of inactivity to enable her to rest both mind and body. The two men seemed to understand her need for peace and refrained from speaking more than a word or two.

When they reached the place closest to the boats Barntredor arranged to meet them again in the morning and they said good bye. Barntredor obviously enjoyed the neat little trap and the smart horse that pulled it. Nemle and Kel watched him go and turned towards the boats, Nemle leaning heavily on Kel's arm.

"You're tired," he said solicitously, taking Marheh's boots from her.

"I am rather," she replied, relinquishing them without protest. "But nothing a good night's sleep won't cure."

"Perhaps you will let me cook for us all this evening," Kel said. "You and Marheh have done enough."

Nemle smiled at him. "That's a very good offer, thank you. Can we help with supplies?"

"I'll let you know when I've checked the larder," he said.

He stood back while she boarded *Day Bringer* then followed her and crossed to *Storm Cloud*.

"Will an hour give you enough time?" he asked.

"Perfect," Nemle said, taking Marheh's boots from him and letting herself into the back cabin. She closed the doors behind her. Marheh was still in her bunk, only now waking with the movement of the boat. Nemle made her way carefully down the steps and opened the curtain then she turned back to sit on the bottom step beside the bunk.

"Your boots madam," she said, holding them up briefly before putting them down on the floor.

"Nemle," Marheh said, and then again. "Nemle, I've been asleep."

"That was the general idea," Nemle said. "How do you feel now?"

Marheh thought for a minute. "Hungry," she said, sitting up and wincing a little as she used her arm.

"Good," Nemle said. "You must be feeling better. We are going to eat on *Storm Cloud* tonight."

Marheh's eyes opened wide. "I'll need to get dressed."

Nemle laughed. "That ought to be possible now that you have your boots."

Marheh gave a little gurgle of laughter. "I'll need to wear more than just boots."

"So you will." Nemle held out a hand to her. "Up you get then. How is your arm?"

"Alright really." She swung herself round and put her feet on the floor.

"Why don't you have a wash and come out by the fire with your hair brush?" Nemle said. "I'll brush it for you while you tell me all about your adventures."

Marheh put her left hand to her head, ran her fingers through the tangle of curls and grimaced. "You'll have your work cut out," she said.

Nemle smiled and stood up. "Call me if you need help," she said. "I'll be in the saloon."

She moved through Marheh's cabin and collected some coal from the store in the engine room as she passed. *Day Bringer* felt cooler than usual and she guessed the fire was low. Once she had made it up she relaxed into the armchair and put her feet up while she waited for Marheh, wondering what she would have to tell her and how she could best respond.

It was not long before Marheh appeared in the saloon. She was carrying her tunic as well as her hair brush and obviously favouring her injured arm.

"Come and let me look at your arm. Is it very sore?" Nemle asked.

"It won't do what I want it to," Marheh said crossly, sinking down on the footstool beside Nemle.

The sling had been discarded when Marheh went to bed and the bandage had slipped. Nemle took hold of her fingers first then gently probed all the way up her arm until she reached the bandage. She unwound it carefully. Bruising was beginning to appear, spreading out from a hard, painful swelling.

"It doesn't look much," Marheh said.

"It will hurt for a day or so till the bruising comes out," Nemle said. "But it won't do any harm to use it a bit. What did you want to do that you couldn't?"

"Put my tunic on," Marheh said, still sounding cross. "It hurts too much when I try to lift it."

Nemle replaced the bandage more firmly and helped her to put her tunic on without further comment. Marheh looked at her feet and muttered a brief apology as Nemle picked up the hairbrush and settled her between her knees, her back against the armchair.

"What a tangle," Nemle said lightly, lifting the long dark hair.

"They did it." Marheh put on SW's voice. "Perhaps we can find you a more grown up hairstyle," she quoted, then in her own voice, "I didn't know myself by the time they had finished."

Nemle began to brush the ends of her curls, making no comment, hoping Marheh would keep talking.

"I suppose that was the idea," Marheh went on thoughtfully. "They tried to take away everything that defines who I am, not just my clothes but," she hesitated, "But my feeling about myself." She twisted around to look at Nemle. "They made Jona and Lithi take off all my clothes and bath me." Nemle nodded and continued her work with the hairbrush. "They call us Silis. I suppose to them we are."

There was silence for a while then. Nemle kept brushing Marheh's hair, now free of tangles, long soothing strokes.

"Are you counting to one hundred?" Marheh asked at last, dreamy and relaxed, conscious of the feeling of warmth and safety that Nemle's care and closeness gave her.

"Sixty seven," Nemle said in answer and Marheh sighed with pleasure and closed her eyes.

For a while the brushing continued then Nemle laid aside the hairbrush and separated the hair into three strands for plaiting.

"There," Nemle said at last. "You're done."

Marheh laid her cheek for a moment against Nemle's knee. "Thank you," she said, then added a little wistfully. "I did look quite pretty with curls."

Nemle placed the long plait deliberately over Marheh's shoulder. "And with your plait you look quite beautiful," she said.

Marheh laughed. "Nemle, you are silly."

"A silly Sili," Nemle said lightly. "Are you ready to go visiting?"

"To *Storm Cloud*?"

"Yes, you said you were hungery."

"I am." Marheh stopped speaking abruptly remembering the young man Kel who had carried her and Sul who had spoken her name. "Do I … do I look like a proper apprentice now?" she asked, blushing a little.

"Entirely proper," Nemle said. "Up you get."

Kel had cooked a savoury vegetable casserole and topped it with mashed potato and cheese. Nemle and Marheh could smell it as they followed Sul through to the saloon. Marheh looked curiously around, interested to see another boat, but it was laid out in much the same way as *Day Bringer*, only the finish was different, not as light and with smaller windows. She and Nemle were given the best seats at the table with Sul and Kel perching on folding chairs that Kel produced from a storage locker.

The meal was served efficiently by Kel and for a while there was not much conversation beyond appreciative murmurs. It was Sul who brought up the subject of the Yareblis, asking Marheh about her experiences and what she knew of Samuel.

"What can we expect when we take him in?" he asked. "What can you tell us about him?"

"Are you really going to take him with you?" she asked.

"I think we have to," Sul said. "For a few months at least to see how we get along and teach him some of our ways. Then we will try to place him with a family."

"He really believes all the things he has been taught already about power," Marheh said. "About using his power to control. He showed me how he could make the servant do what he wanted."

"I feel ashamed to think I kept my eyes closed to what they were doing," Nemle said. "Surely I should have been more aware that they were recruiting, and such young children." She turned to Marheh. "I've you to thank for waking me up to what has been happening."

Marheh looked at her amazed. She opened her mouth and closed it again, blushing furiously.

Sul laughed. "You've made her speechless." He looked at Marheh and then at Kel. "It is one of the good things about having an apprentice, how much you teach us."

Kel and Marheh looked at each other, both lost for words. Marheh applied herself to her dinner while her blushes subsided then she ventured a question.

"I still don't really understand about the Yareblis?" she said. "The way Samuel explained what they think sounded too horrible to be true."

Nemle and Sul looked at each other. "Sul and I were there when it all began," Nemle said slowly. "It was the year I became apprenticed, fifty years ago at the Gathering."

"It was a hundred years since Sila had put forward her idea for the water road," Sul said. "A very special Gathering, for the anniversary and everyone was there. It hardly ever happened that way, but obviously that was an exception. I think people were surprised at how many of us there were, nearly ninety not counting apprentices, though really someone must have known because of the number of boats that had been built. We had not had much in the way of rules up to then, only the promise that we've all made, but that year," he paused and closed his eyes, remembering. "That year, instead of celebrations there were arguments. People who had not appeared at a Gathering for years had developed their own ideas about goodness and beauty and the use of power." He looked at Nemle. "It must have been hard for you," he said. "All that anger and dispute happening around you when you were just at the beginning."

Nemle smiled reminiscently. "Hafa looked after me. You remember what she was like?"

"Terrifying," Sul said. "Forthright, determined, always convinced she was right."

Marheh and Kel looked at each other and then at their mentors. "I always thought those old ones were perfect," Marheh said. "That is the way the stories sound."

Nemle and Sul laughed.

"Hafa wasn't perfect," Nemle said. "Though sometimes she tended to act as if she was. Of course back then I was so over-awed by everything that I was quite ready to worship her."

"She was an amazing woman," Sul said. "But even she couldn't have things all her own way at that Gathering."

Nemle shook her head. "She didn't want us to make all those rules. Said we should be able to judge for ourselves what was right and wrong and how best to act when we needed to, but too many abuses were coming to light. There had to be rules and if there were rules there had to be sanctions and people to enforce the rules."

"But the rules came out of the Great Debate and she was passionate about that."

Kel and Marheh had almost forgotten to eat and Marheh's eyes were like saucers as she listened. "What happened," she asked, as Sul paused for a mouthful.

"The Great Debate was about the disciplines," Nemle said. "And how we should use them." She looked at Sul. "I didn't even know there were disciplines I was so new. You could explain better."

"Some people were practicing the discipline of the mind and ignoring the discipline of the soul," Sul said. "There were even some who doubted that there was a discipline of the soul or that it had any value if it existed. Others like Hafa were convinced that practicing the discipline of the soul was what really mattered, what enabled us to recognise goodness and beauty when we saw it and what kept us straight in our use of the discipline of the mind."

"Samuel told me they give up their names, Yareblis, when they come into their power," Marheh said. "And they never use the soul name."

Sul smiled at her. "More than anything it was the value of the soul that caused the rift," he said. "You saw for yourself what happened to Jona and Lithi. Those who only practice the discipline of the mind begin to believe that anything that can be done is acceptable to do."

Nemle nodded. "I remember Hafa weeping it meant so much to her that the discipline of the mind was being so abused, and that was before anyone really knew how it would continue."

"In the end it came to a vote," Sul said. "Apprentices couldn't vote of course, but we could choose what we would do once the vote was taken."

"Vote about what?" Marheh asked.

"The use of the discipline of the mind," Sul said. "We had to make a rule in the end, several rules really. It could not be used to attain power or to control, that was roughly how it went originally, but perhaps a dozen of the Silberay at the Gathering voted against it. They wanted to be able to control people for the people's good, or that is what they said."

Marheh gasped and the others looked at her.

"Samuel," she said. "He told me he had been given the power to command and it was his right and responsibility to use it." She paused, trying to remember what he had said. "He said making Jona and Lithi into servants was responsible use of ability. He made it sound alright, but when you thought about it, it was all wrong."

Nemle smiled at her. "All wrong," she said. "Though no one, even Hafa, foresaw what would happen. Ten of those who voted against the new rule decided to leave the water road and two apprentices went with them. The rest thought that would be the end of it and we could continue to pursue Sila's dream. Then we began to discover those twelve had turned everything upside down to become Yareblis."

Sul sighed. "And at every Gathering now someone wants to do something about rules, new rules, old rules, amendments to rules, until most of us just want to get on with being and doing. Luckily most of the time we can," he finished. "But I'll deny I said that if I'm challenged," he added, a hint of mischief in his voice.

Nemle laughed and pulled a face. "Such a bad example to my apprentice, who is already too much of a rebel." She smiled at Marheh to show she was joking.

"What sort of rules?" Marheh asked curiously. "I know I'm not supposed to use the discipline of the mind against anyone except Yareblis." She paused and gave Nemle a cheeky grin. "Or Nemle of course, but I don't know any more."

Kel groaned. "You will," he said. "Next Gathering it will be a big part of your apprentice classes."

Marheh made a face. "But what if I break them in the mean time? I easily could. The next Gathering is nearly two years away."

"Then it will be up to Nemle to deal with you," Sul told her with mock solemnity.

"Oh dear," Marheh said. "More spankings I suppose."

Nemle shook her head at her. "Horrible child! Behave yourself."

Having started on Silberay history Nemle and Sul continued to tell stories all evening encouraged by Marheh and Kel. Vegetable casserole was followed by stewed fruit and then cheese with mugs of sperit reinforced by the addition of some vodka that Sul produced. Marheh thought she had never seen Nemle so relaxed. She was enjoying herself too, forgetting the tension and anxiety of the last few days, so she was cross when she suddenly gave an enormous, involuntary yawn that immediately broke up the party despite all her protests that she was not really tired. Goodbyes and thankyous and plans for the morning followed before Nemle escorted her back to *Day Bringer*. She stood a moment at the foot of the steps in her cabin, then moved to let Nemle descend behind her.

"Nemle," she said, then stopped and looked at the floor.

"What is it?" Nemle asked after a moment.

Marheh looked at her. "Kithla's father said, he said… he said you loved me and I didn't believe him," she said, then finished in a rush. "But I do now."

Nemle smiled at her. "Good, I do." She put on an expression of mock severity. "But that doesn't mean I won't apply the back of that hairbrush to your rear if I think you need it."

Marheh gave a little giggle and another big yawn.

"Bed," Nemle said. "Quick smart. Do you need help with your tunic?"

Marheh slept well, helped by *Day Bringer*'s gentle movement, by Nemle's comforting presence and no doubt by the unaccustomed addition of the vodka to her sperit. She was up early and about her normal morning chores, happy to be in her proper attire and at her proper job. Nemle, more tired than she knew, slept late, not even stirring until Marheh scratched on her door with a mug of sperit.

"Here's my apprentice back," she said, smiling at Marheh. "I've missed her."

Marheh grinned. "Porridge in five minutes," she said. "No milk and no bread I'm afraid."

Breakfast was soon over and it was not long before Kel joined them and they went to meet Barntredor with the trap. Marheh was both excited and a little fearful, a response that she had not expected. Apparently all was quiet at the farm, at least as far as Barntredor was aware. Trodkali was making plans for him to adopt Bernard he told them. The boy had chosen to sleep with them and was trying to decide whether Bernardi or Bernardo would be a better name for a Traveller.

"It will be good for my Trodkali to have a friend like himself," Barntredor said. "So we shall see how it works out."

Barntredor's cheerful unconcern was calming as was Nemle's quiet, matter-of-fact acceptance and by the time they reached the farm Marheh was feeling much steadier. She had not expected that her first task would be to help Jona with the breakfast washing up, but a glance from Nemle subdued any incipient grumbles and she found that getting to know Jona was rewarding in itself. She seemed to be fully recovered from the Yareblis' abuse, at least as far as Marheh could tell, and she was exceedingly grateful to Marheh for what she had done. Marheh dried dishes assiduously and basked in her praise.

By the time the dishes were done Barntredor and Lithi had departed in the trap with four small children who were to be taken home. Kel had taken charge of Samuel, who had been sleeping under lock and key and command when they arrived, and Nemle had made sure SP, SW and SM were fed and physically comfortable before going with Min to check the storerooms. Jona went off to the Travellers' camp to see if she could help with the children and Marheh, suddenly deserted, decided to explore. She knew she ought to be looking for Nemle to give her another job, but had no difficulty in ignoring the prompting of her conscience. Although she told herself she was exploring she knew her real intention was to revisit SW's room and look around. She went back through the dining room and up the stairs, walking quietly and slowly and looking around. She had no trouble finding the room and stood for a moment outside it looking at the key. It was her right to go back and look, she told herself. She had had some very unpleasant times in here and she needed to go back. Carefully, looking around to see if she was observed, she turned the key, then the door handle and entered the room.

The sun shone through the window onto the small table where Marheh had eaten breakfast at SW's behest, the screen still stood in the corner, the sofa, the dressing table, the closets and the double bed all continued to decorate the luxurious carpet, but to Marheh's surprise there, sitting upright on the sofa by the window, was SW. She stopped, uncertain, then realised that SW was still, blank and stunned and seemed not to recognise her. Marheh went cautiously towards her and stood over her for a moment, watching the empty eyes and expressionless face. She gave a small, nervous giggle and stepped backwards with little, almost dancing steps, then whirled around and explored the room, looking into drawers and cupboards, bouncing on the bed, staring at herself in the mirror and finally, with a backward glance at SW, waltzing behind the screen to where yesterday's bathwater still sat in the tub, cold, grey and rather scummy.

She studied it for a moment, then a malicious smile found its way onto her face. She moved to where she could see both SW and the tub and gave a little inward shiver of glee. Cautiously she slipped into SW's mind, not quite sure what she would find there. Nothing very much it appeared. Guiltily she set about commanding SW. She could not quite manage it at first, but just a little experimentation had her standing up and stepping forward.

"I'm allowed to practice on Yareblis," Marheh said to herself rather defiantly.

Slowly she instructed SW to walk towards the tub, to step over the rim and into the cold water. Shoes and stockings, the hem of the elegant gown were submerged, but SW made no sign. The blank face remained blank.

For a moment Marheh kept her standing there in the water. She was tempted to have her slide down into the tub, but could not quite bring herself to continue. Instead she moved her back to her former position on the sofa, dripping watery trails as she went. For a minute or two longer Marheh stood and stared, but the blank face revealed nothing and she began to feel a little ashamed. Turning away she walked quietly out of the room, only looking back as she closed the door. She locked it carefully and lifted her chin.

"It serves her right," she said to herself, but underneath she had a feeling that Nemle would not have approved of her actions.

The next door had a key in it also. She opened it cautiously and peered in. Here was SM, sitting in a more masculine environment looking similarly blank. Just to prove she could, Marheh entered his mind and moved him from one chair to another, pleased with what she considered to be her developing ability, carefully suppressing the qualms of conscience that threatened to curtail her activities. This room did not have the same interest for her so she did not spend time poking about but let herself out, locked the door and moved on to the next room.

It did not really surprise her to see SP sitting blankly upright here. This room was larger than the other two and SP was placed behind a big desk with a polished surface clear of everything except a crystal inkwell and a pen holder. Marheh stood in the doorway and stared for a moment then walked across to the desk to stand and study SP. She had not forgotten how he had tried to humiliate her, scolding her in front of all the children, nor had she forgotten that Nemle had had to rescue her mind from his. Standing there in front of him, even though his face was blank, his eyes looking nowhere, Marheh was beginning to feel like a naughty child and she resented it.

She took a deep breath and eased herself into his mind. Having just experienced the result of her own actions on the minds of SW and SM, she was unprepared for Nemle's carefully calibrated control. Here was no emptiness but a mind restrained and too late she recognised that her presence had altered the balance of power. Perhaps if she left immediately she could have escaped, but she had been tempted to try and control him and his skill was greater than hers. He was cunning too, not pressing to destroy her so that she would send Nemle an involuntary cry for help, instead using her to free himself from Nemle's control then binding her mind in sticky thread like a little fly bound by a spider. She understood that he enjoyed her helplessness and also understood that he wanted to crush her and would have done so if his over-riding imperative had not been to escape. He forced her to her knees and detached his mind from hers. She could not move, but she saw him walk to the door. She could not speak, but she heard him say very quietly "Until next time little fly."

"There may be occasions when some kind of punishment is called for. Stern words will be enough for most offences, but the behaviour of an unruly apprentice may call for the removal of privileges or even a good spanking."

Guidelines for mentoring the young apprentice.

Chapter Seventeen

Nemle was in demand on every side. She had been with Min to the store rooms, spoken with Kel about Samuel, visited the Travellers' camp and checked with Barntredor about the children he had taken to their parents. Now it was lunch time and she was hungry and rather tired as well as being uneasily conscious that she had not seen Marheh for some time. Everyone gathered in the dining room where Jona had spread out loaves of bread, wedges of cheese and bowls of fruit. There was the sound of happy chatter from the children, Barntredor's booming laugh and a savoury smell from the bowls of soup Jona and Lithi were carrying in from the kitchen.

"Is Marheh helping you?" Nemle asked Jona as she put a bowl down in front of her.

Jona shook her head. "Not since we finished the dishes," she said.

Nemle frowned. "You haven't seen her?"

Jona shook her head again and continued on with her tray. Nemle looked carefully around the room, but she was not mistaken, Marheh was not there.

Excusing herself to Fliandre who was sitting beside her, Nemle went outside where it was quieter and she could concentrate. Focusing precisely she set her mind to find Marheh's. It did not take her long to become aware of her, although communication seemed blurred and indistinct. Ceasing her mental voyaging Nemle went back into the dining room and crossed to the stairs. It was not really surprising to find that Marheh had wanted to explore but something had prevented her from responding to the lure of a good lunch.

Everything looked as it should when she reached the corridor, three doors all closed all with keys in locks. There was a staircase at the other end leading down to the seldom used front door of the farm, but she could think of no reason why Marheh might have explored in that direction. She opened the door to SW's room and looked in. As soon as she saw the state of SW's dress and shoes she realised that Marheh had been there, but a quick glance around showed her that she was there no longer. She let herself out and locked the door again, her face grave, her lips pressed together as if to control her feelings.

She checked the next room and saw that Marheh had been at work there also, so it was with a sense of inevitability that she opened the door to SP's room to discover Marheh frozen in position on her knees and SP gone.

She studied Marheh for a moment while she gathered herself, dealing firmly with the temper that threatened to flare. It was not difficult to slip into Marheh's mind and untangle her from the threads that bound her. It was difficult to control her anger at the result of Marheh's meddling.

Once she had been released Marheh looked at her beseechingly from her position of supplication.

"I'm sorry Nemle," she whispered.

"Go and have some lunch," Nemle said curtly. "We will speak about this later."

She turned and walked away, not trusting herself to remain calm, not wanting to show her anger or her disappointment.

Rather unsteadily Marheh got to her feet and followed Nemle slowly down to the dining room.

Nemle returned to her position beside Fliandre and began on her soup. Fliandre looked sideways at her and then across the room to where Marheh had entered and found a place.

"There is trouble?" she asked quietly after a few minutes.

Nemle turned to her with a rueful smile. "My girl," she said. "She was trying her power, silly child, and allowed the school principal to escape." She looked across at Marheh whose face revealed a complex mixture of guilt and defiance. "I don't manage her very well at times like this," she admitted. "I'm inclined to lose my temper."

"She is very young," Fliandre said carefully.

Nemle nodded. "Younger than her age in many ways. She has great talent and not much commonsense."

Fliandre laughed. "Commonsense is for old ones, like us."

Nemle laughed too. "Not for the young, you think? But she must learn some soon, for safety if nothing else."

"She wants adventure, not safety," Fliandre said.

Nemle nodded. "All the same I shall need to have words when I have thought what to say."

Fliandre smiled and spent a moment placing a piece of cheese carefully on a slice of bread. She looked across to Marheh who was eating soup and glancing at Nemle between every mouthful.

"She cares what you will say," Fliandre commented.

"Yes," Nemle said. "I believe she does, which makes it all the more important that I find some wisdom before I speak."

"You are Mama Nemle," Fliandre said. "Of course you will find wisdom."

When she had finished eating Nemle went across to Marheh. "I want you to help Jona clear up," she said. "Barntredor will take the next group of children home after lunch and when they have gone and the kitchen work is finished we will go home together."

Marheh nodded without speaking. She looked rather pale, Nemle thought.

"Eat up now," Nemle said. "We haven't much food on *Day Bringer* and you look as if you need feeding."

"I didn't mean to," Marheh blurted out as Nemle turned away.

"It's alright," Nemle said, turning back to touch her lightly. "We will talk later about what's happened."

Marheh finished her lunch and went dutifully to work in the kitchen. She felt a little disoriented and her knees and back ached, but this seemed trivial beside the fact of SP's escape and Nemle's displeasure. There was not very much clearing up to do and she had finished and was busy scraping carrots for the evening meal when Nemle came to the kitchen to collect her. After a word to Jona, Nemle moved across to where she was working. Barntredor had taken the children in the trap so they would have to walk across the fields to *Day Bringer*. Marheh took off the voluminous apron Jona had wrapped her in and hung it up behind the door. Jona thanked her for her help and said goodbye. Marheh, aware of Nemle's grave expression, almost wished she was staying in the warm kitchen.

It was a very silent walk. Nemle spoke seldom, seeming thoughtful and preoccupied. Marheh wished she had the courage to speak now so the scolding she expected would be over quicker, but it was very clear that Nemle had put the subject aside until they reached *Day Bringer*. Tentatively Marheh offered Nemle a hand as they reached the first of the stiles and Nemle's quiet thanks lightened her fears a little. It was hard to respond to

Sul's greeting when they reached the boats and harder still to go obediently through to the saloon at Nemle's request when Nemle stayed behind to have a quick word to Sul where he sat enjoying the afternoon sunshine on the back deck.

Marheh moved restlessly around the saloon, unable to settle, until Nemle came in and stood watching her from the doorway.

"What am I going to do with you?" she said as Marheh stopped her fidgeting and looked up to meet her gaze.

Almost immediately she looked away then up again. "Shall I..?" she hesitated then finished in a rush. "Do you want me to fetch my hair brush?"

Nemle looked at her puzzled for a moment then she smiled. "What a good idea, or perhaps a slipper, either would do," she said reflectively. "Why don't you choose?"

Marheh's mouth dropped open and she stood looking at Nemle. She had not expected to be taken seriously.

"Really?" she asked at last.

"Yes, really. Off you go. Hair brush or slipper, it doesn't matter."

Nemle's face was unreadable as she stood waiting for Marheh to obey her. Marheh looked imploringly at her for a moment then went slowly towards her cabin. Nemle bit her lip and turned to pace the length of the little saloon. Marheh went through the bathroom and the engine room to her cabin and sank onto her bunk. One hand pressed to her mouth she looked wildly from slippers to hairbrush and then, just for a moment, at the door to the back deck.

Without really considering she grabbed the nearest of her slippers and made her way back to the saloon. At the doorway she stopped, her hand behind her back, her face very white except for two red spots high on her cheek bones.

"I'm really sorry Nemle," she said.

"Good," said Nemle. "So you should be." She held out her hand. "What have you got for me?"

Wordlessly Marheh held out her slipper. Nemle took it, held it, flexed it.

"Hmm," she said. "What will be best do you think?" She tapped the sole of the slipper lightly on her palm as Marheh approached. "Perhaps you could lie across the arm of the chair, that should present a suitable target."

Marheh looked at her, saw no softening in the stern face and turned slowly towards the armchair.

"And you'd better take your trousers down first," Nemle added.

The horrified look on Marheh's face almost made her stop there but she gave one last twist.

"And your knickers. Might as well do the job properly."

Marheh stood unable to move, dumb and repentant, tears sliding down her cheeks. For a few moments Nemle was silent watching Marheh struggle to obey her then she said very gently "Marheh."

Marheh looked up from where her hands were fumbling with her belt buckle, saw the love in Nemle's eyes and took a step towards her. In a moment she was being hugged, warm and reassuring.

"All the same, I'm very disappointed in you," Nemle said when Marheh had stopped quivering in her arms. "But I shan't beat you this time." She drew her across to the footstool and sat her down facing the armchair where she sat down herself.

"I didn't mean to," Marheh ventured, looking at her hands.

"Didn't mean to what?" Nemle asked.

"Let SP escape," Marheh answered.

"Perhaps not," Nemle said, leaning forward to clasp Marheh's hands in hers and command her attention. "But you did know that you were supposed to be working with Jona, not hopping about on your own."

"I only…" Marheh began.

Nemle gave the back of her hand a little slap.

"Stop making excuses or I might change my mind about using that slipper." She looked severely at Marheh. "You knew didn't you?"

Marheh hung her head. "I did wait till the dishes were done," she said.

Nemle spoke severely. "Marheh, look at me."

Marheh looked slowly up.

"You knew, didn't you?" Nemle said again.

"Yes," said Marheh, blushing.

"And you had no business to be playing around with SW and SM and you knew that too."

"I…" Marheh saw Nemle's face and stopped. "Yes," she said.

"And you knew what you were doing to SW was wrong or you would not have stopped when you did," Nemle continued relentlessly.

"She deserved it," Marheh burst out.

Nemle raised her eyebrows. "Perhaps, but if we all got what we deserved…" She paused and picked up the slipper.

Marheh's blush deepened.

"So whether you meant to let SP escape is immaterial. You did a lot of things you knew you should not have done and SP's escape was the consequence." Marheh was crying now but Nemle was unmoved. "You have jeopardised our safety, you've been very silly and thoughtless and you have treated the power you have been given as some kind of plaything instead of the precious trust that it is."

Marheh wanted to run and hide, to cover her face, but Nemle still held both hands in a firm grip so her tears ran unhindered down her cheeks and dripped off her chin. Nemle ached to hold her, comfort her, assure her that she was forgiven, but she held back, wanting to be sure she understood the gravity of what she had done. At last Marheh's sobs subsided enough for her to stammer out an apology. She buried her face in Nemle's lap and for a moment or two Nemle stroked her head and let her cry then she lifted her up.

"Go and wash your face," she said gravely. "Then come back here so we can talk."

Marheh went off as she was told. Nemle took a deep breath and let it out in a sigh, covered her face with both hands and waited for her to return. By the time Marheh reappeared she was sitting straight again, calm and unreadable.

"Better?" she asked as Marheh came hesitantly to sit before her again.

"I'm sorry Nemle," she said again. "I didn't think."

"You never do," Nemle said. "Just leap in and do what you want. It's time you learnt better." Nemle's voice softened at the sight of Marheh's woebegone face and red eyes. "You've plenty of courage for leaping," she said. "And curiosity and lots of potential, but no commonsense and not much skill."

They talked for a long time about Marheh's responsibility to the power she had been given, about the balance she needed to develop between curiosity and commonsense and especially about the need for humility in the getting of wisdom.

As she brought the lengthy discussion to a conclusion Nemle said, "What I don't understand is why you were so silly as to take on SP when you had already lost once."

Marheh sighed. "I thought it would be like it was with SW and SM because you had controlled him," she said. "Why wasn't it?"

Nemle looked at her, hesitating, wondering whether she should answer this particular question. She picked up Marheh's hand where it lay on her knee, turned it over to examine the palm then replaced it where it was. Marheh watched her curiously.

"If you understand enough to ask the question then you've a right to an answer," Nemle said at last. "It's really part of what we were talking about before, but I hoped perhaps..." She broke off at the sight of Marheh's troubled face. She put a hand over Marheh's. "It's just that you haven't developed your skill at mind control yet so your response when they threatened you was more of a reaction, an over-reaction really because you were frightened and uncertain."

Marheh was silent for a long time, thinking about this. She was glad that Nemle's warm strong hand still lay over hers.

"Did I do something bad?" she asked at last.

"No," Nemle said firmly after a moment of thought. "You did the best you could when it needed to be done, but if you had known more you would have done things differently, so it's up to me to make sure you know more next time."

Silence ensued whilst Marheh considered this and then a long sigh. Nemle used the ball of her thumb to wipe away an errant tear then gave her a little hug.

"You've enough to think about just now," she said. "We'll put this aside for the moment while we see if we can find enough food to offer guests."

Marheh was very subdued at the meal which followed. They had combined lentils, onions, potatoes and some of Nemle's herbs and a ham bone from the farm to make a reasonably palatable dish. Sul and Kel arrived bringing their chairs with them to enjoy a final evening together. When the main part of the meal was over Nemle looked meaningfully at Marheh. She bit her lip and blushed, but began bravely enough.

"I did something...stupid...this morning," she said and choked a little. "Nemle said I had to tell you myself."

The two men, one old, one young, studied her with kindly interest. Her face burned under their regard.

"I tried...tried to," she looked pleadingly at Nemle, but she had no intention of letting her off. "I tried to control SP," she said in a rush. "And he escaped."

Kel's exclamation of surprise held a touch of admiration Nemle thought, but Sul's grave reproach was exactly right and gave no hint of his prior knowledge. Marheh sighed with relief now her confession was over and busied herself collecting up the dirty plates and putting the kettle on for sperit.

Nemle smiled her thanks at Sul and began to speak of Samuel and their plans for him. They all agreed that managing him would not be easy. Marheh spoke little, not wanting to acknowledge her fear of him or her dislike, but she reddened painfully when Kel wondered aloud whether SP might perhaps be intending to seek him out.

"We need to help him find his soul name again," Sul said to the two apprentices. "To do that will involve demonstrating our concern for him and perhaps eliciting a response. It is not enough just to care for his physical well-being."

"What about the other children?" Marheh asked, thinking of some of the snide giggles and unkind remarks she and Trodkali had experienced.

Sul shook his head. "We can only hope they will respond now the Yareblis influence is removed."

"Now they have been identified, Silberay will keep an eye out for them too," Nemle added. "Lithi and Min have offered to keep those who have no homes, and two of the older ones will go with the Travellers. We won't forget them."

Sul looked kindly at Marheh. "You started something bigger than you expected, didn't you?" he said.

The meal over they said their goodbyes knowing that the two boats would part and go their separate ways during the day following. Perhaps they would see each other again before the next Gathering, but perhaps not. That was the way it was travelling the water road.

"Your apprentice will be your constant
companion for many years. Avoid problems by
early training in obedience. Be kind, firm and
detached. Do not allow excessive displays of
emotion at any time."
Guidelines for mentoring the young apprentice

Chapter Eighteen

One consequence of SP's escape was that Nemle felt Marheh to be vulnerable whilst in the immediate area and was not prepared to allow her to go about by herself. She did not tell Marheh that however, but rearranged her plans to provide suitable protection. Accordingly next morning Marheh found herself squeezed into the trap between Nemle and Barntredor with SW and SM behind. Nemle explained that Marheh had laid herself open to the possibility of official sanctions by her treatment of SW and SM and they were on their way to a hospice where they could be cared for and Marheh could offer her labour for a few days by way of reparation.

"But you said I didn't do anything wrong," Marheh protested when she was told that she was to spend a week away from Nemle and *Day Bringer* working in a hospice.

"Neither you did," Nemle said. "But every action has consequences and you will spend the week learning about the consequences of yours."

She did not dare to grumble, but she packed her few necessities into a small bag with very ill grace and every line of her body spoke of her resentment.

Nemle and Barntredor ignored her as the trap sped smartly along the lanes. If she had been less preoccupied with the wrongs done to her, she would have realised that Nemle at least was amused by her sulks, but, perhaps fortunately, it never occurred to her. The morning was fresh, cool and sunny, and the journey long enough and interesting enough for Marheh to forget herself before it ended in a small village outside a thatched cottage with a pretty garden.

Nemle smiled at Marheh and pointed out the gleam of water almost hidden by the grove of trees behind the cottage.

"It will take me a week to get here by water," she said. "I'll be here to collect you then."

She climbed down rather stiffly and instructed Marheh to wait while she went inside.

There was time for Marheh to think over what Nemle had told her about the place she was to stay. It was run by two Silberay who had left the water road after deciding they wanted to marry. They cared for people whose minds were damaged, mostly Silberay, but not only. It was a noble undertaking but not for her. She looked over her shoulder at SW and SM sitting behind her, blank and empty, and was honest enough to admit that they could no longer look after themselves. She sighed heavily and kicked at the edge of the trap. Barntredor looked sideways at her and a chuckle emerged from somewhere within the matted beard. She looked up.

"I don't want to be here," she said.

"But here you are," Nemle said, emerging from the cottage in time to hear this admission. "Come along. You can manage SW."

Marheh's horrified expression made her laugh aloud.

"You did it before when you walked her into the bath. You can do it again."

Between them they guided SM and SW down from their seats in the trap and along to the front door of the cottage. Barntredor followed with the luggage, two large boxes for the Yareblis and Marheh's little bag. Nemle introduced Marheh to Gip and Deyah, gave her a brisk kiss goodbye and returned to the trap without a backward look.

Marheh swallowed hard as Gip closed the front door, shutting out the sun as well as the last glimpse of Nemle climbing up beside Barntredor. Deyah was kind and businesslike. She led Marheh away to the small corner where she would sleep, pausing to grab a pile of linen from a large cupboard on the way.

"It's only a corner under the stairs at the end of the corridor I'm afraid," she said. "We don't have space to offer you a bedroom, but you'll be used to small places."

Marheh followed without a word, clutching her bag as if to gain reassurance from its familiarity. At the end of the passage beside the stairs Deyah stopped and pulled aside a heavy curtain to reveal a small truckle bed and a little cupboard with a candle in a green candle holder centred on its scratched wooden surface.

"During the day you can fasten the curtain back." Deyah said, demonstrating the loop and hook available for the purpose. "That way you'll get some light. Not that you'll be here much during the day," she added. She put the linen down on the bed and turned to Marheh. "Make up your bed and then come along to the kitchen. You can help me with the lunch."

"The kitchen?" Marheh asked, trying to hide her dismay at the prospect of still more housework.

"Back down the passage and second door on the right. You can't miss it."

Marheh watched her go and bent to examine the pile of linen, blinking back the tears that threatened. It was all very well for Nemle to say she had done nothing wrong but this felt like a punishment.

She made up the bed hastily, not taking much trouble over it, dumped the contents of her bag in the little cupboard and made her way along to the kitchen. It was true she couldn't miss it. The room took up most of the back of the house and seemed to be a combination day room and eating area as well as food preparation place. There were several small tables and a couple of sofas, a wide doorway led into a conservatory with more tables and chairs and in the sunny corner made by the junction of cottage and conservatory was a paved courtyard surrounded by flower beds. Through the big windows she could see two or three figures in the courtyard. There were others in the conservatory and three or four sitting on the sofas or at the tables. They all seemed quiet and calm, not moving much, but not displaying quite the blank emptiness of SW and SM. These two were nowhere to be seen and Marheh assumed they were being settled in, perhaps by Gip. Deyah gave Marheh an apron and a wooden spoon and set her to stirring a large pot of something pale and creamy.

"Don't let it catch," she said, moving briskly from bench to sink to oven in a way that left Marheh feeling distinctly inadequate. As she went she tossed sentences at Marheh, information, instructions, questions, until Marheh felt like an inept juggler trying to keep too many balls in the air.

"We have ten residents, twelve now with your two."

Cabbage leaves were broken into a colander and held under the tap.

"While you're here you'll spend the afternoons making beds and cleaning upstairs in the bedrooms."

A knife and chopping board appeared and the cabbage was quickly and neatly shredded.

"The residents are down here in the afternoons."

In fact there was very little lunch preparation left and by the time Marheh's custard had thickened and been put aside to cool a little everything else was complete. The figures in the courtyard and the conservatory drifted in to sit at the tables, quiet, a little dreamy and introspective, acknowledging no one. Gip came in with SW and SM and sat them down separately. He beckoned to Marheh. She was to help Deyah serve then come and assist him with SW she was told.

"Be quiet and calm," Deyah said when Marheh went to help her. "It doesn't matter if you are a bit slow, no one will worry, but noise and tension is upsetting."

So Marheh took a deep breath and carried bowls carefully, one at a time, as Deyah dished up the stew with cabbage and potato. At first she was nervous of the strange, silent residents and placed each bowl without looking at the recipient for fear of upsetting someone, but after the first couple were served uneventfully she gained in confidence and managed a small smile and even, by the last couple, found she could look them in the eyes with a friendly greeting.

Helping SW was different, her silence was emptiness, beyond the broken mind there was nothing. Dutifully Marheh instructed her to eat and guided the spoon, but she could not care about how she performed the task and SW finished her meal with food on her face and clothes. Gip was disapproving both of the extra work caused and of the disrespect Marheh showed by her carelessness.

"It doesn't matter what she did to you," he said. "You will treat her as you would wish to be treated."

Before she quite understood what was happening Marheh found herself pushing the last of SW's mashed potato into her own face on the end of SW's fork.

"You see?" Gip said when her chin and cheeks were decorated. "Now go and clean yourself up. Then you can come back with a bowl and clean this woman. Whatever she has done or become she could have been Silberay once."

Marheh went to wash her face and came back feeling rather aggrieved. "I thought you weren't allowed to do that to me," she said to Gip, putting the basin and wash cloth down on the table.

"I'm not Silberay now," he said. "If I want to use my skill to make a point or offer a lesson there is nothing to stop me."

"Oh!" Marheh looked from the basin to the food on SW's face and put down the wash cloth. How could she care for SW after what she had done? "Well you've made a point," she said, sounding cross. "But I don't care. I hate her and I can't be nice to her."

"That's honest at least," Gip said slowly. "Do you wish you had killed her then?"

Marheh stared at him. "I'm not a murderer."

"Well without someone to care for her this woman will die because of what you have done."

"That's not fair! I didn't mean it to be like that."

Gip looked at her out of steady grey eyes. "I know you didn't, but that is how it is. So who is going to care for her so you won't be a murderer?"

Marheh was silent for a moment, unwilling to acknowledge the answer. Gip waited patiently.

"You," she said at last.

Gip smiled at her. "So won't you try to help me, just for a little while?"

Marheh stared at him, angry and confronted. She wanted to shout at him in protest, instead she turned and ran, trying to escape from the challenge of his words. But there was no escape. The front door was locked and bolted, but however far she might run the idea was in her mind now and she knew it. She flung herself down on the little bed in the corner, pulled the pillow over her head and battled with herself in the darkness.

When she returned, slowly and reluctantly, Gip and SW were still where she left them, a basin of cooling water between them, a wash cloth waiting. Without looking at Gip, Marheh dipped the cloth into the bowl, squeezed it out and wiped the food from SW's face. She was concentrating fiercely, her lips pressed together, her eyes focused on the work of her hands. When she had finished she let out her breath in a long sigh, looked from SW to Gip and began to cry as if her heart would break.

Gip and Deyah looked at each other across the big room and Deyah nodded. Gip led Marheh out past the silent residents and into the courtyard. He sat her down in a sunny spot and handed her a big handkerchief.

"Take as long as you need," he said kindly and left her alone.

Marheh scarcely knew why she was crying, but alone in the quiet courtyard she managed to pull herself together. Somewhere in her mind she finally acknowledged something of her own responsibility for all that had happened and saw that her adventure was only the beginning. She mopped her eyes and blew her nose and went back to Gip and Deyah. They now sat together. SW and SM were nowhere to be seen and the other residents had moved to the sofas in the conservatory. Marheh sat down with Deyah and Gip to eat lunch and listen to a recital of her duties for the week ahead.

"So you can be a great help to us if you will," Deyah said in the end. "You can give us a little holiday."

"And if you've time after all these jobs," Gip added. "You could try and discover the woman's soul name. She must have had one once."

Marheh's jaw dropped and she looked from one to the other. Wasn't that an impossible task?

Nemle drove away with Barntredor and did not look back, but she left her thoughts behind, wondering how Marheh would manage, hoping her own words and actions had been enough and not too much or to little to help Marheh find sense and direction. She was glad that Barntredor was not much of a conversationalist and rested in his silence until they had almost reached the farm.

"You will miss your daughter?" Barntredor said carefully as they turned into the lane which led to the farm entrance.

"I will indeed," Nemle said smiling at him. "You have been very good, driving all over the place for us."

Barntredor gave a pleased sounding grunt and clicked the reins. "I like to drive," he said. "But we must move on soon."

"Of course," Nemle agreed. "There is not much more for me to do here."

They were soon pulling up in the courtyard at the farm. Min came out to greet them and help Nemle to alight. Jona invited them both to come in for lunch, but Barntredor chose to return to the Travellers' camp.

The children were gathered in the kitchen with Lithi. It was warm and filled with chatter and good smells. There were only half a dozen children left and they seemed very much at home. Nemle listened and watched with a sense of relief. It seemed as if these children would not have suffered permanent harm. Four adults and six children made quite a crowd around the big table but it was a cheerful meal. Then, when it was over, Nemle spent sometime saying goodbye to each child. She knew it would be part of her task and Marheh's to watch over their welfare and she needed to be sure that they each remembered their soul name and would use it amongst themselves.

Jona insisted on putting together a bag of food for her and while she was doing so Nemle went to the Travellers' camp to thank them and say goodbye. She and Fliandre understood each other well and needed little more than a smile and the touch of a hand to convey gratitude and good wishes. Trodkali was there with Bernard, now Bernardo, and, rather surprisingly, with Dyti, who had chosen to become Andyti and not return to the reluctant hospitality of the relative she had lived with. Nemle thought she would be unsettled for some time and made a mental note to keep in touch. She was a little older than the two boys, but seemed happy to be with them, barefooted and scruffy, but free to enjoy the countryside, scrounge for wild food and firewood and learn the Travellers' skills.

Min had harnessed the pony again and soon Nemle was on her way back to *Day Bringer*, a box of provisions on the seat beside her. Min carried the box to the edge of the water road for her and said goodbye, a little reluctant to leave her alone in a field, but trusting her word that a boat on the water was waiting for her there. Kel had already taken Samuel to *Storm Cloud*, but they were still moored beside *Day Bringer*. Nemle understood that they would not leave *Day Bringer* unprotected whilst SP was possibly about the area. She lifted the box of food onto *Day Bringer* then knocked on *Storm Cloud's* roof. Kel came to greet her and invite her in. She indicated the food, offering to share, but the farm had already provided for them. They were about to set out, Kel told her, but they would not have gone without saying goodbye. A day of goodbyes, Nemle thought sadly.

She went on board with Kel and down into *Storm Cloud's* saloon. Sul and Samuel were there and she sensed a degree of tension in the way they faced each other. Sul stood up slowly and came to greet her while Kel beckoned to Samuel to join him while he performed the engine checks.

"You will have a difficult time with him," Nemle said sympathetically once she and Sul were alone.

Sul nodded. "A weary time, but worthwhile if it heals him."

"I will think of you often," Nemle said, clasping Sul's hand briefly before making her way back to *Day Bringer*.

Five minutes later she heard the throb of *Storm Cloud's* engine, felt *Day Bringer* move as the mooring ropes were unfastened and Kel pushed *Storm Cloud* away. She stood in the well deck to wave as they went slowly past, Kel at the tiller, Samuel, still and scowling by his side.

She was alone. Quietly she made her own preparations for departure, the box of food stored away, the fire banked, the engine checked after its long silence. She had just started the engine when *Storm Cloud* came back from the turning place and passed her, resuming their interrupted journey. She smiled and waved and watched them out of sight before continuing, pulling up mooring pins, coiling ropes and wishing for Marheh's loving, challenging presence.

She did not travel for long, perhaps two hours, just what was needed for a change of scene and a change of pace. She moored on the edge of a small wood and sat thinking of Marheh, wondering how she was feeling and later as twilight hung about her listening to the sound of her solitude before going quietly to bed.

Marheh spent her afternoon upstairs making beds. Deyah had gone up with her to show her what was expected. The little bedrooms were narrow and compact, not very different in some respects to her own little cabin on *Day Bringer*.

"It is what Silberay are comfortable with," Deyah explained. "Though I'm sure they miss the ripple of reflected light on the ceiling and sense of being close to the natural world."

Her description gave Marheh a pang of homesickness, but she thrust it resolutely aside. She thought she was going to hate every minute of her time at the hospice, but she was determined to do her best not to let Nemle down.

"Try not to hate it," Deyah said, watching Marheh struggling with the bed clothes and fighting the broom. "It's only you that suffers. Better to just get on and do it without thinking about it." She smiled at Marheh. "Or perhaps you could think about what you are doing for other people, giving me and Gip a holiday, making a comfortable place for someone."

Marheh got up from the floor where she had been pursuing the dust under the bed. Already she looked flushed and dishevelled.

"I'm not such a nice person as that," she said with a flash of insight.

Deyah laughed softly. "I think you could be," she said, going out of the room.

Marheh stared after her, heard her quiet footsteps moving along the corridor then returned to her task with something else to think about.

Evening meal preparation was next with Gip in charge of the menu. A small respite was provided while they ate, but the washing up seemed to go on for ever. By the time she had finished the residents were all in their rooms and she was invited, perhaps requested, to sit down with Gip and Deyah.

"Nemle said you have already experienced the soul song," Deyah said when they were settled comfortably, a mug of sperit in one hand, a big piece of Deyah's special carrot cake in the other.

Marheh looked puzzled for a minute then realised what she was referring to.

"Nemle sang with me," she said, not sure she wanted to talk about the way Nemle had helped her to return from the place SW had sent her.

"These Silberay would like you to sing with them," Deyah said seriously. "They sing very sweetly."

"But I don't know how," Marheh said. "It was Nemle."

"If you practice your discipline of the soul I think they will find you," Gip said. "Will you try?"

"Why do they want to sing with me?" Marheh asked, puzzled and curious.

"Because you are here looking after them," Gip said. "They want to know you the only way they can."

"Now?" Marheh asked after a long pause.

"When you have finished your cake and your drink," Deyah said. "When you are ready."

Consequently Marheh went soon to her little corner under the stairs, lit her candle and drew the heavy curtain. She was very tired, everything seemed strange and different and she was not sure she could find the focus she would need to enter the discipline of the soul. She wanted to try though. The idea of singing with the strange, quiet souls of the residents of the cottage piqued her curiosity and the remembrance of the song she had shared with Nemle made her eager for more. She chose to lie on the floor rather than the little bed, thinking she might go to sleep if she was too comfortable. For a few moments she watched the flickering shadows that played above her, the long slope of the rising staircase, the dark corners bravely held at bay by the candlelight. Then she turned from the real candle to find the flame that would lead her into the discipline. Building it was an effort of concentration but she was aided by the deep silence of the cottage and by something outside herself that seemed to be beckoning. Gradually the candle flame lit its warmth within her and she rested in it. Then the song began. At first it came only as the faintest echo so she scarcely knew when it began, high and far off, a little melancholy. New voices entered, new tones wove together and came closer. This was not the contrapuntal dance she had made with Nemle, but a harmonious choir calling her and if she listened very carefully she could hear the space they had left for her voice to join them. Faltering, a little tentative at first, she began to sing, softly so she could continue to listen for her place, caring only that she did not spoil the harmony. Then she began to understand that the other voices were cherishing her, nurturing her song, drawing music from her she did not know she possessed. Gratefully she responded, forgetting herself in the joy of being part of the beauty that surrounded her.

The music was all time and no time and when it finally withdrew the real candle still shone, gently illuminating her little corner. She rested for a moment, reluctant to move, to break the spell, then she pulled off her clothes, tumbled into bed, blew out the candle and fell instantly asleep.

Next morning she woke early, refreshed and eager. Even the knowledge that it was her job to get up and see to the downstairs fires was a challenge not a chore. She'd had plenty of practice with fires now. She remembered the disastrous morning when Nemle had been so angry with her. They still hadn't replaced all the dishes she had broken then. She thought of Nemle as she dressed carefully and crept along the corridor to the kitchen. The fire in the stove was the most important, that one heated the hot water for the bathrooms upstairs as well. She hummed a little tune under her breath as she worked and was surprised to find that she was enjoying herself.

By the time Gip and Deyah came downstairs she had completed all her before breakfast chores and was busy stirring a big pot of porridge. They smiled at her, but did not comment on her happy face and changed outlook.

"We had a lovely sleep-in," Deyah said as they sat together over breakfast. "Thank you so much."

Marheh glowed with pleasure at this acknowledgement of her efforts and applied herself diligently to her porridge, then whisked around collecting dirty plates and making toast and sperit. All but the most damaged residents were able to dress and make their way down stairs to breakfast if prompted. Marheh went up with Deyah and learned how to slip gently into each broken mind and offer a picture of the outcome she desired, the appropriately clad individual sitting and eating at the breakfast table. Deyah did not comment, but she began to understand something of Nemle's concern for her apprentice when she saw how quickly and naturally Marheh was able to do this. Marheh herself was thoughtful as they approached the last two Silberay, who needed extra assistance. Deyah waited, wondering whether she would speak her thoughts. It was not until they were downstairs again and Gip had brought in SW and SM that she revealed what was on her mind.

"You can't really have rules about it, can you?" she said. She spoke slowly as if trying to resolve some problem that had developed for her.

Deyah waited for more.

"I mean the discipline of the mind," she said. "Nemle and Sul were telling us about the Great Debate and all the rules about not using the discipline of the mind, but there are times you have to use it."

Still Deyah waited, hoping she would find her own answer.

"Do you think perhaps it might be more important to try and be a good person?" she said, her big brown eyes looking from Deyah to Gip. "And then you wouldn't need the rules because you would use it in a good way."

The residents were beginning to drift into the dining area now and it was time for Marheh to begin serving the porridge. She got up quickly without waiting for an answer. Deyah followed her.

"I think you might be right," she said, beginning to ladle porridge into bowls for Marheh to deliver to the tables.

Distribution was quickly accomplished and Marheh sat with Gip and SM and SW and helped SW to eat her breakfast. She was more careful this time and Gip smiled his approval.

"Do you think?" she said to Deyah as she took her the dirty plates. "Do you think that if you don't want to try and be a good person then you can't really be Silberay?"

She filled the sink with hot water and began on the dishes almost without thinking.

"Perhaps sometimes you need some guidelines," Deyah suggested when she was sure Marheh had said all she wanted. "It is not always easy to know what makes a good person."

Marheh thought about this then nodded slowly. "So I have to keep the rules because I'm not very good yet, but you and Nemle don't because you are."

Deyah shook her head. "It seems to me to be a bit dangerous for anyone to think of themselves as a good person," she said. "A bit complacent. Even trying too hard to be good can be dangerous, better to concentrate on practicing the discipline of the soul and let that take care of the goodness."

Marheh put the last bowl in the drainer and began on the porridge pot. It required a degree of elbow grease and for a few minutes she worked hard and said nothing. Deyah dried the cutlery and waited, wondering what Marheh would make of her words.

When she spoke it was unexpected, almost shy. "Last night I sang with them," she said, inspecting the porridge pot so she did not have to look up. "This morning I am happy to be here helping."

Deyah lifted the big saucepan from Marheh's hands and enveloped it in her tea towel.

"When yesterday you hated it, even though you were trying to be good," she said. "Maybe we need both things, the trying and the willingness to be remade."

She dried the pot and put it away while Marheh was wiping down the sink. Then she sent Marheh off to the vegetable garden to see if she could find a couple of lettuces and perhaps an early tomato or two to add to their lunch, giving her time and space to make her own meaning from all they had said.

As the days went past Marheh slipped into the routine that Gip and Deyah had developed to give their residents a sense of comfort and security. She got up early and worked hard until evening doing chores that were boring and uncongenial without complaining and thinking hard about the needs of the Silberay she was helping. Sometimes if she had a free moment she would ask one of the residents if she could enter her mind and though she never received an answer it seemed to her that she was welcomed as she slipped carefully into the damaged space that had once been the receptacle for a wealth of intelligence and skill. Marheh had no thought beyond the desire to attempt some kind of communication with these, to her, almost tragic figures. She understood very little of what they had suffered to reduce them to their current state, but knew suffering and endurance had made them and so felt a kind of reverence that showed itself in her careful gentleness and unaccustomed humility.

Deyah and Gip, very aware of all that affected their charges, watched carefully at first, but soon realised that Marheh's attempts at communication were not harming them. They said nothing to Marheh, but to their eyes, one or two of the residents seemed almost to show faint signs of improvement, though Deyah shook her head when she and Gip first discussed the possibility.

"I think we are just seeing something we long for," she said. "Not something real."

Each evening when the work was done and after she had reviewed the day with Gip and Deyah, Marheh went early to her corner and practiced the discipline of the soul. It came more easily each time and though there were not always souls to sing with, she began to make her own soul song, not a very accomplished melody, but one she could sing and send seeking response. She had not forgotten Gip's challenge to her to find SW's soul name and it seemed to her that if she was to succeed she must be able to initiate a song and not just respond to other's prompting, so she practiced assiduously and in doing so forgot herself.

Nemle, alone on *Day Bringer*, found her thoughts constantly turning to Marheh, not only wondering how she was coping with the new environment, but also turning over and over in her mind possibilities for teaching her and helping her develop. It seemed to her that this task of being mentor to Marheh was the most important work she had ever attempted and there were times when she doubted her fitness for the task. She had thought that a week alone would be just a return to her solitary years of boating, but in fact it was nothing like, for Marheh's absence was almost as strongly felt as her presence, challenging and demanding as it was.

She travelled towards the cottage for several hours each day. The journey included a couple of locks and she thought how Marheh would have enjoyed them as she completed the process of emptying and filling, opening and closing, as she had done for so many years alone. Each day too she worked with her plants and herbs, aware that her financial resources were getting low. She had not spent her usual time plant gathering because of Marheh's coming and she began to see that Marheh would need to help her, even if it was not congenial employment, because she consumed resources, she would have to contribute to acquiring them. Structure and discipline had to be part of Marheh's life with her but she needed challenge too. There was time to browse through her copy of *Guidelines for Mentoring the Young Apprentice* once more before deciding that whoever had written it did not know Marheh and that his advice (Nemle was sure the author was a man) was not only unhelpful, but in some instances likely to arouse resistance. Without giving herself time to re-consider, she put it in the fire and closed the door. She and Marheh would decide together on their own guidelines.

The days went past and *Day Bringer* travelled on. A week had seldom seemed so long. Although she had plenty to keep her occupied and lots to think about Nemle missed Marheh even more than she had expected. Each evening she entered the discipline of the soul, refreshing herself with the stillness, resting in the quiet place that held her so gently. She had felt no need to make her song and send it voyaging, though as always, there was a hint of distant music. One evening however a song seemed to be seeking hers. It was a simple melody, unadorned, almost childlike. Nemle listened as the eager, questing phrase reached out bravely. Then she responded, carefully, tenderly with her own song, muted in deference to the innocent little tune that now seemed to be all happiness. Her own song laughed with delight, its deep chuckle rippling beneath the sweet, clear notes of the other, lifting, nurturing. Outside time they played together, the old soul led by the young, the old soul guarding the young with subtle care. When they parted, withdrew, still filled with delight, Nemle glimpsed Marheh's rapt face and understood who her companion had been.

Marheh, returning to her shadowy corner, had seen Nemle's eyes and shared the moment of mutual recognition. Of course, she thought, it could only have been Nemle who gave her that sense of safety. She stretched and sighed and counted the days and realised that most of the week had gone. The day after tomorrow she would be back on *Day Bringer*. The thought made her smile happily as she changed into her nightdress and snuggled into bed. It would be a new start, she thought, mistakes and reparations past and the future to look forward to.

"Your mentor is responsible for your safety. This may, at times, seem restrictive and you may feel rebellious. Remember that what may be thought of as the physical discipline, the practice of boating, can be dangerous and accidents happen in places where help is not easily obtained."

The Silberay apprentice : a handbook

Chapter Nineteen

Nemle reached the place below the cottage late in the afternoon. She moored neatly and efficiently and made her way up to the front door, looking forward to reclaiming Marheh, hoping she would be happy to come with her. Deyah saw her coming and let her in quietly.

"How's my girl?" she asked, trying not to show her anxiety.

Deyah put her finger to her lips. "She's upstairs doing the bedrooms," she said softly. "Would you like to surprise her?"

Nemle shook her head. "That wouldn't be fair, she might think I was spying on her."

Deyah smiled and shook her head. "I don't think so," she said. "But come into the kitchen and sit down, she won't be much longer. I'll make sperit."

It was perhaps ten minutes later when Nemle heard the quick, light footsteps in the corridor. She turned from her seat in the living area and looked towards the door. A moment later Marheh came in. She did not see Nemle, but went to the sink where Deyah stood with the kettle. She looked content and purposeful Nemle thought thankfully. She saw Deyah say something and Marheh's face turn curiously in her direction, then when she understood who was waiting there her face lit up. Nemle smiled and began to stand up, but Marheh was already by her side, kneeling at her chair. Nemle reached for her, held her briefly, then leaned back to look at her.

"You've been working hard," she said a little unsteadily. She rubbed gently with her thumb at a smudge of dirt on Marheh's cheek. "I can tell."

"I do the bedrooms in the afternoon," Marheh told her, a kind of pride in her voice. "I've really tried not to let you down," she added with a touch of anxiety.

"I've missed you," Nemle said, kissing her lightly. "I'm sure you haven't let me down, or yourself."

167

Deyah came across to them in time to hear Nemle's last comment. She put a hand on Marheh's shoulder and smiled down at her.

"You've been a great help. Gip and I have had a real holiday." She looked from one to the other. "Would you like to show Nemle round before you take your bag down to *Day Bringer* and then we hope you will both come back and have dinner with us before we say goodbye."

Marheh spent a long time taking Nemle round. It was as if she needed to tell her everything; how she had rebelled and wept that first day, how she had sung with the residents, how she had cleaned and washed up and chopped vegetables and not minded too much because she was trying to be a good person. Nemle smiled and hugged her and watched with interest as she shared herself with the residents, entering their minds with grave deference and managing SW capably and without fuss.

She took so long that dinner preparation was underway and they still had not been down to *Day Bringer*. Marheh looked apologetically at Nemle.

"I'm longing to go back," she said. "But I think I should stay and help with dinner. My bag can come down after."

"We'll both help with dinner," Nemle said, her voice revealing her pride and pleasure.

They did not begin their own meal until all the residents had finished and gone up for the evening, so it was quite late by the time Nemle and Marheh finally returned to *Day Bringer*. Marheh was very quiet as they made their way down to the water road. The long twilight had almost gone and *Day Bringer* was just a dark shape, resting quietly on the still, dark water. She smoothed a hand lightly over the hull as they reached the boat.

"Imagine having to leave the water road," she said softly to Nemle. "Those Silberay have given up everything. I think I'd rather die, but they wanted me to sing with them."

Nemle placed one hand gently over Marheh's for a moment then led the way on board.

Next morning Marheh was up early and about her regular chores, taking new pleasure in tidying her little cabin, tending the fire and making the breakfast. She and Nemle had sung together with the residents before sleeping and there was a gentle sadness in leave taking that she had not expected, but now, with the new day, she felt as if she was making a new start. As *Day Bringer* slid away from her mooring she stood in the well deck coiling the front line. She heard the chuckle of water under the bow and the gentle throb of *Day Bringer*'s engine. She watched the pearl coloured sky brighten to blue and the rising sun awaken the shadows that patterned the landscape. Then she made her way along the gunnel to join Nemle on the back deck eager to tell her about the new start she was making. Nemle smiled and encouraged her and thought about new days and new starts of her own.

The days began to fall into a pattern of work and travel and long lazy twilit evenings and the spring moved on towards summer. To Marheh's joy Nemle began to teach her about the engine, simple things at first, just checking oil and water, but moving on to nuts and bolts and bits that needed to be cleaned and oiled.

She was not quite so overjoyed to hear that she was also to learn to help Nemle with her plants, but she was gratified when Nemle explained their financial situation and how she could be involved in earning their keep.

"And you know," Nemle said. "I have never seen that clay you spoke of putting under your bunk. Why don't you take a bit of time to practice like you planned?"

Marheh's face lit up. "I didn't think you wanted me to."

"I was a bit disappointed I think," Nemle said slowly. "Because I hoped you would want to continue my work, but that was not fair of me. I want you to do what makes you happiest. Of course," she added with a twinkle. "You will still have to help me, so maybe you'll come to enjoy it."

Marheh grinned and shook her head. "Maybe," she said doubtfully.

So that evening she brought out her clay from its long incarceration. She spent most of the first evening working it to the consistency she wanted. Nemle watched her intent face and knew she had been wise to encourage her. Then, on subsequent evenings, she delighted in the little pieces Marheh produced, small birds and animals appeared under her clever fingers as well as small figures. Usually Marheh destroyed her work, saying she was just practicing, but once or twice Nemle insisted on rescuing a piece that particularly appealed.

It was not all plain sailing. Marheh still pushed against the discipline Nemle was trying to instil in her.

There were locks on this section of the water road and once Nemle had shown her what to do, Marheh was happy working off some of her energy with a windlass, walking between locks and setting them ready for *Day Bringer*.

Nemle had drilled her carefully and told her she must do exactly as she had been taught, but after a couple of days, when they had successfully negotiated half a dozen locks, Marheh felt she knew enough to experiment.

Next time Nemle brought *Day Bringer* round a corner to a lock she saw Marheh stepping casually across the gap between an open gate and one waiting to be opened. It was a move she had made hundreds of times herself, but it was not one she had shown Marheh, who needed to practice the safer way many times more. As *Day Bringer* came up in the lock Nemle climbed onto the roof and stepped out onto the lockside. She held out her hand for Marheh's windlass.

"You must learn to do as you are told," she said, taking it from her. "You may try that move again when you've worked a hundred locks."

"But it seems so silly to do it the slow way when I can easily step across," Marheh protested, reaching for the windlass.

Nemle kept a firm hold. "Silly or not you practice going slowly first. You may think you know all about locks, but take it from me you know very little."

Marheh still looked as if she would have liked to argue.

Nemle continued to hold the windlass. "I'll look after this for now," she said, tucking it into her belt alongside her own.

"But I can't do the locks without it."

"No," said Nemle getting ready to open the lock.

Marheh turned away, kicking at the grass on the lockside. Nemle watched her struggle with herself.

"I'm sorry Nemle," she said at last. "I'll do it your way I promise."

Together they leaned on the gate to open it. Nemle stood up, lowered the gate paddles and stepped onto *Day Bringer*.

"You don't need your windlass to close the gate," she said, pushing down the throttle and easing *Day Bringer* out of the lock.

Marheh leaned on the gate to close it, and then watched open mouthed as Nemle kept going straight on.

It was not so very far to the final lock for the day, perhaps half a mile. Marheh began the walk angrily. It wasn't fair, she was careful, she wasn't a child. But she was not able to deceive herself for long. Nemle had been very precise in her instructions. She knew what she was supposed to do and she had not done it. Nemle was disappointed in her, it was her own fault and she had spoiled the new start she had wanted to make. She stopped for a moment to rub at her face then she put her chin in the air and quickened her pace. By the time she reached the lock Nemle had opened the gates and was hauling *Day Bringer* into it using the centre line. She leaned back on the rope, braking *Day Bringer*'s forward movement before she reached the top gate, then she looked across the deep chasm of the lock to where Marheh was hurrying up the final steep incline. Nemle looped her line loosely around the top gate and went back to close the lower gate on her side. Marheh, she was pleased to see, was already at work on the other gate. Carefully Nemle began to wind the paddles in the top gate, watching *Day Bringer* as the water gushed in. Marheh watched too, seeing how Nemle kept *Day Bringer*'s bow up close to the gate so she couldn't bump too much. Soon *Day Bringer* reached her new level. Both together they leaned on the gate to open it. Nemle dropped the paddles and stepped on board to take *Day Bringer* out of the lock but this time she waited, hovering in the mouth of the lock while Marheh closed the gate. Once it was done Marheh looked at her, a questioning look. Nemle held out her hand.

"That was the last one for today," she said, gripping Marheh's hand as she made the step onto the back deck.

That evening as Nemle read by the fire Marheh worked with her clay at the table. Nemle had learned to judge the progress of the work by the little sounds she heard, brief sighs, the occasional mutter, a quick catch of breath, sometimes a faint humming. Tonight there seemed to be more sighs than usual, but finally she heard the caught breath that meant the finishing touches. Then suddenly Marheh was kneeling by her chair. In her hands she offered a little figure that was all contrition. The face was hidden, but the slim body was Marheh's own and a long plait lay over the bent back. Nemle looked into the brown eyes that were raised anxiously to hers. Carefully she took the little model and smiled at the giver.

"I see she is feeling repentant," she said, studying her gift. "Isn't it lucky there is a new start to each day?"

"I love my present," Nemle said next morning as they travelled quietly along. "And later I shall ask you to tell me how to look after it, but I'm not really sure that I should accept it. I don't want you to be obedient for the sake of pleasing me."

Marheh turned from her casual examination of the landscape in some surprise.

"Why not?"

Nemle looked at her. "Obedience is part of being disciplined about yourself, not thinking you know best, being able to put an idea ahead of yourself, being humble."

171

"But what if I do know best?" Marheh said. "Why should I be humble? I don't mind doing what you tell me … well not really," she added, grinning as Nemle laughed. "Because I know you care about me and I do want to be a good person, but I don't really see why obedience is part of being good."

Nemle thought for a minute, the hand resting on the tiller automatically making the small adjustments necessary for *Day Bringer*'s safe passage.

"You say you want to be a good person," Nemle said at last. "That is an idea you want to be obedient to, being Silberay is an idea you want to be obedient to. Being obedient to me is practicing for that obedience, that discipline."

Plenty of time was given to practicing the other disciplines too. Nemle was determined that Marheh be challenged and interested and that she develop her skills and her understanding. When she learned that Gip had challenged Marheh to find SW's soul name she encouraged her to practise the discipline of the soul in different ways. Always she must begin with her candle flame and spend time resting in its warmth for this was her safeguard, but then she could stretch herself as she saw fit, sending out her song, making harmonies. Nemle only asked that Marheh tell her when she set out. For the moment Nemle would voyage beside or behind her since there were dangers even in this.

Practicing the discipline of the mind could be a game and Nemle tried to find ways to make it enjoyable without losing sight of the essential seriousness. Speed and subtlety were important as well as strength and skill. Marheh's experiences in the cottage had given her new skills in mind to mind communication and Nemle encouraged her to build on these by making herself a willing receptacle for Marheh's commands. She could not help laughing the day when Marheh chose to do the lunch dishes with Nemle's hands and when she tried to have Nemle's fingers fashion a small plump robin from her clay. She did not allow Marheh to have things all her own way however. It was important she be able to defend herself from such as SP and there were times when Marheh felt Nemle's fingers squeezing her out of shape as SP's had done, times when she had to exert all her strength to release herself only to find that Nemle still held her captive. Sometimes practicing was enough to exhaust them both.

Marheh knew practicing the discipline of the mind was hedged with restrictions, but even here she could not help herself from experimenting.

One day she carried a tray of Nemle's seedlings up to a village close to where they were moored. All she had to do was deliver them and then call into the village shop for some bacon and cheese. She had been away perhaps half an hour when Nemle felt her tempestuous return to *Day*

Bringer. She looked up to see her come into the saloon very red faced and breathing hard. Before Nemle had a chance to ask what was wrong Marheh thrust one of her slippers into her hand and flung herself to her knees.

"You might as well beat me now," she said and threw herself forward to sprawl across the footstool.

"Very dramatic," Nemle said dryly. "But I decline to whack you without knowing what you've done."

Marheh pushed herself up and slid back onto her heels. "You don't want to know," she said. "And even if you do whack me it will be worth it."

Nemle sat on the footstool beside her and shook her head. "Then what would be the point of whacking you?" she said.

"I know you're supposed to punish me if I use the discipline of the mind when I shouldn't," Marheh said fiercely. "So you had better get on with it."

Nemle's presence on the footstool foiled her from adopting her previous position, but she looked as if she would not need much encouragement to put herself across Nemle's lap.

"Stop being melodramatic and tell me what you have done," Nemle said firmly.

Marheh opened and closed her mouth a couple of times like a fish, but nothing came out.

"Take a deep breath," Nemle instructed, giving her hand a little slap. "And another."

Marheh obeyed her and began to look calmer.

"Now tell me what happened."

Marheh took another deep breath and began.

"I delivered the seedlings where you told me," she said. "They were very pleased. So then I went along to the shop. I was just going in when this woman started to come out. I was very polite and backed away and held the door for her. She was all dressed in black with a basket over her arm and a big black hat with dead birds on it."

"Marheh!" Nemle cautioned as Marheh seemed to be getting carried away by her story.

"She did!" Marheh protested. "At least that's what it looked like. I suppose I was sort of staring because she glared at me and said 'Go away you dirty little gypsy. We don't want your sort here.' So then I made her take off her hat and put it on backwards, and some of her false hair came off with it."

Marheh giggled at the memory and Nemle's lips twitched as she tried to hide her smile.

"And then I remembered that I wasn't supposed to, and I thought you'd be cross, so I came back... and I forgot to get the bacon and cheese," she added.

"Oh Marheh," Nemle said, sighing a little and wondering when Marheh would begin to grow up. "I suppose it's partly my fault," she said. "Since I've encouraged you to play games with me when you practice, but surely you know better than that?"

"I do really," Marheh said. "It's just that I did it before I thought because I was angry."

"So what are we going to do to help you remember to think first?" Nemle asked.

"I don't know," Marheh said gloomily. "I suppose you had better beat me."

"I have no intention of beating you," Nemle said firmly. "So don't start feeling martyred. But this is the second time you've used the discipline of the mind to take personal revenge on someone and it is unacceptable behaviour. If you were not a first year apprentice you would get us grounded."

"What do you mean grounded?"

"*Day Bringer* would be lifted out and put on the bank for a number of months or years depending on how bad you were."

"But that would punish you too," Marheh said. "That's not fair."

"Perfectly fair, since I am supposed to teach you what is right."

"You do teach me, but..." Marheh broke off.

"But you don't learn?" asked Nemle. "Then we had better start thinking of what will encourage you." She stood up. "In the mean time you can go back and get the bacon and cheese before the shop shuts and this time if someone calls you a dirty little gypsy you curtsy and agree with them politely."

Spring became summer as they moved slowly onwards. Marheh realised she had never followed the progress of a season so closely as she now was. Every smallest change in the landscape seemed to shout at her to take notice, a change of tone, deepening greens as leafy canopies filled out and took shape, hedges misted over with pink and white before darkening to green. Birds seemed to be busy and noisy and small animals were more evident. The long twilit evenings were a time of developing companionship whether she and Nemle were quiet together, each working contentedly at some task of her own, or whether they sat in the well deck and watched as the light faded and owls and small bats began to emerge for their evening of food gathering. Sometimes Marheh took herself off for long walks, but these were not the driven escapes of former times, instead she studied *Day Bringer*'s charts with Nemle and planned her explorations. Nemle encouraged her to add her discoveries to the log as well as keeping a journal of her own and also gave her hints about how she might begin to listen with her heart to get a sense of the well-being of the places she visited. They seldom went near anywhere larger than a village. Towns and cities had little time for the water road on the whole although there were one or two small towns where the Silberay uniform was recognised, sometimes with respect, sometimes with a kind of pitying patronage that angered Marheh.

"They can't see the water and don't want to," Marheh said to Nemle. "And they speak as if they are indulging me, allowing me my different perception of the world, humouring me as if I was a bit crazy in a harmless way."

Nemle laughed at her vehemence. "And is there something wrong with being thought to be a bit crazy in a harmless way? It doesn't hurt us. It might even help us to be humble and it doesn't change who we are or interfere with what we do."

Marheh made a face. "I'm not humble I know and I want to be … to be acknowledged for who I am I suppose."

"As long as they pay for my seedlings and my medicines and take my money for the goods I need I'm acknowledged enough," Nemle said, giving Marheh the new blank book she had bought for her in the town they had just visited.

Marheh gave her a hug. "I suppose it is better than being a dirty little gypsy."

The route they were taking made a big circle through the countryside before it returned to their original course not far from the cottage. Marheh had missed the junction which Nemle had passed during her solitary week between Fairdale Rising and the cottage, but Nemle had shown her on the map. It had taken them six weeks of slow, steady boating. Half the summer was over before they passed under the bridge that completed the ring.

They were moored up by lunch time. Marheh studied the map and looked at Nemle.

"Could we visit Gip and Deyah? It doesn't look to be more than three or four miles."

"Would you like to?"

Marheh nodded. "I've learned such a lot since I was there. I thought perhaps …" She broke off and blushed unexpectedly. "Gip wanted me to find SW's soul name, perhaps I can now if I see her again."

"Do you think so?" Nemle asked. "Then of course you must try. Would you like to walk or shall we take *Day Bringer*? It would not be difficult to back her up to the junction and turn there."

"Could we?" Marheh was delighted. "I was afraid you might not want to walk so far."

"We'll be there in an hour, or perhaps an hour and a half if we go on and turn before we moor."

So a couple of hours later Marheh shyly presented herself at the front door of the cottage. Nemle had insisted that she go alone although she promised to join her later if it seemed appropriate. Gip and Deyah welcomed her kindly and listened while she explained her purpose.

"I know that normally you don't have to be near someone to sing with them," she finished. "But I think it might be different with someone like SW who doesn't believe she has a soul."

Deyah smiled at her. "We would love you to try, but you mustn't be too disappointed if you don't succeed."

"I'll be disappointed," Marheh said. "But I'll keep trying."

They left her with SW, sitting opposite each other in the little courtyard. Marheh looked intently at her for a while then entered her mind, trying to find something she might recognise in the emptiness. She had thought and thought about what might be possible and what might lead her to find SW's soul name. Her plan was to try and enter the discipline of the soul whilst she was within SW's mind, but she did not know whether she could. Carefully she established herself in SW's mind, doing her best to acknowledge the involuntary hospitality that allowed her to remain there unchallenged. Then she tried to find her candle flame and bring it into the mind she inhabited. At first it seemed like an impossible balancing act and time and again she found her focus slipping, but gradually she found the trick of it. Then she had to begin her song, sing it into the corners of the mind around hers, sing in and through that mind. Almost she gave up. Her song seemed to echo, eerily alone, but as she flooded SW's being with her music she caught the faint hint of a response. It was not a song, not really, more like the wailing cry of an exhausted prisoner, two notes, faint and close together, again and again. Marheh listened and tempered her own song to weave softly around the two notes, beckoning, offering release.

"Come with me," she sang. "Come and be free, be free to grow."

Although she was unaware of them, Nemle, Deyah and Gip had all entered the discipline of the soul and waited around her, protecting her, but now, as she drew SW's starved soul out into the light, they too began to sing, supporting the melody Marheh was making as she carried SW's soul, welcoming SW's faltering notes.

At last Marheh laid down the soul she carried and withdrew quietly back into her own mind and into the care of the loving souls who supported her. Slowly she returned to herself, not really surprised to find Nemle beside her. She looked across at SW.

"Her name is Waila," she said.

"Waila," Nemle repeated, looking at SW and wondering if she imagined a change in the blank eyes.

She turned back to Marheh and saw that she had curled up in the chair and fallen asleep. She looked very young and vulnerable Nemle thought, settling herself to watch over her.

They left her to sleep until dinner time. Deyah brought a light blanket to cover her and tucked a small pillow under her head. She barely stirred. Nemle spent the rest of the afternoon pottering in the courtyard garden so she could be near her. The sunny space was quiet and peaceful and the time passed pleasantly.

Marheh was very quiet all evening as they ate together. The others let her be, smiling and including her, but not pushing for a response. It was not until she and Nemle were walking back to *Day Bringer* in the late summer twilight that she turned to Nemle.

"I'm glad," she said. "I stopped hating her and it grew from there."

Nemle smiled and hugged her and led the way on board.

Next morning they were off again, travelling towards the farm, a quiet, restorative week of summer sun, wide green landscape, birdsong and calm water. Marheh began to talk to Nemle about what she had done, not much, not all at once, but enough for Nemle to recognise just how far she had travelled, how much she had grown during the summer.

There was a sense of anticipation as they arrived at the mooring place near the farm, both of them keen to see Jona, Lithi, Min and the children again. Nemle however decreed that they should not take the long walk until morning. Instead Marheh walked back to the last bridge they had passed beneath and explored in the other direction returning to *Day Bringer* in time for a late supper, tired and happy.

Next morning they were welcomed joyfully as they reached the farm house. All work stopped and they were escorted into the big kitchen for cake and sperit. Nemle was pleased to see how happily the children had settled in and Jona, Lithi and Min seemed to be both loved and respected. Having the three of them to share the work meant that they could all have time for themselves as well, Jona told Nemle, so no one felt over burdened. There were plenty of things for the children to show Nemle and Marheh, a new calf, a new skill, a game that Marheh must join in while Nemle watched and laughed. When it was time to go the two oldest children proudly harnessed the pony with only a little help from Min.

They were just saying goodbye, laden with farm produce, when Lithi dashed back inside and returned with another parcel. She gave it to Marheh.

"It's the things you brought with you when you came," she said. "I found them when I was cleaning out rooms, and the other clothes they dressed you in."

Marheh looked at the parcel almost with distaste, remembering the humiliation she had felt. She wanted to refuse without hurting Lithi, after all she could not wear them. Then Nemle nudged her and she remembered Kithla. Some of the things were hers anyway. So she was able to smile and say thank you and hold the parcel on her lap as they trotted along the lanes and back to *Day Bringer*.

A few more days of boating brought them to the mooring at Fairdale Lading. Marheh was quite excited at the prospect of seeing Kithla and her father and telling them all that had happened. After they had eaten lunch Nemle waved her off, clutching the parcel of clothes.

"I'll come up and see them tomorrow," she said. "We'll stay a couple of days so we can catch up on all the news."

"I'll be quite glad to get my extra uniform back too," Marheh said. "I need more than one pair of trousers."

Nemle laughed. "Go on, give them my love and don't worry about me. Stay and enjoy it if they ask you to have dinner with them."

She watched as Marheh hurried up the hill, turning to wave as she reached the top. Then she went inside to sort through some seedlings she would take to Kithla and her father next day.

Marheh walked happily along the lane. She was not thinking particularly where she was going, sure she would recognise the low stone wall and neat, flowery front garden, so she was surprised when she reached the village green and realised she had gone past the little cottage where Kithla and her father lived. She mocked herself gently for her inattention and turned back, going more carefully this time.

"It should be somewhere here," she told herself, stopping and looking puzzled. This was the right place, she was sure, but the neat pretty garden was over grown and full of weeds.

"Something is wrong," she thought anxiously, pushing open the gate and making her way round the side. "Something is wrong," she thought again as she went through to the back and saw the raised beds had not been tended. Her mind full of dire imaginings she hurried to the back door and knocked. She was about to knock again when she heard footsteps and the sound of someone fumbling with the latch. The door opened and she stepped eagerly inside and turned to greet Kithla, but when she saw her the greeting died on her lips.

Called forth, beckoned by dawn's quiet light
Soft mist and sunrise surround
Sweet silvered waters mirror the world
Held in a silence profound.
                    Songs of the Silberay

Chapter Twenty

Nemle had *Day Bringer*'s roof almost covered with trays of seedlings in various stages of development. Marheh's assistance had enabled her to increase production, but her lack of knowledge meant that Nemle had plenty of sorting out to do. To Marheh one tray of little green shoots looked much like another and although most were now well established and looking more like their adult selves she still could not identify many of the herbs that were Nemle's speciality. Nemle was happy to spend a quiet afternoon pottering, her mind drifting as her fingers worked amongst the little plants. Soon now, she thought, she would teach Marheh to steer as she longed for. She had learned to heed Nemle's wishes, she had practiced the disciplines devotedly, she was happy and loving and there was no longer any reason to hold back. Nemle pictured her delight and decided that if the weather continued fine and calm she would let her take the tiller once they had left Fairdale Lading. She stopped work for a moment to wonder how Marheh was getting on with Kithla and her father and felt an unexpected touch of anxiety, but she put it aside feeling disloyal to Marheh. She was a very different person from the sulky, self-centred young woman she had been then. Nemle smiled at the remembrance and then allowed work to absorb her again.

Marheh looked at Kithla and just had time to register that she now wore the blank, unresponsive expression that had characterised Jona and Lithi when a voice spoke from within the kitchen.

"Welcome, little fly," it said. "I thought you might come to me here."

Startled, Marheh looked around to see SP seated in an imposing chair beside the fire. His hands rested easily on the flat wooden arms, the high back rose behind him. He had a small smile of anticipation on his face that set Marheh's heart beating faster. Kithla walked past her and sat on a stool against the wall. Her father, equally empty of expression, sat silent in his chair beside her.

"What have you done to them?" Marheh demanded, forgetting her fear.

"Nothing irreversible … yet," he said. "But that depends on you."

"On me?" Marheh said apprehensively.

"You must see that you cannot go unpunished," SP said, still with the imperturbable smile hovering.

He made a small gesture and a man, unnoticed until now, stepped forward out of the shadowy corner where he had been waiting. Marheh had a strange feeling that she had seen him before but it was not until SP had introduced him as CP, Canoe Person, that she realised he had been one of the Yareblis who had forced her into the water on her first visit to Fairdale Lading. She stood straighter, put her chin in the air and tried to prepare to defend her mind. SP continued speaking, his voice quiet and controlled.

"CP is directing the mind of your friend," he said. "Should you fail to cooperate with me, he will punish her. Ultimately he can destroy her."

Marheh looked from SP to CP and then at Kithla.

"Demonstrate," SP said sharply.

As Marheh watched an expression of pain crossed Kithla's previously blank face and she whimpered.

"What must I do?" Marheh asked as the sound died away and Kithla's face again became blank. She was trying to contain her fear and think of some way she could defend herself and Kithla.

"First you will allow him to restrain you."

Kithla's father was wheeling his chair forward. He took hold of Marheh's right wrist. His grip was strong, his face as blank as Kithla's. He pulled her towards the heavy wooden table where he and Kithla ate their meals and pressed her hand down onto the table, palm upwards. Marheh looked down and saw that preparations had been made for her visit. Nailed to the table were two short leather straps with buckles. Kithla's father began to fasten one around her wrist. Involuntarily she pulled away. Kithla's father held her easily. Suddenly terrified she used her mind to make him release her. Kithla screamed and everything stopped. Into the silence SP dropped five words, each separate, distinct and completely devoid of expression.

"Allow him to restrain you."

Marheh looked at the restraints that would bind her to the table. Some where inside she thought she screamed a protest, so she was surprised to find herself placing her wrists in the straps and remaining quiet while Kithla's father buckled them tightly. Then with gentle strength he forced her to her knees behind the table. She was shaking with fear, but she continued to look at SP across the table and made herself breath deeply and calmly. For a few minutes nothing more happened. Marheh was aware of her hands, quite small hands, brown from her summer out of doors, strong from wielding a windlass, resting palm upward, fingers lightly curled, looking curiously separated from her outstretched arms, cut off from them by the dark straps. Involuntarily she shuddered, closed her eyes for a moment trying to contain herself. When she opened them again SP was getting to his feet. In his hand he held a thin pointer like the one SW had used to punish her. The point was quite sharp and as he drew it across her wrists next to the straps it left a thin red line. Marheh bit her lip and concentrated on her breathing.

"You cost me my right hand and my left hand," SP said smoothly. "Why should I not take yours?"

It took a moment for his meaning to register and even when she understood the words, and that he referred to SW and SM Marheh could not quite comprehend what he intended. Then he struck her. In her mind she screamed for Nemle, outwardly the small brown hand jerked and someone whimpered. Kithla and her father moved to the table, one each side and held down the curling fingers then he struck again, left hand, right hand, left hand, right hand, sharp and deliberate. Then he was in her mind, tormenting her with images of the indescribable horrors he might inflict on her. She tried to fight him, to keep him out, heard Kithla scream and opened her eyes to see her face twisted in pain. In a confusion of pain and fear she pushed her mind into Kithla's, whether to defend her or to escape SP's torment she did not know. In Kithla's mind she could stand back from the pain of the bloodied hands on the table. She could strike at the mind controlling Kithla and drive him out, disable him. Protect Kithla, she must protect Kithla. She thought her tears this time were tears of blood wept in the empty quadrangle of Kithla's imprisoned mind.

Nemle's plants could not absorb her attention as they usually did. Anxiety kept breaking through. Deliberately she packed away her tools and set out for the cottage, so that when the first wave of Marheh's fear reached her she was already half way up the hill from the water road. She froze and sent her mind seeking Marheh's but encountered only confusion. Fearful now she continued more quickly and she had reached the lane when she received Marheh's scream of despair. She needed all her self discipline to remain calm and collected enough to think rather than react. She continued to the cottage quickly but steadily trying to prepare herself for whatever she would encounter. Here in Fairdale Lading was where it had all begun. Why had she not realised that it was not over, that the enemy would seek to conclude the battle here? The enemy, she thought, picturing SP as she had last seen him, frozen behind his desk before Marheh had so foolishly engaged with him. No longer could Silberay hide their heads in the sand and think of the Yareblis as misguided Silberay. They had adopted different goals and different methods and were unquestionably ready to destroy Silberay if they could.

She reached the cottage and stopped for breath, staring at the sad untended garden with a kind of dread. Quietly she centred herself and walked around to the back. Her mind and spirit were held, steady and firm in purpose against the chaos that she felt all around her. There was so much pain and most of it was Marheh's but she dared not dwell on it in case it undermined her ability to take control. Carefully she lifted the latch on the back door, paused to take a deep breath, then thrust it open.

She thought what she saw would be imprinted on her mind forever. On the floor, almost at her feet, a strange man rocked himself in a foetal position. Kithla and her father leaned towards each other over the kitchen table. Kithla's eyes lifted and a ripple of expression passed over her face. SP stood, his back to the door, his arm raised to strike. Before he knew what had happened Nemle was in and out of his mind, stunning him, scarcely caring whether or not she was using more force than necessary. Then she saw Marheh.

Marheh was still on her knees, slumped against the table, her head between her outstretched arms, her eyes closed. Both hands were covered in blood. The fingers of her left hand twitched a little and began to curl over as Kithla released them.

Nemle stepped towards her, looked at her face, dreading what she might see there. Marheh's expression was calm and still. Inwardly Nemle howled an anguished protest against the thought that Marheh might be maimed, her mind broken, then she drew herself together and began to seek for her.

Marheh's faltering response came from Kithla's mind.

"Mama Nemle."

"Where are you Marheh?"

"Protect Kithla, have to protect Kithla."

"Kithla is safe now."

Nemle longed to touch Marheh, to release the restraints, to hold her and tend her wounds, but she understood that Marheh's link to her own body was so tenuous that the slightest nudge might break it.

"You must come back now. Kithla is safe now."

"It hurts too much."

"I know, but you must try."

"It hurts."

Nemle sent both mind and soul to enfold her, coax her, build her courage.

"Come Marheh, Kithla needs you to return to yourself so she can heal."

The calm quiet face resting on the table changed, twisted. There was a gasping sob and her eyes opened.

"Oh Nemle," she whispered. "Oh Nemle."

Nemle leant over her, kissed her gently and reached to unbuckle the straps that bound her. She was not ready yet to examine the wounded hands, but she instructed Kithla and together they helped her to her feet and into a chair where she sat resting, her eyes closed, her breathing deliberately slow and deep as she collected herself.

Nemle hardly knew what to tackle first now that Marheh was safe, but she checked that the two Yareblis were controlled and directed them into the pantry where they would be out of Marheh's sight. Then she entered Kithla's mind to check her progress and her father's mind to release him. They would find it hard to forget what SP had made them do to Marheh.

At last she felt she could turn her whole attention on Marheh. First she looked at the wounded hands, just looked, without touching them. Beneath the blood stains she saw they were not as bad as she had feared. Marheh was watching her with anxious eyes.

"I will get better?" she asked hesitantly. "I will, won't I?"

"Yes Marheh, you will get better."

Tears came then, tears of relief that she could not hold back or wipe away.

"He said I had taken his right hand and his left hand, so he would take mine."

Nemle stood silently by for a minute then took out her handkerchief, patted Marheh's face gently and held it for her to blow her nose.

Nemle badly wanted to carry Marheh away to *Day Bringer* and look after her there but she knew Kithla and her father needed her too. Both of them were beginning to regain their senses, both were confused and unhappy about what had been done to their lives. She found a basin and a soft cloth and Kithla was able to give her ointment, some of Nemle's own that she had given them, and bandages. Although Nemle was as gentle as possible the process of treating her hands was a painful one for Marheh and she was exhausted before it was over. Nemle helped her upstairs to Kithla's bedroom, undressed her and put her to bed. She sat by her until she slept then went wearily down to the kitchen again.

Kithla was staring at the straps still nailed to the table and the marks of Marheh's blood. Nemle swept her into a hug, felt her stiff posture relax as she began to cry. Thad was angrily wheeling himself round and round the kitchen table. He too had the marks of tears on his face. Nemle stood in front of him to stop him, placed her hands gently over his. She thought for a minute he would wrench himself away and continue his frantic circling, but he stared at her briefly then buried his face in his hands. Gently Nemle pushed Kithla towards him and went to put the kettle on.

By the time the water had boiled and Nemle had made sperit things were calmer. Thad had found his claw hammer and was tugging at the last of the nails in the table. Kithla was scrubbing away the bloodstains. Nemle put the mugs on the table and sat down beside them.

"Tell me," she said after a short silence. "Tell me what happened."

Kithla and her father looked at each other then he spoke.

"It was that Mr Cowper," he said. "I never got on with him really, but you don't want to be on bad terms with a neighbour. He came and asked me if I would help him with something that needed strong hands. Of course I did what I could then gradually he seemed to be coming every day and I couldn't say no to him. Kithla didn't like him either. She kept out of the way at first, but one day he asked her for a cup of tea. What could she say?"

He paused and Nemle nodded. She understood having once complied with a request it became more and more difficult to refuse.

"Then he brought that other one and they moved in. I couldn't do anything about it – or Kithla. It was like we had no will of our own; every day waiting on the two of them, the garden going to rack and ruin, I don't know how long. We could hear the neighbours coming to inquire of us and Cowper told them we had gone away on holiday and let our cottage to that other one. That one just blanked us out."

Nemle reached out to take a hand of each.

"Then she came, your girl, and we knew what he had been waiting for." He shook his head. "A little bit of a girl like that and he went to all that trouble to be revenged."

Nemle waited while he took a gulp from his mug.

"Marheh is a bit special. I think they want to disable her before she develops her talents any more," she said.

"And they made us help," Kithla said, a catch in her voice.

Nemle squeezed her hand.

"Marheh understands you could not refuse them."

"She did something to Mr Cowper so he stopped hurting me," Kithla said. "And all the time the other one was hurting her."

Nemle encouraged them to talk as long as they needed, listening to their story again and again. Then she suggested perhaps they might make some supper for them all while she went back to Marheh. Kithla looked fearfully at the pantry so Nemle got out what she needed and reassured her that the two Yareblis were under control then she went back upstairs.

Marheh lay awake staring at the ceiling. Her hands and arms rested stiffly outside the covers, rather as if they did not belong to her. Nemle sat down beside her, took off her boots and lifted her feet onto the bed. She leaned back against the head board and sighed a little. One finger lightly brushed Marheh's cheek where a single tear was trying to make its way down the side of her face.

"Why?" Marheh said softly as the silence lengthened.

"Why at all, or why you?" Nemle asked.

"Revenge I suppose," Marheh said, her voice strengthening. "Because I got in his way."

Nemle looked down at her. She seemed such a child.

"I think they are afraid of what you might become," she said at last, knowing that despite her looks Marheh was a child no longer.

"Me?" Marheh sounded disbelieving.

"Yes, you," Nemle said firmly.

Marheh was silent then for several minutes.

"I don't feel special," she said at last, then managed a small smile. "Just sore."

Marheh found the days that followed very difficult. She hated being so dependent on the care of others. Nemle tried in every way she could to show her that she delighted in caring for her but to be washed and dressed and fed like a baby made her feel very small and useless. Practicing the disciplines was the best solace. She and Nemle moved back to *Day Bringer* and that helped her too, though they remained moored at Fairdale Lading and visited Kithla and her father each day. What to do with SP and CP was a problem that had to be resolved. CP was known in the village as Mr Cowper and lived in a cottage not far from Kithla and Thad. Nemle discussed solutions with Marheh as she washed and dressed her the first morning back on *Day Bringer*.

"I'm still so angry at what they did to you that I don't quite trust myself with them," Nemle said, hauling Marheh's nightdress over her head.

"We can't send them to Gip and Deyah," Marheh said when she could speak. "It wouldn't be fair."

Nemle dipped the wash cloth into the basin of warm soapy water beside her and began with Marheh's face.

"We haven't destroyed their minds, though I'm tempted."

"But then we'd be no better than they are." Marheh finished the thought in unison with her.

Nemle dried her face and kissed her briskly.

"In the past we would just have let them go with a command to keep walking for a few days," she said.

Marheh held her arms out from her sides.

"What good did that do?" she asked as Nemle passed the damp cloth over her back, under her arms and over her small high breasts.

"Got them out of the way for a few months if we were lucky."

"What would you have done with SP if I hadn't let him escape?" Marheh asked curiously.

Nemle dried her upper body and draped the towel around her shoulders.

"You may well ask?" she said, dipping the cloth and wringing it out again.

She knelt to continue her work and her voice reached Marheh sounding muffled.

"Sent him to the other side of the country and hoped he would stay there I expect."

"That wouldn't have been much use," Marheh said scornfully.

"Not much," Nemle agreed sitting back on her heels and looking up. Marheh shook herself so the towel dropped to the floor. Nemle rubbed her dry.

"Do you want to sit down while I do your feet?" she asked.

"I can balance," Marheh said, proving it. "The best thing would be if they couldn't see the water road any more," she said thoughtfully, standing on one leg. "Or if they couldn't do mind stuff." She changed legs and continued. "Can we do that? Put them out of the water dimension?"

Nemle dried carefully between the last little toe then stood up rather creakily. Impulsively Marheh put her arms around her.

"It isn't right," she said. "You shouldn't be kneeling to look after me."

Nemle gave her a quick kiss and a little slap on her bottom. "Why not, you're my charge to look after." She picked up the knickers from the little pile of Marheh's clothes and held them out for her to step into. "What did you just say? Put them out of the water dimension? I wonder whether we could."

It was an interesting and challenging idea and they discussed it all the time Nemle was putting Marheh into her clothes.

"If we tried it on SP first," Marheh said. "Then if something went wrong, well he deserves it."

She sat down at the table and held out her hands for Nemle to take off the bandages. She was gentle and skilled, but Marheh still needed to bite her lip as her hands were bathed and dressed. Nemle had her bend and flex her fingers and although it hurt Marheh took comfort from the knowledge that she could do so.

When everything was done Nemle left Marheh with instructions to think about how SP and CP might be banished from the water dimension and went to make breakfast. They both agreed that as the Yareblis denied the soul they would need to make a selective foray into their minds.

"But what do we look for?" Marheh asked while Nemle was helping herself to porridge.

Nemle shook her head and picked up Marheh's spoon. "I don't know," she said spooning porridge into Marheh's open mouth. "But I think you might be the one to recognise it if I invite you to look around my mind."

Marheh swallowed hastily. "Me!"

Nemle nodded. "You."

Kithla came down to help Nemle with her plants and together they all went back to the cottage for lunch, but later, while Nemle sat relaxed and comfortable in the armchair, Marheh began the task Nemle had given her. She had been in Nemle's mind before when they practised together, but never like this. During practice Nemle had controlled what Marheh saw of her mind, but now she had given her permission to explore, to poke into all the intimate places in her attempt to understand. Later Marheh was to realise that this was Nemle's gift to her, another kind of naked helplessness offered in sympathy with her own.

Being in Nemle's mind was a bit like inhabiting a large and crowded library, but one without any signs or labels. Marheh hardly knew where to start looking. She felt as if there ought to be a big bookshelf full of her knowledge of the water road, but it was not just knowledge she sought. Being in the water dimension was not learned, but something integral. It could be developed but not unless there was something already existing to develop. Perhaps she should be looking for the bookshelf, not the books.

It was exhausting work, needing all her concentration and after an hour she left Nemle's mind, carefully and respectfully, and returned to herself. Then she could share with Nemle her thoughts and ideas and receive encouragement. Nemle laughed at the idea of her mind being a library without any signs or labels and wondered whether that was the reason why she could not always find what she knew was there. She encouraged Marheh's idea about the bookcase and suggested that she may need to explore another mind, perhaps CP's, to look for similarities. Marheh protested at the suggestion that there should be any similarities between Nemle's mind and CP's, but was forced to admit that this must be the case, forced to admit that there must be similarities between her own mind and the minds of the Yareblis. She wondered aloud why she couldn't look into her own mind like she could into Nemle's, but Nemle told her to work it out for herself.

After supper Marheh visited Nemle's mind again, familiarising herself with the shapes within it. Then next morning they went together to the cottage to try and explore CP's mind. It would need them both to work together, Nemle to control, Marheh to examine and they rehearsed their strategy as they climbed the hill to the village.

"It was easy," Marheh told Nemle when she had finished her exploration. "There was only one shape possible, everything else was too different."

Nemle looked at her, wanting to be sure she was not over-confident, but she was not boasting.

"So somehow we must excise that shape," Nemle said.

"But how?" Marheh asked.

There was silence then Nemle spoke slowly. "I think you had better do some experimenting in my mind. See how difficult it is to dislodge," she said.

"No!" Marheh was horrified. "I might hurt you."

"You might," Nemle agreed. "But this is important and we need to get it right. You'll be careful and gentle I know."

The work was difficult and exhausting for them both, so Nemle decreed that one experiment per day was enough.

"There is no hurry," she said when Marheh protested. "We can't leave yet. Your hands are healing nicely. Kithla and her father still need us. Let's not rush."

Next day Marheh again entered Nemle's mind and rather fearfully attempted to dislodge the shape she had identified. It moved easily, far more easily than she expected. She returned it gently to its place and slipped out of Nemle's mind to find her white and shaken.

"I did hurt you," she cried. "I'm so sorry. I knew we shouldn't have done it."

Nemle held out her arms to her. "I knew it might hurt," she said, hugging Marheh as much for her own comfort as for Marheh's. "For a minute my whole world shifted, *Day Bringer* dissolved around me, so I think you've got it right."

It was such a big thing to have discovered that for a moment they could only look at each other, brown eyes and grey eyes wide with awe at the realisation of their achievement. Then Marheh looked ruefully at her bandaged hands and back to Nemle.

"And I can't even make you sperit," she said.

Nemle's arms tightened around her again. "I'll be alright in a minute," she said, and Marheh sighed and snuggled into her embrace.

Even after this success the next steps were not straightforward. First Nemle then Marheh would question the morality of what they planned and they spent hours discussing the issues they raised. Then Kithla and her father had to be consulted. The plan was that SP and CP would be left in Mr Cowper's cottage once they had been excluded from the water dimension and their power removed, but Kithla and her father may find them too uncomfortable as neighbours if they remained in Fairdale Lading.

Marheh's hands continued to heal and she was promoted to lighter bandages that enabled her to use her fingers for holding a spoon, doing up buttons and best of all, she told Nemle grinning, for pulling up her knickers.

At last the day came when they could talk no more. SP and CP had already been taken to CP's cottage so that Kithla and Thad could complete their recovery. Marheh and Nemle went together to see to their physical well-being each day but Nemle was beginning to feel they could move on again and only the need to finally deal with the two Yareblis was keeping them. Thoughtfully, a little apprehensive, they climbed the hill to the village and entered Mr Cowper's cottage. The two men were sitting motionless in separate rooms. Visiting CP first, Nemle entered his mind to continue controlling him before Marheh entered, grasped the shape she had identified and carried it away back into her own mind. Quite how she would rid herself of this extra burden they had not discussed and Marheh was aware of a degree of discomfort as she returned to herself, but she was able to put it aside without too much difficulty.

Marheh was much more fearful about entering SP's mind, remembering her previous experiences. Even though he was under Nemle's control, for a minute or two she could not find the focus she needed. She kept hearing his taunting "little fly" and drawing back, but at last she managed to make the step from her mind to his. She found it was not so different from CP's though everything was a bit bigger. It was harder to move the shape of the water dimension and harder still to return with it to her own mind. The discomfort had increased and she could not help wondering how she would get rid of it.

The two men continued to remain under Nemle's control although Marheh had done her work. She and Nemle returned to CP.

"Do you think we should try and restore their soul names?" Marheh asked. "It would be something."

Nemle was looking at CP, who sat quiet, eyes open but seeing nothing. He did not seem to have suffered from Marheh's activities.

"Yes, I do," she said. "Though it will be up to them whether they use it, but I would like to see what happens when I release him first."

Marheh nodded. "We have to be sure that it has worked," she said.

"And that he can function as an ordinary adult," Nemle added.

Mr Cowper emerged from Nemle's control belligerent and seemingly unaffected by what Marheh had done. They followed him as he led the way down stairs to his kitchen. Once there he turned towards them and a look of surprise passed across his face.

"What have you done to me?" he demanded.

Nemle and Marheh looked at each other.

"What do you think we have done?" Nemle asked cautiously.

"I'm different… there's something…," he tried to articulate what he felt but ended by yelling at them. "I don't know."

"We'll go now," Nemle said kindly. "We will come back and see you tomorrow. SP is upstairs and I think he will need us."

It was Nemle who suggested how Marheh might rid herself of the two shapes she had garnered. She encouraged Marheh to imagine a box, strongly made with a hinged lid and a latch to fasten it. Then when she was sure about the box, she could put the two shapes into it and close the lid. Then she could imagine herself putting the box away in a corner of *Day Bringer*'s engine room.

"Later," she said. "You can drop it off at Silberay Harbour."

It worked admirably and Marheh was very relieved to be rid of her burden.

Next day, back they went to release SP. Neither of the men had the slightest interest in their soul names so that Nemle discouraged Marheh from attempting to restore them. Both were short tempered to the point of rudeness, but seemed not to comprehend the loss of their power to control.

Nemle and Marheh left them without any regrets and went to explain what they had done to Kithla and Thad. They were both hard at work in their garden which was beginning to look more as it should. Nemle worked alongside them while Marheh talked, not just about what they had done to disable the two Yareblis, but also about everything that had happened since they had left Fairdale Lading back in the spring.

It was leave taking and they were all aware of it. Nemle and Marheh would move on in the morning and it would be months before they returned. First however they would celebrate and say goodbye by sharing in a meal together. They all helped with preparation. Marheh was given the task of setting the table. Delicious smells filled the kitchen as the food cooked. Nemle ceremonially unbandaged Marheh's hands for the last time. She held them up and waggled her fingers joyfully and the kitchen lost its power to remind them of what she had suffered there.

Together they ate and talked, drank sperit and talked some more so that it was almost dark when Nemle and Marheh made their way back to *Day Bringer*. Marheh thought she would be too excited to sleep for Nemle had promised that tomorrow she could take the tiller, but Nemle insisted on staying to be sure she could manage by herself and on practising the discipline of the soul with her and on tucking her into her bunk. She fell asleep almost as soon as her head touched the pillow and it was Nemle who lay awake, comfortably reflecting on what had passed and imagining the future.

Next morning they were up with the day. Marheh resumed her usual chores, happy to be able to. Soon they were ready to go, *Day Bringer* tidy and clean, engine checks done. As Marheh was about to take up her usual position with the front line, Nemle called her back to give her a pair of fingerless mittens she had made her. The palms were padded with thin leather and would protect Marheh's hands from rope and windlass. The engine started and settled into its usual patient throbbing, Marheh took up the front mooring pin, put it on board and stood holding the line until Nemle was ready. She pushed out the bow and stepped on board and they were away.

Kithla, just too late to say goodbye, watched from the top of the hill. She saw Marheh coiling her line and making her way along the gunnel to Nemle. She saw Nemle take Marheh's right hand and place it on the tiller. She saw Marheh straighten her spine and lift her head. Her plait hung down her back, her feet were firmly planted a little apart. She looked forward. Nemle was beside her, watchful and caring. Then they were round the bend and out of sight.

Forthcoming title - September 2013

Marheh of the Silberay Book 2

Apprentice Still

"Rules and regulations! If we were really pursuing the aims we believe in would we need them? It seems the answer is yes."

Sila's Journal: the early years

Chapter One

"Marheh Carron, we find you guilty of using your mental ability for the purpose of exploitation."

There was a small gasp from somewhere in the room and Marheh's face drained of colour.

"Stand while sentence is pronounced."

Obediently she stood, straight and still. Only Nemle, her mentor, knew her well enough to recognise the tension in her clenched hands.

"The proscribed penalty is that you be grounded and Day Bringer lifted out of the water for ten years."

Marheh stared down the emptiness of ten years imprisoned on land.

"However, in view of your youth, I am authorised to offer you the choice of a beating and a two year extension of your apprenticeship."

Silence.

She stood motionless, determined to reveal nothing, but she dared not meet Nemle's anxious gaze. Those nearest saw her close her eyes for a moment, saw her swallow with difficulty. Everyone in the room heard her clear soft voice when she said "I choose to be beaten."

There was an exhalation, as if the room had been holding its breath.

"Very well."

The voice paused. A page was turned in a large book.

"Sentence will be carried out in this room on Tuesday next at 10.00 am."

The owner of the voice left the room and a babble of sound rose from the spectators, but Marheh still stood motionless as if any action would break her fragile control. At last Nemle went to her, took her by the hand and led her away to Day Bringer.

The Harbour was looking particularly beautiful in the spring sunshine. Light played on the water and the shining brass of the Silberay boats gathered there. The trees that bordered the moorings were veiled in new green. A gentle breeze touched the water, the trees and Marheh herself, but she was isolated from it all, encased in a hard shell that prevented feeling.

It was not until they reached the haven of Day Bringer's cosy saloon that her control broke and she began to shake so much that it seemed easier to drop to the floor than force her legs to carry her further. Nemle crouched beside her holding her in her arms while she sobbed.

At last, when her trembling had ceased she looked at Nemle.

"I won't let them force me from the water road, no matter what it costs."

Nemle's arms tightened around her.

"But you don't have to do it this way. Accept the grounding, that will give us time to find the truth. Tuesday is only three days away."

"And if we don't find out, if the sentence is not overturned? Ten years could be the rest of your life and if we are off the water we will never learn who hates me so much."

Nemle closed her eyes, opened them again. There was nothing to say. Marheh sighed and snuggled into her arms.

"Hold me a bit longer Mama Nemle," she whispered. "Then I'll be brave."

Nemle held her and kissed her and helped her to wash her tear-stained face so that when a businesslike rap on the roof demanded entrance she was in control of herself again. Their visitor was the man who would carry out her sentence. He was matter-of-fact, even cheerful, like a doctor with a pleasant bedside manner. He carried folded garments of white cotton and a small piece of blue rubber, half moon shaped. He put the things on the table and waited for Nemle and Marheh to sit.

"You will present yourself at 9.45 wearing these clothes only. They fasten at the back," he said. "You may have this to bite on."

Marheh looked at the blue rubber in horrified fascination.

"Nemle will prepare you by fastening your wrists and ankles to the frame that will be constructed. She will then uncover you. You will receive fifty strokes of the cane in the space of an hour."

Marheh shivered and Nemle heard a tiny whimper from deep in her throat.

"Now you need to come outside so I can measure you for the frame."

Obediently Marheh followed him out to the back deck. She stood on tiptoe with her arms stretched above her head when instructed. She waited while he made this measurement and that. Nemle stood on the back step watching with anxious eyes. When he was done he rolled up his tape measure and nodded to her.

"I'll see you on Tuesday," he said. Then, as he was stepping off the deck he turned back to add. "Best if you don't have breakfast and be sure to empty your bowels and bladder."

Nemle thought Marheh would faint she became so white. She sprang up the steps and supported her into the back cabin, held her through spasms of uncontrollable shaking. She was still trembling when they felt Day Bringer move as someone heavy came on board. Nemle looked up angrily, afraid of some new refinement of mental torment, but relaxed when she realised it was Marheh's Uncle Jik. He came down the steps and took in the scene in the cabin.

"Wrap her in a blanket and I'll carry her through to the saloon," he said. "I saw that pantomime on the back deck."

Hastily Nemle pulled a blanket from Marheh's bunk and wrapped it around her. Jik gathered her in his arms and carried her into the saloon as if she was a baby. He put her onto Nemle's lap in the big chair. Nemle cuddled her until she was calm while Jik perched beside them on the footstool.

"I'm sorry," she said at last. "I didn't know … how it would be." Nemle still held her, but now she tried to get up. "I'm too heavy for you Nemle," she said.

"You stay here my darling, just let me hold you."

Jik reached out to take one of her hands in his. Marheh held it tightly.

"I didn't do what they said, Jik, truly."

"I know you didn't."

"You won't tell them at home, will you?"

He shook his head. "Not that they would doubt you, but it would hurt them."

Marheh nodded. "That's what I thought."

"Marheh," Jik said. "You know there will be people watching don't you?"

"I guessed there might," she said, cuddling in to Nemle again.

"Will it make it better or worse if Uncle Jik who loves you is there?"

Marheh clutched his hands.

"Oh, better. I can be brave for you and Nemle."

You are the old, our wisdom our strength,
As you pass let our love wrap you well
Let it nourish and warm as you journey ahead
To enrich all the stories we tell.
Songs of the Silberay

Chapter Two

Marheh had known she had enemies. She and Nemle had been involved in a confrontation with Yareblis in the first months of her apprenticeship. Now it seemed there was an enemy within the Silberay. It hurt almost more than the prospect ahead of her.

"My own people," she said, looking at Nemle with tragic eyes. "Who I've chosen to spend my life with."

Nemle held her. "I feel as if I've been blind," she said

She put Marheh away from her and moved impatiently around the saloon.

"This is about power, but the Silberay have never been about power. How could things change so much when I wasn't looking?"

Marheh stood at the window. The Harbour looked as it always did on a fine spring afternoon.

"It's like a stick that gets stuck in the water," she said, trying to work it out. "There it is and the water flows around it. If you notice it at all it's to enjoy the pattern it makes. Then another stick comes and gets trapped against the first. Then there's another and another and before you know it the water is breaking the banks trying to get past."

She turned back to Nemle.

"No one cares about one stick," she said.

The first inkling that Marheh had become a target should have been at the Gathering two years ago, Nemle thought, but neither of them had realised that the trouble then was anything more than the passion and curiosity of youth rubbing against caution and conservatism.

Like all whose vocation was to be Silberay, Marheh made her life choice at twenty. She became apprenticed to seventy year old Nemle, to live with her on the boat Day Bringer and travel the water road learning from her and serving her. Nemle had quickly discovered that Marheh was exceptionally talented at the Silberay disciplines of mind and soul and it became an imperative for her to teach Marheh how to control and develop her natural ability. Now, although she hesitated to say so, she could not help wondering whether someone wanted to stop Marheh from reaching her full potential.

Gatherings were held only every second year, in the first weeks of spring, and were a time of discussion and reflection, of sharing difficulties and joys and for the apprentices an opportunity for formal instruction.

Two years ago was Marheh's third Gathering. She was twenty-four, idealistic, passionate, adventurous, inclined to be arrogant and impulsive. It had been a hard winter and the journey to Silberay Harbour and the Gathering had been challenging, but as the boats began to converge, conquering the bitter weather became a source of pride. Marheh had wanted to push on in all weathers hoping for a good mooring at the harbour, hoping to be amongst the first to arrive. Nemle had laughed and let her have her way only making sure there was a hot drink and a warm fire when she came in from the tiller, blue and shivering.

"You know there is room for us all at the harbour," Nemle teased as Marheh's teeth chattered against the mug she held with both hands. "You don't actually need to do this."

"Yes I do." Marheh was determined. "We are going to get a mooring in the old part, where it's quiet, but not too far from the meeting room."

Nemle shook her head and watched to see that Marheh's competitive spirit did not lead her to inconsiderate behaviour, but she kept her speed legal, slowed when passing moored boats and achieved her aim by early rising and stamina.

The old part of the harbour was the nicest, the trees were established, the jetties were wider and seemed more stable and by arriving early they not only got a good place, but an extra day to enjoy it. Marheh was out with the brass polish first thing, making sure that Day Bringer was at her very best. As they sat together over lunch Nemle ventured a word of advice.

"This is a Gathering, not a competition," she said carefully. "We're not putting on a special effort to be on show."

Marheh flushed. "But Day Bringer has to look her best," she protested.

"Of course she does, but she has to look her best every day and I don't often see you quite so enthusiastic with the brass cloth."

Marheh made a face acknowledging the truth of Nemle's words. "But I can do it today, can't I?"

Later, as more boats arrived, Marheh went striding around the harbour looking for her own particular friends, the two apprentices who made their choice the same time as she did, her Uncle Jik on Autumn Wind and Storm Cloud where Kel and Sul lived. Nemle was happy to stay by the fire for the most part, but she did make her way to the main meeting room early in the day to see what had been planned for the Gathering and consider what contribution she might make. There were Mentor discussions scheduled that she should attend although she was always reticent about her experiences. She had never confessed that she had burned her copy of *Guidelines for Mentoring the Young Apprentice* within the first six months of trying to apply its precepts to her relationship with Marheh.

Marheh came back to help prepare the evening meal full of enthusiasm and news. "Jik's just arrived. He's been boating all day so I invited him to come for supper. That's alright isn't it? I got an extra chop from the store." She grinned. "He sent you commiserations and hoped you'd been giving me plenty of spankings."

Nemle smiled at her. "And Sul?" she asked.

Marheh shook her head. "Not here yet, but Tippa said they passed them moored up a couple of days ago, so they must be on their way."

Nemle moved to set the table as Marheh peeled potatoes and carrots. "The big welcome breakfast is tomorrow morning so they'll want to be here for that."

Marheh nodded. "And then classes for us in the afternoon and singing and stories by the fire after supper."

There was a knock on the roof and Day Bringer rocked gently as someone stepped on board. Nemle called a welcome and Jik made his way through to the saloon. He was a big man and seemed to fill the narrow space, his head scarcely an inch from the ceiling.

"I've left my coat in the engine room," he said, coming closer to the fire. "This is good of you."

"You're very welcome," Nemle said. "I remember well what it is like to feel too tired to cook after a day at the tiller." She indicated the one big armchair by the fire. "Sit down. Marheh's got dinner under control, but it will be twenty minutes or so. Can I get you some sperit?"

He subsided gratefully into the chair and the saloon suddenly seemed less crowded. Marheh grinned at him from the galley.

"You'll never be able to have an apprentice," she said. "There won't be enough room for two of you on Autumn Wind."

"I'll have to find a little scrawny one and starve him," Jik said. He stretched lazily and reached for the mug of sperit Nemle had made him. "This is good of you," he said again.

He rested the mug on the arm of the chair and closed his eyes. A few minutes later Nemle lifted the mug to safety on the bench.

When the meal was ready Nemle woke him gently and they squeezed around the small table, Marheh balancing on a folding stool, while the others used the fixed seating.

"So what's the news?" he asked when the first hunger was sated.

Marheh ran through what she had discovered so far.

"Sunrise needs a whole new floor, she got flooded in a lock. Tippa said it was touch and go whether she would sink. Tomorrow my classes start and we're going to take down an engine." Her eyes sparkled at the prospect. "Storm Cloud still hasn't arrived. I hope they're alright. Oh and there's a new tutor for Silberay law. His name is Hud. Do you know him?" She paused and looked from Nemle to Jik.

"Are you sure?" Jik said.

"That's what it said on the notice board."

"It seems odd," he said and Nemle nodded.

"The tutors are always taken from the older mentors, the ones whose apprentices are past the need for formal classes. Hud is not old enough to even have an apprentice."

Marheh shrugged. "Perhaps he has done lots of study or something." She wrinkled her nose. "I can think of better things to study though."

The next afternoon Marheh came back to Day Bringer very grubby and full of the joys of engine maintenance.

"It's just the three of us," she told Nemle. "Tippa and Pon and me, and we've practically taken the engine apart. I don't think Tippa likes it very much because we do get dirty, but I love it."

Nemle smiled at her. "A wash before supper might be a good idea."

"I've put my name down for one of the bathrooms. Imagine a real bath."

Nemle laughed.

The bath on Day Bringer was a large tin basin with the sole advantage that it was portable enough to be moved from the bathroom to the hearth on very cold days. The half dozen bathrooms at the Harbour were always very popular during the Gathering. Marheh collected her towel and washing things and raced off for her bath and Nemle smiled and enjoyed her enthusiasm.

The days passed busily and Nemle's friends commented on Marheh's delight in all she was learning and doing.

The classes in Silberay law were not scheduled to start until the second week of the Gathering and were for all the younger apprentices, not just the three at Marheh's level. Silberay were of course expected to know and obey the laws of the land, but Sila, founder of the Silberay, had set down guiding principles for the appropriate use of the discipline of the mind.

There were perhaps a dozen young men and women gathered in the smallest of the meeting rooms awaiting the arrival of their tutor. Marheh could not help being a little apprehensive about this class. She had been practicing the discipline of the mind without really knowing what she was doing even before she became apprenticed and in the early days of her apprenticeship her skill was not developed enough to control her instinctive response to situations where she was angry or afraid. She knew she had not always acted according to the law, but Nemle knew and understood and was teaching her the techniques she needed. Marheh realised it was time she understood the law better and had even provided herself with a note book and pencil to make notes of what seemed important.

Hud came sweeping into the meeting room a few minutes after everyone else had arrived. He was not a particularly tall man, but carried himself with such an air of confidence that he seemed to fill the room. He was wearing tunic and trousers cut to the traditional Silberay pattern, but the material was much richer and more luxurious than any Marheh had seen before. The midnight blue fabric had a subtle sheen to it that gave the folds mysterious darks and glowing highlights. His belt gleamed silver against the deep blue tunic. Marheh wrinkled her nose disdainfully. He obviously never wore these clothes when boating and the belt would not have held a windlass.

Unaware of Marheh's disapproval he surveyed the class with an air of condescension that did nothing to dispel her first impression. Then he began to speak. Marheh got ready with her pencil. His voice was beautiful; colour, light and shade, sometimes soft and caressing, sometimes sharp and biting, sometimes deep and strong. The class was transfixed. For a few minutes Marheh listened with the rest, spellbound by the brilliance of his elocution, but she had her pencil in her hand and she was writing nothing. She tried to focus, to find the gold amongst the glitter that was spilling out before them, but for all the clever technique it seemed to her that he was saying nothing. She really tried, but all too soon her pencil drifted into little doodles, then she began to draw in earnest, and the mellifluous voice was just music in the background.

"It wasn't just me," she said later, trying to explain to Nemle why her note book was full of sketches. "Some people thought he was wonderful, but even they could not say what they had learned about Silberay law."

Nemle turned the pages of the notebook smiling a little at Marheh's clever drawings.

"Just be careful," she said. "I think he could be a bad person to cross."

Marheh nodded. "Maybe it will be better tomorrow."

She went next morning, hopeful, armed with her notebook and pencil and found that in some respects it was better. Certainly there was more content to the flow of words, but what dry, narrow, nit-picking content it seemed to be and delivered not in the colourful persuasive tones he had used to woo them the previous day, but dictated from an important looking tome full of handwritten lists.

"It's all the wrong shape for Silberay," Marheh said to Nemle again displaying her notebook, this time full of scribbled oddments. "There are so many little picky prohibitions it's surprising we ever do anything. It doesn't seem a bit like Sila's dream for us."

Nemle looked at her thoughtfully. "I suppose most of us older ones just go along with what we think is right and forget that every Gathering someone wants to add to the rule book."

"Well I think we should have another Great Debate and see if we can make things simpler."

Marheh was very much in earnest. Nemle remembered how she and Sul had shared with Marheh and Kel their memories of that long ago Gathering where rights and wrongs had been debated and affirmations made. Some of the Silberay left the water road to become Yareblis, denying the value of the discipline of the soul and challenging the way the discipline of the mind should be used. It had been important then to take a stand, but now, perhaps, it was time to re-think.

Nemle looked at Marheh. "So you think we have let things slip since then."

Marheh flushed but returned Nemle's gaze bravely. "I suppose I do a bit," she said. "Not you, but …"

Nemle smiled at her. "You're quite right. I ought to know what the book of rules has turned into and I don't and I doubt whether many of the other mentors do either. Perhaps that's why Hud is teaching you."

Marheh made a face. "It doesn't seem like teaching, not proper teaching, just lecturing."

"Only one more class," Nemle said sympathetically. "Perhaps he will give you the opportunity for questions and discussion then."

"Perhaps," Marheh said doubtfully.

She went off to visit Tippa looking thoughtful and determined.

Nemle watched her go and resolved to ask her own question when the mentors met again that evening.

It was a comfortable, easy group she met with, all of them over seventy, confident of who they were and of their place in their world. Although there were twenty-three mentors at the moment only fifteen were there in the small lounge. Apprenticeship for the Silberay lasted twenty years and during the last five or six years the aging mentor was often physically dependent on the apprentice, who thus learned practical service along with the disciplines. These older mentors were usually respected and consulted for their wisdom, but did not necessarily join the mentor discussions. Nemle looked around the room, most of the fifteen were her contemporaries, some her friends. Sul, six years older than she, had been a particular friend and guide. She wished that Loma had joined them, but at eighty-eight she suffered from arthritis in her hips and knees and was often in pain. Nemle pictured Hafa, her own mentor and wondered what she would advise. The oldest person present was eighty-five year old Yin and he drew them into silence. It was the only formality and once he broke the silence a few minutes later they were ready to listen and talk.

"Has anyone else been hearing about the classes for law?" Nemle asked. "Do we know why Hud is taking them?"

It was enough to spark a vigorous discussion.

"It should have been Loma but she felt she could not manage this time."

"Tippa thinks Hud is wonderful."

"Yin would have done a better job."

"There seem to be so many rules now. I don't know them all."

"Marheh spoke of a large book, full of lists."

"I can't help wondering whether I'm missing something."

11

"If we don't know all the rules does that mean we are breaking them?"

"Perhaps we should ask to see this rule book. How can we mentor properly if we don't know?"

"Perhaps it is time for us to take another real look and try to simplify," Nemle said at last.

There was a brief pause while the others thought about this.

"I think it is too late for this Gathering," Sul said. "But we need to think seriously between now and the next."

There were nods and murmurs of affirmation.

"And we need to see the rule book," Yin added.

"Before the Gathering is over," Nemle said firmly, and again there was agreement.

Next morning Marheh went off to her class with a determined look which Nemle observed with a degree of concern, wondering what she was planning. She was early and chose her seat carefully so she could watch all the others as they came in. She wished Kel was part of the class because she knew he would understand the reason for the question she planned to ask, but he had moved beyond the need for classes.

As he had on the previous mornings Hud swept in last, the big, ornately bound book of rules clasped to his chest. He laid it on the table and stood back from it dramatically. His peroration began as an elaborate defense of the book. Marheh wondered suddenly in the middle of it whether Nemle had raised the issue in her mentors' meeting. When it seemed that he might be coming towards the end of his diatribe Marheh raised her hand politely.

At first Hud ignored her, but she persisted, and once the students near her realised and began to cast covert glances in her direction he could no longer pretend not to have seen.

"Yes young woman," he said at last, his voice patronising.

Marheh was aware that he knew her name, but she responded politely. "My name is Marheh. I belong to Day Bringer. I wanted to ask why we need so many rules and whether the rules sometimes stop us from doing what we think is right?"

There was a moment of silence. Faces turned towards Marheh and then back to Hud.

"I presume you have been listening while you have been sitting in this room," he said.

"Yes sir," Marheh said.

"And you still need to ask that question?" He raised his eyebrows and looked around the group asking them to share his surprise.

"Yes Sir," Marheh said again, controlling herself rigorously, knowing she must not let him provoke her into an unconsidered response.

"Am I to assume from your questions that you are of the opinion that there are too many rules and that these may stop us from acting rightly?"

"Yes Sir."

"Then perhaps you will give us all the benefit of your reasoning," he said. "With examples from your own experiences of course."

"Really?" Marheh asked, surprised and pleased to be given the opportunity.

"I insist," Hud said.

Someone giggled and Marheh flushed, unaware that none of her audience thought she had any experiences to draw on.

"We have a rule that we must not use the discipline of the mind to coerce or exploit," she said. "And that was one of the first rules, one of Sila's rules. I think that is like a guiding principle, but underneath that are all those little rules you told us about, like not entering a Silberay mind without asking and receiving permission, or not speaking mind to mind if you haven't spoken voice to voice first. But sometimes that is not possible. We have no "do" rules, only "don't" rules, but when we become apprenticed we chose the active pursuit of goodness and beauty." She paused and looked around at her fellow apprentices. "Nemle and I go for a week each year to help at Haven Cottage. People live there whose minds have been partly destroyed. We have to enter their minds to show them even simple things like how to go downstairs and eat breakfast. It seems to me we must be breaking some of the rules, but they would starve if we didn't." She stopped abruptly, aware that she had allowed her feelings to overcome her discretion. "You said to speak from my experience," she muttered.

Hud looked scornfully at her. "From your experiences, not Nemle's," he said. "An apprentice at your level is hardly likely to be directing minds."

Marheh managed to bite back an angry response. How she would love to enter his mind and prove her ability by making him do something silly, but she refrained, closing her mouth and spending the rest of the lesson deciding what the something silly would be, supposing she were to allow herself to take that kind of revenge.

The class ended soon after, Hud sweeping out of the room in much the same way as he had entered. Tippa turned to Marheh as they stood to leave.

"You can't really do that mind stuff, can you?" she asked.

"Yes," Marheh said, not wanting to elaborate.

"I don't believe you."

"Give me permission to enter your mind and I'll prove it," Marheh said.

"No way!" Tippa moved back from her a little.

"Then you'll just have to take it on trust," Marheh said lightly, turning away a little to hide her hurt.

Marheh was rather quiet for the rest of the day and Nemle received no report of the events in the class. She wondered a little, but did not ask, trusting Marheh would tell her when she was ready. Instead Nemle spoke of the Mentor meeting and how they had all felt challenged to investigate the rule book.

"We have asked to see it at tonight's meeting," she told Marheh as she put on her big coat ready to go.

Marheh's face lit up. "Good," she said emphatically.

Nemle smiled and came across to kiss her. "You're looking a bit tired. Why don't you have an early night?"

"Mmm, I might." She looked down at the doodles in her notebook. "I'm not doing much good here."

"Last day celebrations tomorrow," Nemle said. "Practice the discipline of the soul for half an hour or so then get a good sleep, alright."

"Mmm," Marheh said again and stood up to give Nemle a hug before making her way to her cabin. She was in the habit of obeying Nemle and although this last instruction was merely advice Marheh knew it was good advice. She lit her candle and lay quietly on her bunk until she felt Day Bringer move as Nemle left her. Then she began to build the image of a candle flame in her mind, carefully, painstakingly until she was lifted out of herself and into the space where her soul could sing.

Next morning she seemed to have recovered her good spirits and talked happily over breakfast about the forthcoming celebrations. These would include the presentation to the apprentices of their new tunics, a different colour to show their progress. This Gathering Marheh's tunic would be a deep claret colour, a great improvement she thought on the mid-grey she had been wearing. The most important ceremony though was the

Consigning. Two mentors had turned ninety and would leave their boats. Their apprentices would become full Silberay and take over the boats they had lived and trained on for the past twenty years. There was sadness and joy mingled, for the mentors seldom lived for long once they had relinquished the boat that had been home for seventy years, where they had learned, cared, struggled and lived. Yet they seemed content to let go, Nemle thought, remembering past ceremonies and wondering how she would feel when her time came. Only yesterday she had been as young as Marheh, now she was a mentor and the years in between had gone, sunrise to sunset and then the night.

She and Marheh spent most of the morning cramming every available space on Day Bringer with non-perishable foodstuffs; flour, cereals and pulses. They had filled the diesel tank early in the Gathering but the water tank needed continual topping up. They planned to make an early start next morning. Marheh was looking forward to being on the move again, especially as they would be travelling a section of the water road that was new to her. Just before lunch she went off to the store to pick up the order Nemle had made for the more perishable foodstuffs. It was always cheaper at the Harbour and the Harbour Master knew there would be large orders needed during the Gathering.

There was a short queue in the store. Marheh and Nemle were not the only ones preparing for an early departure. Marheh smiled and greeted the other customers, most of whom were apprentices. There was another grey tunic nearer the counter. Pon turned round to smile and waved a pair of new boots at her.

"New ones," Marheh said. "You are lucky, I had to have mine re-soled this time."

"You were pretty brave to tackle Hud," Pon said. "He didn't treat you very well."

Marheh shrugged. "I should have known he didn't want questions."

A blue tunic turned around. "You were showing off, of course he squashed you. Silberay don't show off."

"I asked a question," Marheh said angrily. "How is that showing off?"

"Pretending to have done all that mind stuff with Nemle," the blue tunic said severely.

Marheh studied her accuser. She was a young woman of twenty eight, blonde and blue-eyed, quite heavily built. Marheh did not know her well but remembered her kind but rather condescending manner from the previous Gathering when she had appointed herself guide and instructor to the younger apprentices.

"Lati," she said carefully. "It would have been wrong of me to pretend."

"Of course it would," Lati said. "I'm glad you recognise that."

"But you weren't pretending, were you?" Pon asked quietly.

Marheh smiled gratefully. "I wasn't actually."

"Pretending or lying if you like that better," Lati said. "You should be ashamed of yourself."

"What gives you the right to accuse me of lying?" Marheh said. "I never lie."

Lati shook her head sorrowfully, a response that angered Marheh more than speech would have done.

"I suppose you think I can't do it because you can't." She tossed her head. "If there were not so many stupid rules I'd prove it to you."

Pon put a hand on her arm but she shook him off impatiently.

"I don't need to lie," she announced.

By this time everyone in the store was aware of her anger. One of the older Silberay turned to look at her, caught her eye, spoke her name. She flushed and took a deep breath.

"Sorry," she muttered, controlling herself with difficulty.

Fortunately at that moment Lati's order was called and she involved herself in the transaction at the counter and departed with her bundles, giving Marheh one more sorrowful head shake as she went.

Marheh took another deep breath and let it out in a sigh. "Sorry," she said more calmly. "I shouldn't let her get to me."

Pon gave her a bit of a grin and departed with his new boots and Marheh looked at the floor and tried to be invisible. She was conscious that her outburst had resulted in general disapproval quite unrelated to the question of her probity. She was glad when she could collect her order and go home to Day Bringer. Nemle would probably be disappointed in her, she thought, knowing she must confess before the story reached her in magnified form.

Nemle listened gravely as she explained what had happened.

"Silly child," she said affectionately, when Marheh had finished. "Getting angry just rebounded on you, didn't it?"

Marheh nodded and Nemle gave her a hug. "I would have been angry too," she said. "Perhaps it's just as well I wasn't there."

"I wish you had been," Marheh said. "She would not have dared to call me a liar then."

They watched the Consigning together late that afternoon. Marheh, happy that Nemle understood, had forgotten the troubles of the morning. Nemle had not quite forgotten, but thought the difficulty would blow over before the next Gathering.

The Consigning ceremony took place in front of the dry docks and around the waters of the Harbour. The two boats that would be handed on had been thoroughly overhauled and the front cabin of each, that used by the Mentor, had been re-modelled to provide a work area appropriate to the needs of the two apprentices who were about to graduate.

The ninety odd Silberay stood in silence as the boats were refloated and bow hauled out of the dry dock to the empty loading dock. There the two retiring Mentors waited with their apprentices. Carefully the Mentors stepped on board and held out a hand to their apprentices, offering an invitation to join them. The Mentor started the engine, the apprentice went forward to take the front line and the two boats began a slow lap of the Harbour. The gathered Silberay began to sing. Marheh felt close to tears as the two old Silberay, standing straight and proud steered their boats for the last time. Nemle found she was watching Marheh as well as the boats. She was singing with attention, words and music rendered with thought and feeling. She had an expressive face and Nemle saw that she was deeply moved by the occasion.

As the boats drew up again at the loading dock the song ended. Apprentice and Mentor embraced. The Mentor carefully removed the tiller arm and handed it to the apprentice who bowed and took it in both hands. There were words too, spoken quietly between them then the Mentor stepped ashore to stand and watch as the apprentice refitted the tiller arm and made another lap of the Harbour. The Silberay began to sing again, a song of welcome for the newly graduated ones.

Marheh turned to Nemle, still singing, a single tear visible at the corner of one eye, her face revealing a complex mixture of feelings. Nemle hugged her as the song ended and the boats returned to be carefully moored before the former Mentor and the former apprentice greeted each other again and made their slow way towards the Harbour buildings where the oldest Silberay made their home. The gathered Silberay parted to allow them passage and clapped softly as they went.

As the crowd began to disperse Marheh sighed and turned again to Nemle.

"How can something be so sad and so happy at the same time?" she said.

Nemle smiled sympathetically but said nothing, knowing she did not expect an answer.

"One day it will be me," Marheh said, then looked quickly at Nemle.

"And me," Nemle said. "And one day it will be you and your apprentice, but we've both got a way to go yet."

"And now a party," Marheh said gleefully, her mood changing again. "And goodbye to my grey tunic."

Nemle laughed at her. "What a baby you are," she teased.

Marheh spun around, her long dark plait flying out behind her. "I'll wear the grey one to get the coal in and check the engine," she said. "It won't show the dirt."

Nemle laughed again. "Go on, run if you want to. I can see you can't wait to get there."

Marheh danced off laughing. Nemle followed more slowly, smiling at Marheh's enthusiasm.

The big meeting room was transformed. Chairs had been moved to the edges and two long tables were laden with food. In one corner, near the dais, a small group were making music. Violin, flute and guitar played folk tunes and Silberay songs. The room quickly filled with happy chatter as Silberay took the opportunity to speak to friends they may not see again until the next Gathering, two years away. There was a moment of quiet while the Harbour Master welcomed them and invited them to enjoy the food then the cheerful conviviality continued.

At last came the concluding ceremonies. Marheh brought Nemle her grey tunic to hold and went to stand in line with the other apprentices. First the two new apprentices received their gold coloured tunics and spoke the words of the Silberay choice and their mentors went forward to sign their indentures. The Apprentice Master welcomed them formally and the assembled company sang as they walked with their mentors across the dais and back into the group they had joined.

The ordinary apprentices came next, Marheh among them. Nemle positioned herself where she would see Marheh's face. Four apprentices came to stand before the Apprentice Master and have grey tunics pulled over their heads. To each the Apprentice Master spoke words of congratulation and encouragement. Nemle smiled to herself, remembering that Marheh had been enthusiastic about her grey tunic two years ago. Then came Tippa, Pon and Marheh. The deep claret colour was lovely

Nemle thought, as first Tippa then Pon put on their tunics. It would suit Marheh too. At last it was Marheh's turn. She was very white and her eyes were alight with excitement. The tunic was pulled over her head. Suddenly the warmth and conviviality disappeared. For a second or two Marheh's face registered hurt, bewilderment, betrayal, then set into the blankness of stone. The longed for claret coloured tunic was disfigured by a large yellow P sewn on front and back. Nemle stared, not quite sure what she was seeing, then bit back a cry of protest.

"The P is for Probation Marheh," the Apprentice Master said. "One of your tutors does not feel you are ready for promotion."

"I see."

Marheh's little stiff voice wrenched Nemle's heart.

"It's not right," she said loudly.

There were mutters around her and Sul touched her arm.

"Later," he said quietly.

Nemle glared at him then accepted the sense of his advice. Marheh, holding herself rigid, walked carefully off the dais and the ceremony continued.

Nemle saw very little of it. All she could think of was Marheh. She watched her walk stiffly across to the edge of the room then lost sight of her as she began to make her way towards the back.

"How dare they," she thought angrily. "How dare they treat her like that."

The apprentices filed on and off and received their tunics, then the two newly graduated Silberay were given badges and certificates and finally the two retiring Mentors were honoured. Nemle, who normally had her temper under control, felt her anger growing through it all. The Harbour Master had barely completed his final greeting, the Apprentice Master had scarcely stepped down from the dais when Nemle was confronting him, but to her surprise she was not alone. Sul was beside her and she might have expected that, but several of the other mentors gathered around including the woman who taught engine maintenance and there, with his mentor, was Pon in his red tunic.

"If she doesn't get promoted then neither should I," he was saying earnestly to his mentor.

"You hear that?" Nemle said to the Apprentice Master, her small, stocky figure standing firmly in front of him. "What could she possibly have done that deserved public humiliation? What kind of people are Silberay to let it happen?"

The Apprentice Master looked anxiously at Nemle, his blue eyes worried. "Hud said she was lying, boasting about using mind control at Haven Cottage. I'm sorry Nemle," he finished regretfully. "But you know we couldn't let that pass."

"Hud said!" Nemle bit off the words. "Hud said! What would he know?"

Sul put a hand on her arm. "Marheh has no need to lie or boast when it comes to mind control," he said quietly. "She has been using the discipline of the mind very capably for a number of years."

"But she's only twenty four," the Apprentice Master said. "She is hardly old enough even to know what is possible."

"I don't think age has anything to do with it," Sul said. "She is very talented."

"And she wasn't boasting," Pon said.

The Mentors all turned to look at him and he reddened slightly but held his ground.

"She was asked to give examples from her own experience. I was there."

Nemle looked disgusted. "You let that posturing lawyer manipulate you because Marheh asked a question he didn't like," she told the Apprentice Master. "You believed him and didn't even think to verify what he told you. Who is the liar would you say?" She turned away. "I need to find her," she told them. "You need to think of a way to give her back what you've just taken away."

She pushed through the group around the Apprentice Master and made her way to the door, heedless of the glances, curious, sympathetic, occasionally mildly disapproving, that came her way from those Silberay who had lingered in the meeting room.

It was almost dark outside. Nemle made her way along the jetties to Day Bringer where she hoped she would find Marheh. Day Bringer was showing no lights and for a moment she worried Marheh might have gone to hide somewhere else. She stepped on board and into the back cabin, Marheh's cabin, and there she was lying on her bunk on her back staring at nothing, only visible in the dim light because she had shed the new tunic and was wearing only her light coloured shirt. There was a small movement from the bunk and a small voice said. "Go away Nemle please."

Nemle did not answer, only moved quietly into the cabin, lighting Marheh's candle, drawing the curtains, picking up the claret coloured tunic from the floor and folding it. Then she sat down on the bottom step beside Marheh's bed. Marheh turned her head away.

"It won't go away Marheh," she said. "And neither will I. You have to deal with it."

There was a long silence.

"In front of everyone," Marheh said at last, still not looking at Nemle, speaking so quietly Nemle had to strain to hear.

"It was unkind and unjust," Nemle said matter-of-factly.

"I was so looking forward to getting my new tunic."

"Yes, I know."

Nemle had the tunic on her lap. She looked at the stitching around the yellow letters, saw that it would come away without much trouble.

"Now it's all spoiled."

"Only if you let it be. You knew when you asked your question that there might be repercussions."

"I didn't know it would hurt so much," Marheh said, looking at Nemle for the first time.

Nemle smiled at her, touched her cheek lightly with one finger.

"That's life," she said. "Things do hurt." She stood up carefully. "Now you will practice the discipline of the soul while I find some scissors. I think you will find there are souls wanting to sing with yours."